HASTY (DO-OVER BOOK #4)

JULIA KENT

Cover: Hang Le

Editor: Elisa Reed

I have to thank a lot of people for their help while I was writing Hasty. Half of this book was written as COVID created a lockdown situation, and as my husband experienced a harrowing set of health issues.

I won't go into detail, as you're about to read a romantic comedy and who wants to start in a sad mood? Let's just say I am deeply grateful to a wide range of people in my life who helped me as I wrote this book.

You know who you are. <3

And writing romantic comedy gave me a world to escape into. I hope you get that same escape as you read about rabbit breastmilk and the kind of glove you wear to birth a cow. :)

HASTY

I never thought my perp walk would lead to true love.

Then again, I never thought I'd be arrested on RICO charges and hauled away in zip ties on camera for the world to see, minutes after closing the most amazing deal of my career.

And all of it in front of my biggest rival, billionaire wunderkind Ian McCrory.

I am broke.

I am disgraced.

I am alone.

I am a sucker.

But the worst part? I have to go back to my hometown and live in my bedroom filled with relics from my childhood.

Lisa Frank never made me so mad before.

Just when I needed a rescue, I got one — in the form of help from my biggest rival.

He can't bring back my money.

He certainly can't bring back my reputation or my pride.

But there's one thing he can bring back to me.

A sense of hope.

Maybe even love.

Ian sees something in me no one else does, and he's relentless about making me see it, too. As we grow closer, I'm starting to see that while my entire life used to be a lie, the truth is staring me in the present — and it's a truth I like very, very much, hot eyes and gorgeous smile and all.

But I have to be careful.

I can't be too —

That's right.

Hasty.

Read the final standalone book in the *USA Today* bestselling Do-Over Series (*Fluffy*, *Perky*, *Feisty*), as Mallory's sister, Hastings "Hasty" Monahan gets her turn at a happily ever after that starts off with an arrest.

Hers.

And ends with a surprisingly cheesy happily ever after.

Audiobook narrated by Audie award winner Erin Mallon.

Today is the best day of my life.

I know people say that, and they mean it, but they don't mean *this*. My best day is better than anyone else's. Trust me.

I *know*.

I'm sitting at a table at Essentialz, a five-star restaurant in San Francisco. Everyone at the table watches me as I tuck the signed paperwork away in my black Bottega Veneta woven leather brief bag.

I, Hastings Monahan, just signed a nine-figure investment deal on behalf of the venture capital firm I work for.

Full partner, here I come.

Of course, lawyers will handle the majority of this. The signatures are symbolic as much as they are legal. But the fellow diners at my carefully crafted table will go back to China with an exciting opportunity for their company, Zhangwa Telecommunications, to enter the North American market with climate-change technology projecting yields that are the best aphrodisiac *ever*.

As I sip from my glass of Montrachet Grand Cru, I catch

the eye of Ming Bannerton, a consultant with Zhangwa whose father is a high-ranking U.S State Department official in China, a woman who has a hunger for financial success that I can spot in anyone in three seconds flat. There's something special about a fellow hustler–and when I use the word *hustler*, I don't mean it pejoratively.

People who hustle get things *done.*

We connect. We network. We pattern match. We ruthlessly apply what we intuitively feel to what we operationally know in order to produce optimal outcomes.

In short–we *hustle.*

And we win.

But in competition, there can only be one winner.

One.

Tonight, I'm it.

Her smile mirrors mine, red lips stretched over perfectly white teeth that are as straight as a new picket fence. The smile doesn't reach her eyes, but an intensity infuses her. She's about five years younger than me, with a knowing eye that tells me we need to stay in touch. Someday soon, she may shoot past me, and that's where all the legwork pays off.

In this business, you network *down* as well as you network *up*, if you want to get anywhere.

And the manila folder resting in my brief bag, the one that feels like a warm gold ingot pressed against my lips? *That*, ladies and gentlemen, is how you *get* somewhere.

"Where is Burke?" Mr. Zhao Bai asks, his head at a slight tilt, a gesture of genuine curiosity as his eyes survey me, looking for information that doesn't come directly from my mouth. He's the youngest of the four men at the table, a fast talker who looks around the room like he's a mob boss. Negotiating with him took a steady hand I didn't know I possessed, but now I understand.

Burke is part of the deal, and I didn't realize it.

The contracts are signed, though. That makes my husband an off-the-books addendum. No matter what, this is *my* accomplishment.

My husband, Burke Oonaj, is one of the hottest market makers in finance right now. Even he will have no choice but to be impressed by the deal I've just put together.

But the inquiry about my husband makes my uterus fall.

And it's not like he's around to catch it.

"Good question," I say before taking another sip of wine, needing to buy myself a smidgen of space and time. I only need a split second.

Normally.

For some reason that I can't explain, my emotions are tangling in my mind, and that's an unpredictable variable I have to weed out.

Fast.

My heart feels strangely heavy in my chest, a sense of dread filling me that has no right to be here. *This is MY night,* I tell that sense of dread. *This is MY deal. This is my culmination of six years of careful work, all coming together, right now.*

Go away, dread.

But Mr. Zhao's question is a good one, because Burke isn't answering any of my texts or emails or phone calls, and hasn't for the last three days.

My husband has disappeared.

Not literally, of course, because husbands don't just *do* that. Business travel can be intense. Plenty of stretches of time have gone by without hearing from him. They involved twenty-four hours or less, though.

Not eighty-one hours and thirteen minutes.

Not that I'm counting.

I can't admit any of this to anyone at this table, of course, so instead, I give what my pattern-matching brain tells me is the optimal answer, designed to make me look good.

"Burke's fine," I say with a grin, the glass of wine still full enough to make more sips look like an appropriate response. "He sends his best regards. He would have been here tonight, but… you know."

Two of the men share a look I don't like. It's a fleeting glance, the type that is practiced and meant to look like nothing. You think I'm paranoid, that I'm inventing it all?

Wrong.

I'm in a state of hyperarousal.

No, not the sexual kind. Haven't felt *that* in a long time, at least not with Burke. *My* hyperarousal is based around the stress hormones pumping through me from the excitement of what I just accomplished.

Me. Myself. Alone.

Independent of Burke.

As workday smiles stretch to become the more casual, intimate grins of people enjoying bottle after bottle of excellent wine, I loosen up. The answer I gave them sufficed. We can move on.

My body feels numb and excited at the same time. I'm on top of the world. The pinnacle.

I am Peak Hastings.

Which is why, when the maître d' approaches my side, I don't pick up on the gravity of his whisper. No one would. Because learning that my credit card has been declined for this business dinner is definitely *not* part of the plan, and the areas of my brain assigned to processing language literally can't comprehend it.

"It's *what?*" I whisper, standing carefully, legs still steady, my alcohol consumption measured, even if my table-mates have made their way through more wine than an entire wedding party back home.

The maître d', José, gives me a wide-eyed but polite look. "I'm sorry, Ms. Monahan. This has never happened before when you've dined with us. But the credit card company was very firm. You cannot use this one."

Mr. Zhao gives me an inquiring look. My stomach sinks. Did he overhear?

"Will you all excuse me?" I tell them, hating the disruption, my legs turning into two steel beams covered in chilled skin.

"Something must be wrong with the credit card processor," I snap at the maître d' as I hurry away from my group. I want to get the taint of this failure out of the way and get back to my stellar success.

Once we're out of sight of my table, I rifle through my purse and find another business credit card. "Use this one. And let me be very clear, to you and to your boss, that this is absolutely, abjectly unacceptable."

He inserts the card, chip side in. "I realize this, Ms. Monahan, but we cannot…"

Beep.

He stares at the credit card terminal.

I read the display upside down. "Declined!" I hiss. "This is impossible! That card has no limit!"

"Perhaps you've had your identity stolen, or there are fraud alerts on your account? Perhaps you're the victim of a financial crime?" José suggests.

"I can't be the victim of a financial crime!" I snap at him. "I'm a financial *expert!* This doesn't happen to people like me. Here!" I shove a third company card at him. This one better work.

I only have one more.

My mind races ahead, conjuring contingency plans, even as my cheeks burn with shame.

Shame.

Why would *I* feel shame for someone else's mistake? And yet, there it is, and I have to override it fast. Because if I don't, it gets a toehold.

And that is the fastest way to lose your edge.

José closes his eyes and lets out a sigh through his nose, a split second before the display terminal beeps.

Again.

"Your computer system is down*,"* I declare, pulling out the fourth card and my phone, texting my office manager. Maybe something went wrong. Maybe José is right. Maybe we were hacked. But this is surreal enough to let the dread come inside me and have a seat, as it decides whether to become an overnight guest.

It doesn't matter. What matters is that I'm staring at a mid-four-figure bill that I owe, right now, and have no way to settle.

This cannot be happening.

As he runs the fourth card, the main door opens. My spine straightens, calves stretching tall, and not just from the five-inch heels I'm wearing.

I know that man.

I *hate* that man.

And he's the last person on Earth I want to see in the middle of this debacle.

Ian McCrory cannot see me like this.

"You need to fix this!" I hiss at José, whose demeanor is rapidly changing.

"Ms. Monahan," he says, "this does not appear to be a credit card *machine* malfunction. This appears to be a credit card *account* malfunction."

Our eyes meet, his with a challenge I am unaccustomed to experiencing. Because I am unaccustomed to my credit cards being declined.

"Hastings!" Ian says, walking toward me with the casual

confidence of a man who has it all. Yes, 'the man who has it all' is a cliché, but clichés exist for a reason.

And Ian McCrory is a walking cliché. He's hot. He's rich. He's smart. He's charming.

And he's alpha to the core.

All of that works against me as I find myself in the least favorable position *ever*.

And if I were to choose a position with Ian, it wouldn't be this one.

Fury at my husband for not answering my calls and texts and emails for *days* rises up in me, tangling with the anger I feel at the inevitable attraction toward Ian, combining with my deep embarrassment.

There's a lot happening inside this toned, successful body.

Ian comes in for the requisite hug, holding it a little longer than he has before.

"You're trembling," he says, his voice textured and nuanced, the concern something I've never heard in past encounters. We've sparred at conference tables that feel like they're the size of football fields. I've lost countless deals to him, some of them reasonable, some of them not. Ian's a favorite of the old boys' network.

Me? Hastings Monahan is not exactly an old boy.

Then again, neither is Ian.

His cologne cuts through the low-grade panic that I'm trying to hide from him as José continues to stare me down. It must be a custom blend. I can pick out notes of cherry, burnt oak, and something spicy. Inhaling the air around him is like experiencing the bouquet of the finest bottle of Screaming Eagle cabernet you've ever tasted, at a private retreat, with people who know how to *live*.

Like me.

His suit fabric under my hand is a weave that can only come from a tenth-generation tailor, the kind whose DNA has been honed by craft and time. Deep brown eyes, so close to the color of his hair and brows, make a ring of chocolate around the edge, the opposite of most people's irises. Even Ian's body doesn't follow the rules.

Ian is the exception in everything, even in how God constructs eyes.

"I'm just worried," I say, deflecting. "I haven't heard from Burke in days, and—"

"Burke!" His entire stance changes, tension filling his body. "Is he here?"

"No. Why would he be here?"

"Aren't you two doing a deal?"

"I'm doing a deal." I bristle inside at the implication that I need Burke for anything.

Ian peers around me, instantly making eye contact with Ms. Bannerton at my table. His eyebrows shoot up. "You scored *that* deal?"

"Yes. Ink's on the papers." I glance distractedly at the credit card still in my hand.

"Congratulations." Now his eyebrows are in a different position, one corner of his mouth curling. I know that feeling. He knows he can't win *all* the deals.

That doesn't mean he doesn't fantasize about them.

"Thank you."

"I can't say I'm surprised. I worked my ass off on the regulatory issue. Zhangwa Telecom couldn't get past that until I pulled some strings with elected officials."

"You groomed the path," I say smoothly, knowing damn well he did forty-nine percent of the work on this. "But you couldn't close."

"Let me guess. I got them close, but you took it all the way." His eyes narrow. "How many personal contacts did you work to get port access for Zhangwa?"

"I did nothing untoward, Ian."

His eyes comb over me. Creepy guys abound in our business, but Ian's gaze is anything but gross. In fact, I like it.

Like it too much.

I'm a very married woman, thank you. I don't stray. Vows matter, even when my husband ignores me for days on end and doesn't sleep with me for...

Far more than a few days.

"I'm sure you were completely above board and legal in every action you took, Hastings. But I also know you have a mind like a steel trap and a nose for gossip. How much dirt did you have to collect on adjacent property owners to guarantee port access?"

All I can do is grin.

It feels remarkably good to have someone *understand* me so well. Emotion swells in my chest, raises my temperature, makes my pulse quicken, a high of accomplishment spreading throughout my body.

It's unfamiliar.

It's unbounded.

And it's Ian McCrory who is eliciting it from me.

"Good work. That's taken you..." his voice fades out as he thinks, "...six years."

"Yes. Yes, it has. And now it's *done*."

"Nice little deal you've made."

"Don't do that."

"Do what?"

"Little. This is anything but *little*, Ian. Don't act like this deal is some sort of a consolation prize for me because you decided you didn't want it enough."

"Don't tell me what I want, Hastings."

Suddenly, it's clear we're not talking about business.

The sound of a man clearing his throat makes us both turn to look at José, who cocks one eyebrow, gives Ian a glance, and then looks at me pointedly.

Ian's not stupid. "Is something wrong?" he asks José, instantly protective. The tone change is one that I would normally admire, but right now, panic is scrambling all of my sensors.

"Ms. Monahan and I were dealing with a business matter, Mr. McCrory. Your room is reserved in the back. Most of your party is there already." José's smile is ingratiating. I can feel the shift in how he treats me versus how he treats Ian in my salivary glands. A bitter taste fills my mouth as I realize I've been instantly relegated to some social trash heap as a result of a computer glitch.

Their glitch.

Ian bends down to kiss my cheek, startling me, his clean-shaven face so smooth, hot, and dry, making my pulse skip.

"Congratulations, Hastings. A job well done. Give my best to Burke when you see him next." He opens his mouth slightly, as if to say something more, and then shuts it quickly. I want to ask him what he started to say, but I know that no matter what, he's sealed up tight, like a drum.

Men like Ian McCrory don't equivocate. If he changed his mind, his mind is *changed*.

I can't help myself as he leaves, my eyes taking in the back of his body, that bespoke suit jacket perfectly molded along the lines of his tight, wide shoulders. His legs are long, shoes shined, a deep Italian richness that you can't buy with just money.

You need taste, too.

Real taste.

José's eyes jump from Ian, to me, back to Ian. The man is clearly making decisions based on social importance. If I am important to Ian McCrory, then upsetting me could upset the alpha.

Social calculations take microseconds for people like me, Ian, and even José. You can't be the maître d' at one of the hottest restaurants in one of the hottest cities in the world and not be people smart. Emotional intelligence isn't just for softhearted church ladies, preschool teachers, and therapists.

We need every advantage we can get in this world.

"Isn't Ian wonderful?" I murmur as I bring José into my space with a confidante's wink. "We go back ages."

José's eyes narrow. He's trying to figure out if by *ages*, I mean we've slept together. It can't hurt to pretend that's the case, so I lean in and lower my voice. "He's a good friend to have. Comes through when you need him. I'll bet he's a great tipper, too."

That elicits a chuckle, something in my gut unclenching at the sound.

"Will you excuse me?" I say to him, my hand on his. "While you figure out the computer glitch, I need to get back to my guests."

As if I weren't deflecting, I give him a flirty smile and move away quickly… but not *too* quickly. I can't be...

Hasty.

"Is there a problem?" Ms. Bannerton asks, batting dark eyes at me that make it clear she knows damn well there's a problem and wants to watch me squirm.

"No problem. Just dealing with—" I hold up my phone and jiggle it. "You know. The husband."

"Everything's okay with Burke, I hope?" Mr. Wang Min asks. He's the senior person from Zhangwa and his silence thus far has been a great contrast to Mr. Zhao.

That same strange look passes between him and Mr. Zhao, though.

"Oh, he's fine. Just had a personal-life question. You know. Marriage."

"My wife texts me twenty times a day when I'm on trips," Mr. Zhao says, lips pressed in a tight smile. "And she doesn't care about time zones, so I get the texts at two in the morning."

"Mine pretends I'm dead when I'm gone," says Mr. Wang. Everyone halts. He laughs. "Not literally. She decided that it's easier to have no contact when I'm away than to have only a little. As long as I bring her back real maple syrup from Vermont, she's fine with all the travel I do."

"It's not as if she has a choice," says Mr. Zhao. That comment elicits the heartiest laugh from the men at the table.

Ms. Bannerton and I give each other sympathetic looks, but not *too* sympathetic, because we can't telegraph weakness in a crowd like this.

Suddenly, the men all stand in unison, Ms. Bannerton struggling to join them in her high heels. My skin breaks out in gooseflesh as I realize something has changed.

Pressing my palms into the arms of my chair, I rise to my feet and turn.

Even before I see him, I know *exactly* who is drawing this reaction from them.

"Ian!" Ms. Bannerton says, her lips spreading in a grin of joy, eyes devouring him. She bypasses all of the men to launch herself into the arms of the ninth richest man in the world. Mr. Zhao and Mr. Wang are only ranking in the high 'teens these days.

Ian accepts her hug with the gracious formality of a man who knows exactly what to do, then works the table, shaking hands. When he's done, he turns to me, arms stretched out in a gesture of gentlemanly acknowledgment, and says, "I don't need to hug you."

Ms. Bannerton's eyebrows shoot up.

"We already took care of the intimacies earlier," he adds.

Normally, that sort of comment would get him a high-heeled spike through that beautiful Italian leather on his size fourteen (I'm guessing) feet, but I'm grateful tonight. It cuts through the tension of my declined credit cards and gives everyone at the table something to whisper about later, long after this dinner is over.

On the other side of the group, José appears, making eyes at me. My heart jumps up into my throat, clawing its way into my sinus cavity, beating like it's in the Tour de France and about to wipe out at the bottom of a steep hill.

I reach for my purse, the universal gesture of going to the ladies' room, and I step away, grateful for Ian's presence. He'll keep them all busy as I go and untangle this very private mess.

My phone buzzes. I look at the text, hopeful.

It's a reminder from my carrier to pay my cellphone bill.

Dammit, Burke. Where are you?

Those words have rushed through my brain hundreds of times in the last three days. He's never gone this long without answering, even if it's just a single letter, "K," when I ask him if he's alive.

I find my way back to the concierge desk, where José is now standing with even less warmth than he had before Ian appeared.

"This is *not* a credit card machine failure, as I suspected," he informs me. "You need to pay the bill."

"I'm a good customer. I'm sure this is some sort of an error. Can't I just—"

"I'm sorry, Ms. Monahan. You have to settle the bill immediately. Do you have a debit card?"

"Oh! My personal account. Of course! I can pay it, and I'll have my company reimburse me once this is all sorted out. There's plenty of money in our personal accounts." I pull out the debit card and hand it to him, relieved to have been given an out, still furious to be in this position at all.

He runs it. I stare at the machine. At the same moment, my skin does that prickly thing again, goosebumps everywhere. If I weren't in this state of abject terror that I'm working so hard to cover, I would think that I was aroused.

Aroused in the most delicious of ways.

Ian McCrory's entirely at fault.

The light on the machine turns red, the word looking like Hebrew, although at this point I know damn well what "decline" looks like upside down.

"Hastings," Ian purrs in my ear, his hand resting between my shoulder blades. His eyes flit down to take in the machine, then the cards gripped in my hand. He looks at José. An extraordinary expression of sympathy that makes me want to rip my own liver out and eat it in front of him covers his face.

"Oh, Hastings. I had no idea."

That is the exact moment I learn how much I *hate* Ian McCrory.

"Had no idea of what?" I challenge.

He looks at the debit card as if it were a limp penis. "That you and Burke were in financial trouble." The words come out of his mouth as if they're in slow motion, in free fall, BASE jumping without a parachute.

"We are not in financial trouble," I snap, hating the edges of my words, how they vibrate out into the waiting area. Two people turn, microscopic shifts in the way that their ears tilt. I know full well about eavesdropping on other people's drama– and I know *damn* well that I don't want to be someone else's funny story for later. "We're fine. This is some kind of computer glitch."

"Ma'am, you have now attempted four credit cards, all from different issuers, and your personal debit card. Everything has been declined," José says, completely obliterating my cover story.

The shift from Ms. Monahan to Ma'am is the *worst*.

The spray of shock that radiates through my body as his

words hit me makes it hard to breathe. Something really *is* wrong. How can the greatest moment in my entire life implode like this?

"José," Ian says to him, making himself a human shield between the prying eyes of my dinner party and me, "put it on my account."

"You can't do that!" I protest.

"I *am* doing that."

"But this is *my* dinner. This is *my* responsibility. And *my* contract," I growl.

"I'm not trying to take your contract away from you, Hastings. I'm trying to save you from embarrassment."

"I don't need you to rescue me."

"It sure as hell looks like you do."

"This... this isn't... I'll pay you back," I hiss, furiously grateful, but filled with more fury than gratitude.

"Of course you will."

"And–I'm *not* in financial trouble."

"Of course you're not."

Condescension is my kryptonite. It's what I use against other people as a weapon, a cover for my insecurity.

Yeah, yeah, I'm not supposed to be that self-aware. I went through enough therapy to know I don't give a damn what other people think about me, but I certainly give a damn about how *I* feel when someone else perceives me as weak.

And that's exactly what Ian's doing right now.

"First of all, you're a jerk. Second of all, thank you."

"That's the worst thank you I've ever received in my life."

"I'm sure you've been subjected to worse."

"Well, there was that one time in Sydney when I was in bed and—"

"I don't want to hear about your sex life!"

Especially when mine is non-existent.

"Look," Ian says, grabbing my upper arm gently, pulling me out of the view of my dinner guests. "I don't want you to win this contract any more than you want *me* to win the ones that I take from *you*."

"You admit it? I'm a competitor of yours?"

"You're an annoyance, Hastings."

"Annoyance?"

"You're so much smarter than you give yourself credit for, and you've attached yourself to that slimy piece of overblown ego masquerading as a finance expert."

"How dare you talk about my husband that way!"

"You knew instantly who I was talking about, though, didn't you?"

We're both breathing harder than we should be, and a flush of heat wanders around my body like it's looking for something to burn.

I straighten my spine and let out a deep sigh. "I am *not* having this conversation with you."

"Actually, you are. We're literally exchanging the words right now."

My phone buzzes in my hand. I look at it. It's from Burke. It's two words:

I'm sorry.

My eyebrows drop, my face twisting with horror. "I'm *sorry?*" I whisper.

"That's better."

"Not you! I'm reading my text from Burke–'I'm sorry'? At least he's finally contacting me, so I can stop worrying."

A second text follows:

Don't tell them anything.

I frown. Before Ian can rudely ask me what the new text says, his phone buzzes, too. Over at the table, everyone's phone buzzes at the same time.

The timing is too coincidental.

A snake begins to uncurl along my tailbone, rising up my spine between my shoulder blades to the base of my neck, splitting in two and going to each ear, crawling up over the crown of my head.

Something is terribly wrong.

Burke doesn't apologize for *anything*.

Behind me, the door to the restaurant opens, bringing with it a cool blast of evening air that should be refreshing but feels more like death. The sound of heavy steps makes me turn, and a clink-clink-clink that is distinct and unfamiliar.

"Hastings Monahan," says a man behind me. He's not asking if I'm her.

Because he knows.

I look at Ian. His eyes are wide, hand gripping his phone, thumb on the unlock position already. When I turn around, I'm faced with uniformed police officers and men and women in black, all of them wearing weapons and expressions of doom.

"Yes?"

What happens next is a blur. Words float into my brain, like *under arrest* and *charged with* as Ian punches the glass screen on his phone like a jackhammer on concrete, barking orders to some person named Irene on the other end. My purse is taken out of my hands, my wrists pulled behind me. I catch Ms. Bannerton's eye, and her whole expression melts into one of mocking delight.

The men at the table do not move, do not defend me, do not protect me, do not interfere in any way.

I can't blame them.

Ian, on the other hand, *the* Ian McCrory, my biggest competitor, my outright nemesis, reaches through the molasses of the moment as my hands are zip tied behind my back, forcing my breasts out, my feet teetering on the platforms of my shoes, my soul slithering out of my body.

"I'm getting lawyers on this. Whatever's going on, I've got you, Hastings," he says grimly, the stark emotion in his voice cutting through the horror of what unfolds.

"You *what?*"

"I've got you."

And those are the last words anyone says to me as police officers remove me from the restaurant, my perp walk the ultimate free-fall from Peak Hastings to Freak Hastings.

Less than an hour has passed since we signed the contract for my nine-figure deal.

The only pen in my life now is going to be a holding pen.

2

*O*ne month later

"Honey, I am so glad to have you back, but what on Earth have you done to your *hair?*"

My mother's hug should be reassuring, but it feels like yet another way I've failed. It's been a month since I was hauled out of Essentialz in handcuffs, with my Chinese colleagues, Ian McCrory, and what felt like half the world watching.

A month is a lifetime *and* a blink.

"I dyed it."

"I can see that." She cradles my face in her hands like I'm a wig mannequin and she's checking out the newest line. "But that color is so *dark*. You're a beautiful, natural blonde! It's almost chestnut now. What's the shade called?"

"Evaded Felony."

She frowns. "Huh. Does Madison Reed carry that?"

"Mom."

"Between that dark hair and those boxy sunglasses, I'd have never guessed it was you!"

"Good. That's the whole point."

"Why would you… oh." Her face falls. "You don't want anyone to know who you are."

"I don't want to *be* who I am, Mom."

Here's what I've learned in the last thirty-two days: My husband, Burke Oonaj, is a festering boil on the back of a rat. He is pond scum, and he can take his "Don't tell them anything" text, print it, roll it into a tiny little ball, and shove it up his ass so far that it hits his prostate and then jabs his throat, where he chokes to death.

I, ladies and gentlemen, am a sucker. I've been taken. I've been fooled.

Me, Hastings Monahan.

While I was closing a nine-figure deal, turns out Burke was handling nine figures of money, too.

Just illegally.

Burke was committing financial crimes left and right, using me as leverage whenever he could. The man convinced investors to fund companies that didn't exist, to make wire transfers to offshore banks, to invest in gold that was as real as the paint on a Buddha statue in a Manhattan gift shop.

And so much more, all of it deeply illegal and cravenly predatory.

I have seven figures in revolving lines of credit for accounts that I never opened, all using my social security number.

Every penny of savings, 401(k), personal defined benefit pension plans: You name it, it's all wiped out.

I am *not* a stupid woman. I have safeguards on everything. What I didn't plan for was the complete, utter, malignant sociopathy of a man who spent more time manscaping at a spa than he ever did learning computer security protocols.

Even worse than all that, it turns out, I'm not really married to him.

Oh, I have the marriage license to prove it. I have the big wedding Mom and Dad paid for to prove it. I have photo albums, and a minister who filed our marriage license with the state of Massachusetts after we got married at the local country club five years ago–all proof.

What I don't have are the names of his other wives.

That's right, *other wives.*

I have no idea who his first wife is—and by "first wife," I don't mean in serial, I mean in parallel. Somebody in the world *is* legally married to Burke Oonaj.

But it's not me.

I've spent the last five years acting as if I were, which means I've spent much of my adult life living a lie.

A lie I never agreed to.

"We kept it just the same for you, sweetie."

"Kept what?" I ask Mom, who is stroking my hair absent-mindedly, like I'm a pet ferret.

"Your room! Of course, you could take Mallory's old room if you'd like. She doesn't, you know, need it." The drop in her voice as the words come out with painstakingly earnest horror almost makes me laugh.

Almost.

The stairs of my childhood home are carpeted. Not a stylish carpet runner over wide, polished oak treads. Oh, no. Wall-to-wall carpeting, all the way up the stairs and into most of the bedrooms.

It's quaint.

Mom and Dad aren't hurting financially, but their home is nothing like the life I've been accustomed to since I moved out to the Bay Area after graduation. In Massachusetts, every-thing old is treasured.

In the Bay Area, everything smart that can be monetized is king.

Or, in my case–*queen*.

Memory makes me kick my shoes off, toes sinking into the thick carpet as we go upstairs. I'm laden with baggage, literally and figuratively. Everything I'm allowed to own is in the three pieces of luggage I carry upstairs. One big backpack with a newly scrubbed tablet, one large checked item of luggage, and one carry-on – a cooler filled with precious cargo. My purse is tucked inside the backpack.

This is all I own.

This is all I'm *allowed* to own, by court order.

Following behind Mom, I make the right turn into my bedroom and stop short. She wasn't kidding. This room is *exactly* as I left it when I moved out after college, twelve years ago.

"See, honey? We even kept your Lisa Frank notebooks and pens and all the paraphernalia. You used to love this stuff!"

I drop the backpack, careful not to crack the tablet. I shove the large suitcase up against the end of the bed. The carry-on fits nicely into the corner near the closet as I turn and take in the room. Sure, I've been home plenty of times in the last twelve years, but I haven't really paid attention to anything in the house.

This is it. *This* is what I've become.

This, and seven hundred dollars in a single bank account that I had to open on my own, attached to a secured credit card that uses five hundred of that to provide a five-hundred-dollar spending limit, is all I have.

Everything else is gone.

It's been seized by the federal government, taken by state

agencies, or is part of lien after lien coming after anything Burke touched.

My lawyer tried to argue that because it was revealed that we were not technically, *legally* married, those assets needed to be separated so that I could preserve mine, but RICO charges don't work that way. Burke was part of something enormous, and I was suspected of being a part of it. A financial scandal that journalists will still be talking about ten years from now.

Hopefully, I'll just be a footnote. A footnote on a footnote.

Unfortunately, the name Hastings Monahan stands out. This is the first time I have ever wished my name were Jane Smith.

No offense to Jane Smiths.

"You must be so tired," Mom says, looking at me nervously.

I don't know what to say to her. This is the first time since I graduated from college that I've been dependent on my parents. Even when I would come into town, I would stay at hotels, so I literally haven't slept in this room in twelve years.

It's not because I don't love my parents, of course.

It's because I hate being dependent on *anyone*.

And I hate not having control of my environment. If I'd stayed here when I visited, Mom would've shaped my time. In a hotel, I could be on endless calls, work into the night, do what needed to be done to set up the next big deal. Keep the momentum going.

Work. Right.

All that work, twelve years of it–*poof!*

Gone in an instant. Gone with a single strip of plastic that wrapped around my wrists and tied a knot in my life, between two worlds.

"Hastings?" Mom says, her hand on my wrist.

I look at her, jolting, realizing that I'm really here. "Yeah?"

"Coffee? I can go brew some downstairs."

"Oh. That would be nice. I'll take a macchiato."

Mom blinks. "We don't have one of those machines, honey. We just make it the good old-fashioned way. Drip drip drip."

"Oh. Sure, right."

"If you want, we can go to Beanerino. I'm sure they have macchiatos and lattes and cappuccinos."

Dread fills me. "No, Mom, no. I'm good. I'll just take a cup of coffee here."

Mom goes downstairs, and I sit on the edge of my floral print-covered bed. It's a twin. I haven't slept in a twin since…

College.

My phone buzzes. It's either my lawyer or an investigator, and if it's an investigator, I'm supposed to refer them to my lawyer.

"Hastings?" Mom calls from downstairs. "Your dad's coming home from the agency. He would love to sit with us and have some coffee."

I groan. That's code for, *Sharon and Roy want to sit down and have a Serious Talk.*

I can't blame them. If my thirty-four-year-old daughter were hauled away in handcuffs, the arrest televised as a great coup on the part of authorities in San Francisco and federal agents who handle financial crimes, I'd want to sit down and talk, too.

For the last month, they've paid for lawyers—more lawyers than you could ever possibly imagine, private investigators, and consultants I didn't even know existed until now.

Did you know you can hire people to come and clean up your home after it's been purged of everything by federal authorities? Not just regular cleaners, but people who seem to understand the delicacy of these situations.

You can hire PR experts. I don't have any of those. Why bother? There's no coming back from this. Burke screwed me royally in every way but one.

In bed.

And now I find out I was never really married to him.

The front door opens, the sound of Dad shuffling in. I can tell he's taking his shoes off, hanging up his coat, and heading straight to the back of the house, where the kitchen is. I've been gone more than a third of my life, but I still know the rhythm.

Flopping back on the bed, I stare at the ceiling, wondering if the glow-in-the-dark stars are still there from when I was little. Knowing my parents, they probably are.

Mom's nostalgic that way. It's like all of the nostalgia that's supposed to be spread out among a general population got collected into Sharon Monahan. Mallory has a little bit of it, too.

They're both so happy here in Anderhill, Massachusetts. There's no part of them that wants to claw their way up. There's no achiever who strives for more, even when *more* is a moving target. They just *are*. They like what they like, and they know what they like.

And that's why I find them both so infuriating.

"Hastings!" Mom calls up. "Coffee's ready!"

I breathe, a deep inhale that goes down into my belly, pushing it up until I can see it, like a whale breaching the surface. I pull more air inside me, pressing the base of my spine down with each breath, down, down, down. I imagine a basketball centered in my pelvis, my arms out, legs splayed and bent at the knees, and I let it out, all the way out.

Then I do it again, this time holding my abdominal muscles flat with my hand.

It's a calming technique.

It's also a sharpening technique.

Right now, I need calm over sharp.

Facing the inevitable, I grab the small cooler and walk downstairs, expecting to find my mother and father at the kitchen table. My phone buzzes again. It's in my pocket. I grab it and look at it.

Ian McCrory.

Again.

"I bought that almond-milk creamer that you like," Mom says when I walk into the kitchen. "I know almonds are supposed to be bad for the environment, but you don't drink cow's milk, and we can't get sheep's milk easily."

"I would never put sheep's milk in coffee, Mom."

"Oh, I know. It's just that you used to use it when you made cheese."

"Not in my coffee, Mom."

"Oh! Why did I think you did that?"

"I used to do coconut milk in my coffee. But thank you. This'll be fine."

"Well, good, dear." She's getting increasingly nervous. "I just want to make sure that whatever you need, we provide, and I just want to make sure you know that we love you, and…" Her voice descends into a tearful, shaking tone that sets my spine on fire.

"It's fine." I hold up the cooler. She brightens.

"You got to keep that?"

I set it down, press the buttons on each side, and open it. Thirty pounds of accomplishment.

The seven wheels, each four pounds, give or take, have a tang to them that cuts through my existential horror and fills me with a faint hope.

"Can we find room in your fridge?"

"Of course! I knew you still made manchego sometimes, but I never expected this!"

"It's the one thing Burke couldn't take from me," I say, hating his name on my tongue. Between the two of us, we get the wheels in the back of the fridge, where I give them one last loving look.

Mission accomplished.

Couldn't save my money, my reputation, my marriage, or my dignity, but by God, I saved that.

"Hastings," Dad says, standing and putting his arm around my shoulders as I stir the almond milk into my coffee. "This is going to take a long time for you to get over."

"Get… over? Dad, you don't 'get over' something like this."

He frowns at me. "Something's different about you."

"I lost my husband, my job, my home, most of my worldly possessions, and every shred of pride?"

"No. That's not it." He studies me, then snaps his fingers. "Eyelash extensions? Mallory did those a few weeks ago and they really make her eyes pop."

Mom sighs. "Roy." Eyeing his blond hair, she clears her throat repeatedly.

Fishing in his front pocket, he removes his balled-up hand and extends it to her, unrolling his fingers.

A cough drop.

"Roy! She dyed her hair brown!"

Dad studies me. "Nah. That's not it."

In spite of myself, I laugh. We're being played.

"ROY! Are you going blind?"

Giggles take us over as Mom stares at us blankly, then joins in.

Bzzzzzzz

I ignore my phone.

"You will get over this, honey," Mom interjects. "I

promise you will. Burke may have screwed you over–well, he didn't just screw you, he fu–"

"Mom!" I cut her off before she can finish.

"I can say that word sometimes. If there's any time to say it, it's now. Look what he did to you!"

"Mom, stop."

"But he *completely* snowed you. All the while, all those years, he lied to you, and he convinced you, right under your nose, that you—"

"MOM!" The shocked look on her face makes me feel bad, but the rage inside me takes over. "Quit talking about how stupid I am."

"No one said anything about you being stupid."

Dad gives me a look of understanding. "No, you didn't, Sharon. But Hastings *feels* stupid right now."

"Of course I do! Wouldn't you?"

"Yes."

"No!" Mom chimes in, the two of them neutralizing each other. "This could happen to anyone."

"Has it ever happened to you?"

"What? Of course not. I'm married to Roy. We've been married for—how many years have we been married, Roy?"

"Thirty-six."

"I've been married to him for thirty-six years. You don't have four extra wives and a hidden identity, do you, Roy?"

"If I did, Sharon, you'd know."

"I didn't know," I say, holding the cup of hot coffee to my lips and sipping, the action mechanical, devoid of any sense of personhood. "And every time anyone talks to me about this, it's like another piece of my soul gets put through a cheese grater."

"Wow!" Mom says, looking at Dad, then turning back to me. "Thank you."

"For what?"

"For telling us how you feel."

"You're *thanking* me for that?"

"Hastings, you don't talk about feelings. *Ever*. I think the last time you told me about your inner state, you were nine, and it was after you ate a bunch of Girl Scout cookies that you had bought out of your allowance so that you would be the troop's top seller. You just don't *do* this."

Bzzzzzzz

In anger, I pick up my phone and hit Accept. Before he can say a word, I snap, "Leave me alone. I don't need anything from *you*."

"I'm just trying to check in and see how you're doing," Ian says.

"I'm fine."

"Look, Hastings, I wanted to talk to you about—"

I end the call. The last thing I need is to have my former nemesis rub my nose in it.

"Was that your lawyer?" Mom asks.

"No. Just someone who needs to leave me alone."

"*Burke?*" she screeches.

"What? No! I'll never hear from him. Ever. That SOB has disappeared entirely."

"Are you sure the charges are dropped?" Dad asks. "I hate to ask, and I don't want to pick at a raw wound, but..."

"It's all in process. I'll get a formal report soon, but it looks like it. My lawyer advised me to provide testimony about Burke. I shared everything that I know, including personal details you just don't talk about with your parents."

Mom turns bright red.

"I'm sorry that you had to get that, um, intimate, dear," Mom says before gulping half her cup of coffee in one big, long, muted gesture.

Dad's eyes narrow, his lips pursed. Roy Monahan is a

pretty mild-mannered guy, but when it comes to us–me, Mallory, and Mom–we always know he has our backs.

I just hate that I had to learn it the hard way.

"It sounds like you have a good team," Dad says. "We've combed over any insurance policies to see if you had any protection from some of the corporate director's and officer's liability." A hangdog expression makes it clear that he found nothing. He turns his hands up in a gesture of helplessness. "And beyond that, it's all about the lawyers."

"It's always about the lawyers, Dad. Burke was a lawyer."

"Burke was a piece of—"

Before Dad can finish, the front door opens. In walks Mallory, followed by her fiancé, Will. Bright red curls bounce into the kitchen atop round, compassionate eyes.

My sister is here for my homecoming. Of course she is. That's what good people do in small towns, right? Shame burns through me as she smiles the standard-issue Smile of Pity.

You know that smile. The one people give you when they're secretly glad they're not *you*.

"Hasty—Hastings, I mean," Mallory says, coming in for a hug. The last time I saw her, I was here in Anderhill for a dress fitting. She and Will are getting married in June, just four months away.

As if my life weren't bad enough.

As if I haven't lost every single bit of money except for that seven hundred dollars in my bank account.

As if being dragged through the mud weren't bad enough.

As if I weren't humiliated enough.

Life converged my scandal with my baby sister's wedding.

She's marrying Will Lotham, the younger brother of Veronica Lotham, whom I hated with a passion in high school.

Why? Because she was so much like my sister.

Mallory has no ambition. She's happy with her life as is. She's barely ever left Massachusetts or our small town, and Veronica's similar.

Even worse–Veronica's happy with her life *and* ambitious.

That one-two punch was just a little too much, even back in high school. She was that super-nice, sharp young woman who had an internal line she wouldn't cross, and who lacked the killer instinct when it came to final negotiations.

I eat those women for lunch now.

Or at least, until a month ago, I did.

"Will!" I exclaim, pretending to be chipper as he comes in for a hug with eyes that have the same pity in them. It's worse somehow, being looked at like this by him, because he *is* ambitious. And successful. Unlike Mallory, he gets it. He knows what it feels like to go out into the world, climb up a ladder, maybe even build the ladder itself, rung by rung, until you're at the top.

Unlike me, he's still up there.

We all sit down at the small table, Mom pouring cups of coffee and pulling milk and sugar out as we settle into an awkward group. This is what daily life is going to be like until I can get back on my feet.

I'm going to sleep in my childhood bedroom. I'm going to sit at my childhood breakfast table. I'm going to drink coffee from a coffee maker.

I'm going to get the look of pity.

Sartre says that hell is other people, but there is no hell like coming home with your tail between your legs after you've been suckered by a high-end con man who is wanted in six states and three different countries.

A high-end con man you gave your best years to.

This is a special kind of hell, custom-designed for *me*.

"Hastings was just telling us about her…" Mom halts as she realizes maybe I don't want to talk about it.

"Everything's looking good on the legal end," Dad says, rescuing me.

"But how are you? Emotionally?" Mallory asks.

She's so predictable.

And then I do something I didn't predict.

I start to *cry*.

Alarm fills Dad's face as he looks at me. Speechless, Mom's hand goes to the base of her throat, fingers intertwining with her necklace. Will looks uncomfortable, eyes anywhere but on me.

Furiously trying to cover my tears, I grab a napkin from the holder in the middle of the table and dab my lower lids.

"Did you get a cat?" I ask Mom in a nasty, accusatory tone that makes me feel more shame. "These allergies..."

"Hasty…"

"Don't call me that," I snap at Mallory.

"I'm sorry. I'm just going back to… it just feels… well, you're…" Her words come out in fits and starts as she tries to figure out the right way to say it.

"Just spit it out. Go ahead. Call me a loser. A failure. A *sucker*. Use all the words you say behind the scenes when you talk about me with Perky and Fiona. I know how it is now. I'm not just your sister. I am a *topic*."

Acid fills my words.

It has to. Otherwise I'd burn right through from the inside out.

"No! You're not! I don't! Hastings, it's just… I'm so sorry."

Niagara Falls bursts out of my eyes.

"I'm just… so… tired," I say, the tears making my voice shake, "of having people feel sorry for me. Stop saying you're sorry. There's only so… much… pity… I can absorb!"

Stricken, Mallory leans back and takes in a sharp inhale that pauses. She's holding her breath. Have I offended her? Did I cross some line?

The old me wouldn't care, but right now, I don't even know which me I am.

"You're not a sucker." Will's words surprise me, his gaze catching mine. "Burke is the asshole here, Hastings. He snowed a *lot* of people. You're not the only one."

"I was his wife. Or was I? Apparently, I wasn't, but I *was*, so I spent all those years as his closest associate. That's what the investigators stressed. I shared a *bed* with him. Not enough," I huff, making Mom's face turn red. "The asshole didn't even sleep with me for the last year that we were together, but I observed our wedding vows. Wedding vows that didn't even exist. But they did, because we have video of it. So who is the sucker, Will? I think if anyone's the sucker, it's me!" I slam my hand on the table, making the sugar spoon leap off the saucer Mom put it on, the thunk on the table like a guillotine slice.

Why am I doing this?

I'm falling apart, in front of the people who are most likely to…

To what? To hurt me? If I can't fall apart with my mom and dad, and my sister and my future brother-in-law, who *can* I fall apart in front of?

"And, Dad?" This is the part I'm most ashamed of. It wasn't my fault, at all, but I have to tell him, and it's killing me.

"Yeah, sweetie?"

"I, um… they took Great-grandma's ring."

Mom gasps. Mallory's eyes go to my left hand.

"The Feds did? I thought you could keep wedding and engagement rings, even if they take other stuff," he says, shocked.

"I wasn't wearing it. Burke asked for it a couple of weeks before, to get it cleaned and re-appraised, and make sure the insurance was up to date."

Dad's eyes narrow, a cold anger coming over him that terrifies me. "*I* carry the insurance on that ring. He never said a word."

All I can do is blink, as I process what Dad's saying.

"Do you have a complete inventory of all of the assets they seized?" Will asks firmly.

"Not yet."

"I suspect that cheating son of a bitch took it," Dad says, face turning red in anger. "Not the Feds."

"Oh, my *God*," I gasp, then sob, my sounds turning atavistic as I hang my head, feeling even more shame than I thought possible. Not only is a family heirloom gone, what I thought happened to it, didn't.

Yet another way Burke screwed me over.

Only this time, he hurt my poor dad.

"I gave that ring to him when he told me he planned to propose. Said it was sentimental and highly valuable."

"He only heard the last part." I look at Mallory. "I'm so sorry."

"Why are you apologizing to me?"

"Because I would have given it to you. You're the one who's about to have an intact marriage."

Mal just blinks.

Bzzzzzz

I look at my phone. It's Ian, yet again. I don't read the text.

"Look," I say, in the silence I've created around us. "I'm tired. It's been a long day. Sorry for getting emotional."

As I wipe my eyes, Mallory makes a face. "You never have to apologize for having feelings, Hasty."

"Don't call me that," I snap.

"Of course." Mom stands. "Take your coffee up to your room." She chuckles. "You're a grown-up now, so you're allowed to eat in your room."

Something in me dies a little. She sees my face.

"You're allowed to do whatever you want in your room. Of course. It's your room. It's your space. You can eat in there. You can redecorate. We can help you out, sweetie. We can give you a budget so you can go to Bed Bath & Beyond, and—"

"Mom." Mallory stops her. "This isn't helping."

"You can even bring *men* home if you want."

"Mom! Stop!"

"Or women," Mom rushes to say, making Dad start coughing in surprise.

"MOM!" Mal and I say in unison.

"I... did I say something offensive?"

Mallory stands and physically puts her hand over our mother's mouth. Dad just blinks. It's Will who finally cuts through my moment of unreal shame.

"You're not a loser," he says to me. "You're the victim of a con man who operated on the level of Bernie Madoff. Plenty of very smart people got taken in by him. You're Burke's victim."

I flinch.

"Lots of people are. We have a system that allowed him to operate the way that he did for as long as he did. Parker is working on some legislation that will help make it so that financial criminals like Burke can't get away with this." His eyebrows go up and he reconsiders. "Or at least can't do it as *easily*."

The mention of Parker jolts me. Parker Campbell is an up-and-coming member of the House of Representatives from Texas, who happens also to be partnered with my sister's best friend, Persephone. It feels like forever ago that I was in

Boston and we rubbed elbows. He's smart, charming, and comes from money.

For the last month, I've been aided by a team of legal experts, attorneys sent in who refused to tell me the name of the person funding their work. Given the countless hours they've put in, and their hourly rate, it has to be someone with serious money.

Either that, or my parents mortgaged the house to the hilt.

I knew this moment would come. Might as well get it over with.

"Thank you," I say, making eye contact with Mom, Dad, and Will. "I don't know which one of you has been paying for my lawyers and consultants, but they've done an extraordinary job, and I really appreciate it."

The words *I'll pay you back* stick in my throat because, of course, I can't.

I can't even pay for a manicure right now.

Confusion radiates from all of them. "What do you mean?" Dad asks.

"Uh, I mean, thank you to all of you. The lawyers. The consultants. The financial experts. The forensic accountants who've been helping me with everything. They won't tell me who's funding it, but I just assumed it had to be you."

All around the table, heads shake.

"Will? No?" It dawns on me. "Parker? Could Parker be doing this?"

Will shakes his head firmly. "Absolutely not. Frankly, it would look bad for him to have the taint of this scandal attached to him."

The taint of this scandal.

The words echo in my head. That's all I am now. I'm just a scandal to be avoided.

"If it's not Parker, and it's not Mom and Dad or Will," Mallory says, perplexed, "then who is it?"

"Perky? She's rich. Could Perky be the one?" I ask Mallory.

"God, no. Perky hates your guts."

"Mallory!" Mom chides.

I look at her. "I'm not offended, Mom. It's true. I can't stand her, either."

Bzzzzzzz

I look at my phone.

Ian.

Another text from *Ian*.

"Oh, *noooooooooo*," I groan, elbows on the table, fingers lacing their way into my unwashed hair. "*Noooooooooo*."

"What's wrong?" Mom asks.

"I think I know who's been funding everything."

"Who? It has to be someone with significant resources, Hastings, because what you've been describing to us... we wondered, but we didn't want to pry."

Mallory cocks one eyebrow. "Who is it?" A smirk of amusement plays at her lips. I'd almost think it was catty, if I didn't know my sister better.

I finally look at the string of texts that have been coming in steadily from Ian McCrory:

TALK TO ME.
Call me back.
Answer your messages.

THESE ARE ORDERS. COMMANDS.

They're not requests.

I've been ignoring them all along.

"Will you excuse me?" I say to everyone, standing abruptly. I march down the hall, turning to the left, padding my way up the carpeted stairs and back into my bedroom, where I slam the door like the fourteen-year-old I am on the inside right now.

"Ian paid for my team?" I hiss in the privacy of my ten-by-twelve bedroom. "How dare he? Who does he think he is? I never asked for anything from him! Why is he doing this?"

Images from the last month wash over me.

Sitting in a holding cell with my arms behind my back. The press of my bladder and realizing I had no control over when I could even go to the bathroom. Being restricted from taking a sip of water. Having a schedule for food I didn't choose and couldn't eat.

The lawyer who showed up wearing a suit that cost more than my entire net worth–now, at least.

How quickly and swiftly he was able to get me out. Ian is well connected. He would know people.

"Oh, no," I groan, pounding my fists into a pillow. "How could I be so stupid?"

The group of security guards who came for *me*, not for the authorities cleaning out my home but to protect *me*. The financial consultants. The forensic accountants, all of them combing through my personal and corporate records, explaining exactly what I could and could not keep.

It was a short list.

All of that was funded by Ian McCrory.

My phone rings. I stare at it. I have to answer it, don't I? I have to get down on bended knee, hands up in prayer, staring into the wide brown eyes of Ian goddamn McCrory and thank him profusely for everything he's just done for me.

I let the phone go to voicemail and contemplate.

A good person would do that. Gratitude is the appropriate human emotion, but he's the last man on Earth I want to subjugate myself to.

Why would he do this? Why would he spend so much

money on me, *rescue* me, mitigate the damage that my husband—not-husband, ex-husband, never-husband, whatever word you use for that snake, Burke—did? What leverage is Ian trying to gain by helping me?

And what the hell does he expect as *payment* for this?

Fine. I pick up the phone and just do it. I go into Contacts and hit the number, and it rings… and rings… and rings.

Finally, his voicemail kicks in.

"Ian. Hastings Monahan here. I want to thank you. I've just discovered that you're the one behind all of the funding for the help that I've received. The legal team, the forensic accounting, all of it. I appreciate it. Thank you. Goodbye." Pressing the button to end the call feels clean.

Done.

There's no subtlety in my words. I've met the letter of the law in acknowledging what he's done for me and thanking him. Now I would like to have a date with a bottle of Tito's vodka and the first season of *The Witcher.*

Date. The word *date* makes me laugh.

And then it makes me cry. Because today, everything makes me cry, right?

It's in the middle of that crying that the phone rings, the display with the words *Ian McCrory* in big letters making me choke-sob.

Might as well answer it, right? What do I have to lose?

Nothing. I have absolutely nothing to lose.

Literally, *nothing*.

"Yes?" I say, wishing for that Tito's bottle.

"Hastings?"

"Ian?"

"What's wrong?" he asks, picking up on my distress.

"What's wrong? You're asking me what's *wrong?* The Tesla dealership put the wrong floor mats in my new delivery." I laugh through the tears. "What the hell do you *think* is wrong, Ian? Everything. Everything is wrong."

"I got your message."

"Was it a good enough thank you? You've critiqued me on that before."

"I could feel your pain in your words."

I drop the phone like it's a poisonous animal. I haven't set it to speaker, so his voice is tinny as he says, "Thank you for finally contacting me. I wanted to see how you're doing."

I grab it and click Speaker. "You know how I'm doing. You have all of these people working for you, telling you how I'm doing. I'm sure they're sending field reports."

"They tell me the operational aspects of your case. Only *you* can tell me about your emotional state."

"Why would I share that with *you?*"

"Because you sound like someone who needs a friend right now."

"Friend? I saw the news last week, Ian. You stole the deal from me."

"Hold on, now–"

"I can read the newspapers."

"The newspapers can't be trusted on this."

"I'm supposed to take your word for it? Is that how this works? Look, I really appreciate everything that you've done for me over the last month. But that doesn't mean that your slimy little trick is something you can get away with."

"It's not like they were going to work with you after the arrest," he says, the words rolling out of his mouth as if he doesn't want to say them.

But he does.

"I know that."

"Someone had to get the deal, Hastings. And it couldn't be you. Don't begrudge the fact that it was me. It's purely business."

"Don't tell me how to feel. Don't tell me what to think. Don't tell me who to believe. In fact, Ian McCrory, thank you very much for all of your help, but don't tell me *anything* ever again."

I hit the red button.

Silence.

3

It's my wedding day. The gown is soft and stiff against my skin, stretching down, the train ten feet long. Every part of me feels clothed, cloaked in love. My hair is swept up in a twist that leaves the back of my neck exposed to the wind, which kisses me in delight.

A breeze flies, the wisps that didn't make it into my tight knot rising up until I'm looking at the sky, laughing. I take a deep breath. It's like inhaling goodness.

Love has a scent, and on my wedding day, it perfumes everything.

The minister's at the front of the church, and I'm far in the back, my shoes on the slate floor. The bouquet is in my right hand, my left hanging loose by my side. The church is completely full, the ceiling soaring up, up, up, impossibly high, until I realize that this isn't my wedding.

I'm not the bride. But I'm wearing the dress.

Why am I wearing the dress?

Faces turn backward, all of them the same.

Burke.

It's the old Burke, the one who charmed me when I met

him on the docked yacht of an up-and-coming social media titan in the Bay Area. Ten years ago, I was a mere babe, just finished with my MBA. His wild, overgrown curls captivated me as the ocean breeze swept them to one side, our hands holding our cocktails, our eyes meeting, mouths dimpling with a grin of shared connection.

Five hundred–five thousand–faces, all of them Burke, stare at me as I look out into the crowd, the aisle to the altar telescoping.

"You don't have to do this," my father whispers in my ear, suddenly standing beside me, gripping my arm with an intensity that is unlike him. Dad looks so good in a tux, but as I reach up to touch the unfamiliar bowtie at his neck, he turns into a penguin and waddles away.

"Mom!" I cry out, searching the crowd for her.

"The florist is late!" I hear her call from one side. "I'm getting the pew flowers ready right now."

It's too late, *I think, my mouth opening to say the words, when suddenly, five greased pigs come running down the aisle, straight for me. They crawl under the crinoline of my skirt, quickly forming a circle that spins around my calves, the slick oil that covers their bodies making my skin warm.*

I squeal with them, too.

All of the Burkes in the audience laugh, their chins tipped up, broad chests wracked with mocking amusement. That's all I am.

Something to laugh at.

The scent of love turns sour as I twist in place to find a door to escape. The only door is the door to my childhood bedroom.

I grab the doorknob and pull hard, the pigs still whirling around at my feet, thousands of Burkes laughing, my mom shouting about lily of the valley from one side of the church.

When I open the door, a giant squid appears. Tentacles

43

reach all over my body, sucking onto my arms, my legs, the pigs long gone.

The squid's face turns into Burke.

I look down at my body. Thousands of leeches cover it as Burke's eyes bore into mine and he says, "Don't tell them anything."

BEEP BEEP BEEP

I wake up to the sound of a trash truck backing up in my parents' driveway.

I stand and run to my window, looking out. A guy with a tape recorder is chatting with what looks like Tommy, if I remember the guy's name correctly. He's been collecting garbage from our side of the town since I was in middle school. The guy with the tape recorder looks up and sees me in the window, his mouth shifting to an O of surprise. Waving wildly, he tries to get my attention.

I turn away.

"Don't tell them anything," I mutter in a snarky tone, still stung by the end of my dream. I hear someone run quickly down the stairs of the house, flinging open our front door, and then my dad is yelling.

Yelling.

Roy Monahan doesn't yell.

"You get out of here and you leave her alone!" Dad shouts.

"I was trying to tell him, Roy," Tom says, a certain quality in his voice making it clear I *need* to watch this.

Unable to help myself, I peek out the window. The sight of two late-fifty-something guys intimidating the newshound doesn't give me the pleasure it should. Thirty-three days ago, the appearance of a journalist would have filled me with glee.

Being covered in the news represented success, attention, discoverability, visibility.

When you're seen, you can be known.

And when you're known, people want you.

But I don't want to be wanted *this* way.

The media attention has been atrocious. Especially when even Saoirse Cannon hunts me down for a quote. The woman was fired from the region's biggest newspaper and cable news channel after a few back-door whispers from Parker and Perky took care of that when they learned she was behind the release of Perky's famous two-dogs-humping photo.

Now she works for a snarky online gossip site, her interviews on a YouTube channel that hasn't even cracked 1,000 subscribers.

The front door slams shut. Dad doesn't come upstairs. I crawl back into bed and close my eyes, willing my heart to slow down.

I look at my phone. It's not the same one I owned a month ago; that's been taken into custody. I was warned by one of my lawyers that there was no way I'd ever get the same hardware back.

This one, at least, has my contacts. I was able to hand-type all the basics in a too-short window of toe-tapping impatience from some law enforcement officer who treated me like a criminal.

Migrating *everything* over wasn't allowed, though. Someone like me, who's worked in the finance industry for years, relies on a wide circle of acquaintances. I had thousands of contacts in my phone. Have you ever tried to manually move an entire database over, one tap at a time?

I had to prioritize.

I was also naïve. Painfully unaware of how fast I was in free-fall.

I assumed people would call me and I'd be able to capture

their information. Do you know who, among my thousands of contacts, actually called me? Guess.

That's right.

One person.

His name starts with an I. His whole world starts with an I.

Self-centered Ian McCrory.

Tap tap tap

"Hastings, it's Dad."

"Who else would it be?" I muttered to myself. "Come in!"

He's standing there with a mug of hot coffee. "Made it with almond milk. Here," he says.

"How'd you know I was up?"

"Lucky guess. We got rid of that reporter." He eyes me uncertainly. "Third time that's happened, but first time since you got home. It was nonstop back in San Francisco, wasn't it?"

"Yes."

"I'm sorry."

Bzzzzzzz

My phone rings. We both ignore it.

"I knew that you were being pursued by the media, but I didn't realize it would be like this."

"The worst of it's over, Dad. That guy's just a bottom feeder."

"They all are, honey."

Ring

We both look at my phone. I grab it. It's Ian. I hit Decline on the screen.

"Who's that?"

"No one."

Dad backs away. "When you're ready, there's more coffee downstairs. I think your mom's making breakfast."

"I don't want breakfast. No one has to do anything fancy. I'm still just—"

"You've got jet lag, honey."

"I'm pretty sure I have *life* lag, Dad."

We share a smile. I've forgotten how good this feels. How good it feels to just talk to him. To wake up in the morning and have someone bring me a cup of coffee. To be asked about myself.

How am I? The question is a recognition that I'm important. That I exist.

That I *matter*.

Most of my interactions in San Francisco are transactions, not an exchange of caring or compassion. We connect in order to use.

Not to matter.

Ring

Dad's hand is on the doorknob, ready to leave, when he looks at my phone and says, "Whoever's calling is persistent."

"Just an old colleague."

"Is it a job offer? Because you know you don't have to worry. You're fine here, honey. We're taking care of everything you need."

"Dad, stop."

"Okay. I just want you to know, you need to recover, and this isn't about going out and making money—"

"Dad."

Ring

He backs out of the room without another word. The door makes a clicking sound that triggers shivering in me. I rotted in a jail cell just about a month ago.

Suddenly, my childhood bedroom doesn't look so bad.

Ian's going to keep calling me, but I'm done with him.

Beep beep beep

The garbage truck outside maneuvers itself yet again. I sit up in frustration. Might as well go downstairs.

Cup of coffee in hand, I walk down to find Mom making eggs with fresh herbs. It looks like she's assembling some kind of omelet, with shredded cheese and various fresh veggies. Watermelon chunks are in a bowl on the table, with feta and what I imagine is crushed mint on top.

"Morning, honey! Before Dad and I go off to work, I thought we could start with a really nice breakfast."

"I don't eat breakfast."

"Then you can just sit with us at the table and watch as we do."

Ring

I put my phone in my pocket as I was leaving my bedroom. I ignore it now. In fact, I take it out of my pocket and turn it off completely, smacking it down on the counter a little too hard.

"Did you ever find out who's funding all of these lawyers and consultants?" Mom asks, eyes cutting over to Dad. It's clear what they talked about last night.

"No." The lie slips out easily.

"Honey." Mom leans forward, eyes filled with concern. She touches my hand. "Whoever is calling and texting you, if they're a nuisance, you can block them. Or we can do something legal if we have to, to get them to stop."

"It's not that, Mom."

"Then what is it?"

"It's… this business colleague from back in San Francisco."

"What's her name?"

"His name, Mom." I sigh. "His name is Ian McCrory."

Dad sits straight up in his chair. "Ian McCrory? *The* Ian McCrory?"

"You've heard of him," I say, my voice filled with sarcasm.

"Of *course,* I've heard of Ian McCrory. Who hasn't? *Forbes, GQ...* and his predictions on trade policy and how it affects insurance are just stellar. You *know* him?"

"I beat him," I tell them.

Dad's eyes light up with pride. "Beat him? In a deal?"

"Yes."

"Which deal?"

"The Zhangwa deal."

"I'm confused. I read that McCrory just closed that deal last week."

"Yeah. After *I* closed it, the night I was arrested."

"Oh, honey!" Mom says, spearing a piece of watermelon and popping it into her mouth.

"Tell us the whole story, hon," Dad asks.

"I spent the better part of six years putting together a sequence of events that led to a nine-figure deal with Chinese investors. Zhangwa is a Chinese telecom company, and they needed port access, and warehouse and office space, for some climate change products and services. I used hundreds of contacts. Working those led to a network of small deals that I put together to make the big deal happen. Zhangwa was shopping this around for that whole time, and no one else could pull it off. But *I* did!"

"Aren't there regulatory issues that would stop a Chinese firm from–"

I cut him off. "That's Ian McCrory's forte."

"Sounds like the two of you would be a killer combo if you ever worked together."

My eyes widen so much, it feels like my lids are clapping behind my back.

"Er, sorry, hon. Go on," Dad says, burying his nose in his coffee mug.

"The night that the contracts were signed, we were sitting at Essentialz when the Feds came."

Dad nearly chokes on his mouthful of eggs. "He was there?"

"Yes."

"Sniping your deal?"

"What? No. Just..." My voice trails off.

I never thought to ask why Ian was there at the very same restaurant that night.

"What does Ian McCrory have to do with this?"

"He's a scavenger."

"I don't know if that's the right word," Dad replies. "The guy's a self-made billionaire."

"He's a bottom feeder, just like that journalist on the lawn, Dad. He happened to be in the restaurant at the worst possible moment in my entire life. I don't think that's a coincidence. It feels like a setup. And then weeks later, he steals *my* contract."

"That's not what the news says, honey. They said Zhangwa was ready to go with a Russian firm, and Ian was able to broker the deal and keep it in the US."

"What?"

"That's what the *Financial Times* says." Dad's hairline jumps back three inches as a thought occurs to him. "Is Ian McCrory the one bankrolling your defense?"

I let out another sigh. "Yes."

"Why?" Mom and Dad gasp together.

Ring

The house phone. Mom and Dad still have a landline.

Mom jumps up from the table, goes over, and picks it up. "Hello, Monahan residence. This is Sharon speaking. Yes?" She immediately looks at me. "Oh. Yes." Her voice drops. "Hastings, it's for you. It's Ian McCrory's assistant on the line."

"Tell Ian McCrory's assistant that Hastings Monahan is not currently available."

"Honey, *I* am not Hastings Monahan's assistant." Mom thrusts the receiver at me. "Take it," she hisses.

"Tell Mr. McCrory that I am not available," I inform the person on the other end.

"Too late. Caught you in a lie." Ian's deep, amused voice vibrates through the earpiece.

"Why are you stalking me?"

"If I were stalking you, Hastings, you would know it. This is me being friendly."

"Your idea of friendly is close to a surveillance state."

"All you have to do is answer the phone, or return my texts, and I'll back off immediately."

"What do you want?"

"I want to know how you're doing."

"I appreciate everything that you did for me, but please, Ian, back off."

I end the call. It's less satisfying than it would be under other circumstances.

"Honey, that was a bit rude," Mom says. Those words have come out of her mouth hundreds of times, maybe even thousands, over the years that I was raised by Sharon and Roy.

"Maybe tone it down a little," Dad says, as if on cue.

"If a man were to speak that way to another man, you wouldn't second-guess him. Who are you two, the tone police?"

"You're my daughter," Mom says. "It's hard to see you treat people this way."

"What way?"

"The way you treat people."

"I don't treat people in some poor way."

"You can get kind of nasty, Hasty."

"Don't call me Hasty!"

"Isn't it funny? Those two words are spelled the same way. Nasty. Hasty. But they're pronounced differently," Mom muses, as if she's decoding the English language single-handedly.

"Did he do something to deserve all this scorn?" Dad asks, puffing up slightly, a protective aura coming into him.

"He's Ian McCrory, Dad. I'm sure he has plenty of sins in his past. No, he didn't do anything directly to me that's negative. He stole my nine-figure contract, but you explained that."

"Maybe that's why he's calling you. Maybe he wants help with it."

I scoff. "I am the *last* person on Earth Ian McCrory needs to help him with a big deal."

"Then why is he calling you?"

"Why do big game animals play with their prey?"

"You think his motives are that warped?" Mom asks, sitting down at the table and staring at me. "If he wanted to ruin your life or destroy you—"

I let out a little huff. "What's left to destroy, Mom? Besides, the investigators know exactly why my life is ruined. *Burke*."

Dad moves over to the television and flips to a news station. As if conjured by the mere mention of his name, my ex-but-not-ex-husband's face appears on the screen. The caption underneath says:

Burke Oonaj, largest financial fraud scandal in US history.

Dad snaps the television off.

"Can we talk about anything–*anything*–other than Burke, or Ian, or the fact that I can't afford a manicure and my split ends are ridiculous and—"

"I know!" Mom says, cooperating. "I have the perfect topic."

"Great!"

"Let's talk about Mallory and Will's wedding."

My gut aches as I curl it in. "You know," I say, standing, "I think this is a good time to go for a run."

"You still run?" Dad asks.

"Of course. I try for twenty miles a week. Most of the time I fit it in around Pilates, but it works."

Pilates.

All my personal training sessions are something from the past. Even a basic gym membership is out of my financial reach right now. I have workout clothes in the handful of suitcases I was allowed to bring.

Running is free. All it costs are shoe soles.

I walk away before Mom and Dad can say anything else, and thump up the stairs. It takes three searches through each of my bags to assemble all the layers I need for a winter run, plus running shoes. My hundreds of pairs of shoes are consolidated now to a pragmatic set of five, and by "consolidated," I mean, the rest were *seized*.

But these running shoes are fairly new. I pull them on. I go downstairs and realize I don't have a Fitbit. I don't have airpods. I don't have–

I don't have *anything*, do I?

Might as well run in silence.

As my feet hit the sidewalk that leads out to the main road, I take deep breaths of the cold mid-February air. It's at least another six weeks before spring rolls around, and when you live in New England, you never know when a late-winter snowstorm will dump two feet on you.

I've been in Northern California for twelve years, so it hasn't been a consideration.

I look up at the sky. The clouds are gray, like sad, dirty cotton, a bank of them threatening something sinister. No flurries dot the air, though. As I start to run, my calf muscles screaming, either in pain or gratitude, I let the cold penetrate me.

My body isn't used to feeling. It hasn't been allowed to express itself for a long time.

The great thing about running is that you don't have to express anything other than one foot in front of the other.

By the time I come back two hours later, bladder full and body parched, there's an Audi SUV in the driveway. Must be Will's car.

Sure enough, when I go in, Will and Mallory are at the dining table. It's eleven a.m., so I'm guessing they're breaking for lunch with Mom, but then again, Will works for himself, Mal works for him, and Mom and Dad own their own insurance agency.

Their time is theirs to rearrange.

So is mine, but for very different reasons now.

I chug sixteen ounces of filtered water, missing my fortified, electrolyte-balanced water from home–er, my old life. Five weeks ago, a run like that would be capped off with a macronutrient-optimized protein shake, a salt-scrub shower, and ten minutes of breathing technique designed to pump oxygen into every tissue in my body.

Instead of *that*, I'm drinking filtered tap water and eyeing a jar of peanut butter and a nice Honeycrisp apple in a bowl on the counter.

"Hey!" Mallory calls out to me with a wave, Will on his phone. They're seated next to each other with a series of battle plans spread out in front of them. Tiny taster bottles of wine, little candies in twenty-seven different foil colors, and ribbons galore are laid out like a vision board.

This is Mallory's thing.

She loves the way objects can be arranged in space to evoke emotion.

And she's *good* at it.

I've made fun of her for years. Not for what she does, but for her lack of ambition. Who takes natural talent and doesn't use it?

Then again, what would I know about natural talent? I don't have any. Everything I do has to come from great effort. Everything I do has to come from outperforming everyone else.

I don't understand my own sister. Never have.

But as I watch Will, Mallory, Mom, and Dad, all around the dining table, talking animatedly about wedding details, it hits me.

Maybe *I'm* the one nobody understands.

✂ 4 ✂

I hate to admit this, and don't ever tell Mallory I said it, but...
　　She's right.
But only about Taco Cubed.

Ever since that dinky little Mexican place opened up, just as I was leaving the East Coast, Mallory has raved about how good it is. I resisted.

First of all, the name is stupid. Who names a restaurant TacoTacoTaco?

Second, there's no way that Mexican food can be better in Anderhill, Massachusetts, than it is in California.

Third... the guy running the counter is *hot*.

Wait. Where did that come from?

Mom and Mallory insisted that we have lunch here. Mom's picking up the tab. A few months ago, I would have come, pulled out a platinum Amex, and paid for everything. Why?

It made me feel good to have that kind of money. It made me feel good to know that I had accomplished something.

Also, there's a certain kind of control that you have when you're the one picking up the check.

I'm sure a therapist would have a field day with me, but I can't afford one now.

"Mallory!" says the heavily tatted-up dude at the counter. "The blushing bride."

"Pedro, stop!" Mallory says.

He has a teardrop along the side of one eye, every bit of the backs of his hands covered in ink. Thick biceps threaten to split a cut-off flannel shirt cuffed at the ends, right over the largest bulge of his arms. He smells like fresh lime and a heady, masculine cologne.

The guy is totally not my type.

Our eyes meet.

"And who is this?" he asks, one eyebrow going up, expression morphing instantly into lust. Think I'm exaggerating? His eyes go straight to my left hand.

I took the wedding ring off long ago. Burke had my engagement ring for reappraisal when he ran off, and it looks like the feds confiscated it. No remnant of my marriage is on my finger right now.

I am a free woman.

And yet...

I could sleep with this guy. I could go to his apartment with him when his shift is done and screw his brains out, then head back home, climb into my twin bed next to my Lisa Frank posters, and...

And *what*?

I wouldn't be breaking any wedding vows, would I? Because it turns out I was never married in the first place. All these years I've been with Burke, I've held myself to an ethical standard based on a vow that didn't exist.

A *husband* who didn't exist.

Possibility hangs in the air between us as Pedro stares me down.

"You must be Mallory's sister," he says. "What kind of meat do *you* like?"

"What kind have you got?"

"I've got a lot."

"I'm sure I'll leave as a satisfied customer."

Mom gives me a wide-eyed look designed to paralyze me. "Hastings," she hisses.

"What? I'm putting in an order."

"I don't think you're ordering the same thing we are," Mal says under her breath.

"You've got a fiancé and I've got a court date, so you do you and I'll do me."

"I think you're trying to do *Pedro.*"

Mom looks at Pedro. "*I* will do the daily special. Chicken soft tacos."

"Mom!" Mallory practically screams. "Never soft taco. You never go soft taco."

Pedro's eyes jump from Mom to Mallory. Mine, mean-while, are pinned to the ceiling. "Mom," I say, laying a hand on her elbow, "Mallory's right."

They both freeze.

"I am?" Mal gasps.

"Soft tacos are an abomination." I turn to Pedro. "I'll take three crispy tacos with cubed chicken, lettuce and tomato, shredded cheese, sour cream, guacamole, and mild salsa on the side. Green salsa, actually." I change my mind at the last second.

"That's *my* order!" Mal says.

"It's not the *order,*" I explain to her. "It's the *ratio.*"

Her mouth goes into a perfect O. My sister looks like a blow-up doll.

Mom closes her eyes slowly. "You, too, Hasty?" she whispers.

"Me, too–what?"

"Two Crazy Mals comin' up!" Pedro shouts to the back, where workers wearing plastic hair caps and gloves start moving fast.

I look at Mallory. She shrugs.

"That's what Pedro calls my order." She looks at me uncertainly. "Do you… do you eat yours with peanut butter?"

"Peanut butter?"

"I know, it sounds really weird, but Fletch—oh, never mind."

Mom hands her credit card over to Pedro, who eyes me as if my chest is a glass screen and he's swiping right nonstop.

"You in town for long?" he asks.

"I'm in town forever." Feels like it, anyway.

"If you ever get bored, or you just want, you know, some good meat, come on by."

"I'll keep that in mind."

"She's *married!*" Mom interrupts.

He shrugs. "That never stopped me before, Sharon."

"Pedro! Does your father know that you—"

"Mom, I'm not married. Remember?" I interrupt her.

A lightbulb goes on in Pedro's eyes. "Wait a minute." He looks at Mallory, Mom, then me. "Monahan. You're *Hastings* Monahan, the one that's all over the news! I never made the connection before. Oh, man, I am so sorry."

What had been naked self-interest, with an emphasis on the *naked* part, suddenly becomes pity.

Pity eyes are a tool of the devil.

I walk down to the order pickup section, ignoring him. Mallory's on my heels. We get to the end, where I start tapping my toe.

"I'm sorry," she whispers.

"About what? Mom's soft tacos?"

"Oh, no. I *am* sorry about that, but no. I mean, I'm sorry about Pedro."

"It's fine. I get that a lot. I got it back home—" I correct myself. "California,*"* I say, emphasizing the word with my body: hands out, palms up in supplication.

"It's not like you came back here a lot. I mean, people remember you, but—"

"Hastings!" Amelia Wissen walks up to us. "Oh, my goodness! I heard about what happened to you. I am so sorry."

I accept her pity hug.

There's no pity in Mallory's expression as she watches us, thank God. There may even be a dawning understanding of what the last month of my life has been like. Empathy was always Mallory's strong suit, and it made me view her as weak.

With brains, no ambition, and piles of empathy, how did she even function?

The comfort I feel in her presence is making me rethink everything I know.

"Amelia! So good to see you. I think I heard you're running a preschool?"

"Oh, I do that on the side. It's my grandmother's foundation. I'm actually the director of a nonprofit that brings injured children over to the United States for reconstructive surgery after they lose a limb from a land mine."

High-quality global philanthropy in *that* narrow a niche? I don't know what to say. I'm speechless.

I just stare at her. Nervousness kicks in and she says:

"It started with a simple donation and went from there when—well, it's a long story."

"I'm curious. Really."

"Oh!" She seems surprised that I would be interested. "I

saw a GoFundMe for someone who had adopted a child who had lost a limb, and the reconstructive surgery was going to be expensive to help this child have the best chance to walk, and I donated and learned more, found out about the success, and... I don't know how to explain it."

"You've always loved children," Mallory says, smiling at Amelia and giving her a quick hug.

"Can't be on the board of a preschool and not."

"And you're a mother," Mallory adds.

"Yes."

"How many kids?" I ask, knowing how this works. Most of the women my age, at my level–well, *former* level–of business, don't have kids. Yet. Like me, they engaged in egg retrieval and freezing in their early twenties. Late thirties, at best, is when I'll be ready to...

Right.

Damn.

All of my plans dissolved when they arrested me.

Amelia's joyful grin shakes me out of my thoughts. "I have two. They're four and three. What about you, Hastings? Do you have kids?"

"No."

"And—oh, right."

The way she closes off is a reminder that–*oh, right.*

I have no life.

From behind the counter, someone calls out her name. She turns and looks at the tray. "I'll see you around!"

"Okay. Bye."

Shallow encounters used to be my forte. It was part of how I networked, the social glue of connection being a way to make money, to gain power, to have influence, to *matter*.

None of that works here, at least not the way that it did in the Bay Area.

It especially doesn't work now, because I am radioactive.

What do you do with radioactive waste? You contain it. You let it sit and sit and *sit* until it degrades, but it takes thousands of years.

I don't have thousands of years, and I certainly don't want to be *contained.*

"Sharon!" calls someone from behind the counter.

I look over. Our trays are there, Mallory staring at me with concern.

"What?" I grab my tray and move.

She takes hers, Mom appears, and the three of us head for an open table as Mallory starts talking to me.

"You're going to experience that over and over. It's not going to stop until some other scandal kicks in."

"How would you know?"

"Because I went through it when I was caught on that porn set. And Perky went through it when her two-dogs-humping picture was everywhere. Fiona went through it when she had to disable the attacker in her preschool classroom. It's how this works."

"It's not *my* fault Burke did what he did."

"Fault doesn't matter, Hasty."

"Stop it. Call me Hastings."

"Fine. Hastings. Fault doesn't matter. You know that."

Fault doesn't matter.

"What matters is keeping your head down."

Mom takes the chair to my right, Mallory sits across from me. Like a mirror image of myself, she shifts the position of everything on her tray: the sour cream, the salsa, the guacamole. A separate knife for each one. The tacos themselves set up just right.

As we organize our ratios to be perfect, a little voice starts whispering in my head. *When did Mallory and I ever have something in common?*

"You, too?" Mom moans, looking at my carefully assembled tray. "Can't you just *eat* tacos?"

"That would be a waste," we say in unison.

Mallory jolts, eyes wide, a curl bouncing over her eyebrow. "When did you—"

"When did *you?*"

"Really? All this time?"

"Maybe you learned it from me," I tell her. "This is just another one of those annoying little sister things, where you watched me create the perfect ratio and then you decided that you were going to be just like me, and—"

"No! We never ate here together during my formative years, when I was learning how important the ratio was. By the time this place opened, you were gone. You came here for my wedding dress fitting, but other than that, *no.*"

Mom purses her mouth, fingertip touching her lips, tapping slowly. "You know, Mallory's right. Dad and I have never taken you both here at the same time. Maybe it's a genetic thing, a recessive gene that skipped right past your father and me, but when we conceived you, it just—"

"Mom! Stop! *Stop!* We don't wanna hear about our conceptions when we're staring at sour cream, of all things!"

Mallory's words make me choke. Mom starts banging on my back with a closed fist while Mal shoves a glass of water at me. I sip it, laugh-choking. Water shoots up into my sinuses, and now I'm burning, choking, and laughing at the same time.

The very same body that doesn't feel anything, suddenly feels too much.

It takes longer than it should for me to calm down, but when I finally do, my throat is raw and ragged as I say, "Natural selection is at play, Mom. We're making a species shift, like going from Neanderthals to humans."

"How can you eat soft tacos like that? How can you not

take into account the ratio, the mouth feel, the macronutrients?" We turn toward the man's enquiring voice to find Chris Fletcher standing there, holding a takeout bag, grinning at our mother as his words sink in.

"Fletch!" Mallory says.

Mom turns around. "Christopher! Good to see you."

"Good to see you, too, Mrs. Mon—I mean, Sharon."

"Nice catch," she says. "What're you doing here?"

He holds up his bag. "Loading up on macronutrients."

"Aren't you worried the taco shells will be too damp by the time you get home?" Mallory asks, mirroring my thoughts exactly.

"That's why I gotta go. Just wanted to say hi." His eyes meet mine. "Hey, Hasty. Hope things are going well. See ya." He takes off.

The use of my nickname, the one that I didn't pick, one that was imposed on me by the apparently irresistible human need to stick a *y* on the end of a dignified adult name and thereby reduce its owner to toddlerhood, makes me bare fangs I don't possess.

"You really hate that," Mom says to me.

"*I* hate when hard-shell tacos get damp," Mallory says as she carefully assembles her sour cream, her guacamole, and her salsa on the edge of her taco shell. Her technique is exceptional.

I'm viewing my sister through a new lens.

"I do. Hasty is a stupid nickname. Hasty rhymes with pasty."

"That's a little porny," Mal says.

I glare at her.

"Hasty rhymes with tasty," Mom says.

"Tasty Pasty. *That* sounds like a porn name."

"Mallory," Mom chides her. But her eyes float up to the

ceiling, as if she's thinking. "Hmm. Basty, daisy, faisty, gaisty, hasty, jaisty, kaisty…"

"Mom, what are you doing?"

"I'm running through the alphabet to see all of the words that rhyme with Hasty. Maisty, nais—nasty, pasty, sais—"

"You forgot q."

"Quaisty? That doesn't work."

"As if any of the other ones do?"

"Tasty, vaisty, waisty, yaisty—"

"That's a little too close to yeasty."

"And zaisty. Hmm. Nope. Tasty Pasty Hasty it is."

"You've just found an even worse nickname that has absolutely nothing to do with Hastings."

"Well, I'm Fluffy," Mallory jokes.

"Can we just focus on the ratio? Let's ignore Mom, but you and me–" I gesture across the table, waving in the air between us "–can we just eat in peace? Because you're ruining my taco nirvana."

There's that O face again from my sister.

"You call it that, too?"

"I called it that *first.*"

Anger sparks between us. Perhaps the sparks are from my teeth grinding together like two pieces of flint. I don't know why I'm suddenly livid. I can feel my pulse pounding in my hands, Mallory an easy target, low-hanging fruit I need to pluck. It's not fair. I know that.

But emotions are never fair.

Studying me like I'm her dissertation project, Mallory takes her time, watching as I munch on my perfectly layered taco, before finally saying, "You look tired."

"Mnx," I mumble through my mouthful.

"No," Mom interrupts. "She looks depressed."

"Urf?"

Great. Now I sound like Scooby Doo.

I swallow long before I'm ready and regret it immediately.

Mal adds, "I'd be tired, too, if I were you. *And* depressed. I can't imagine Will doing to me what Burke did to you."

I didn't know that pity was one of the sides that come with your lunch here at Taco Cubed. Didn't order any of *that* from the menu.

Especially not the extra-large size.

"I am fine," I inform them. "I'm not in a jail cell. No civil suits. Paparazzi aren't chasing me, much. I was allowed to keep five whole pairs of shoes. I," I say through the appalling tear storm that hits me, "am just *fine*."

I sob.

"Shit," Mom mutters under her breath, which makes me realize just how far gone they all think I am, because when Sharon Monahan utters a dirty word like *that*, you're a lost cause.

Mallory hands me a paper napkin for my tears. I use it. I take a deep breath, the scent of cumin and fresh tomatoes giving me life.

Enough with depression.

I'm done.

I did not attend an expensive Hawaiian retreat with one of the best motivational speakers in the world–a guy who appeared on *Oprah* numerous times–just to let myself wallow like I have since I got home. I've run a hundred and seventy-two miles, cleaned my bedroom at least twice, taken seventeen bags of old clothes to Goodwill, and organized the shelves in Dad's garage to the point of being banished from his workshop refuge.

It's time to get my act together.

"I've got to look for a job."

"Do you want some help?" Mal asks gently. "Will could–"

"No. Thank you." Gratitude was never, ever my strong

suit, so this feels awkward, like stretching a too-tight bra over a too-big chest. I do it anyway, because it's all I've got. "I–I appreciate it."

Mom and Mal stare at me, leaving space for my words, open swaths, football fields of space. I'm drowning in my own feelings, arms flailing, begging for help to get to shore, to stop swimming in these dangerous waters.

Emotional oceans are so, so deep.

"We're here for you," Mom and Mal say in unison, making me feel like I'm not even related to them, as if my DNA splintered off somehow, the branch my development took so distant that I'm another species.

My hand goes to my heart. "This… my..." I stutter, fighting to find words.

"That's called your heart, Hasty," Mallory says, making me laugh.

But when I look at her, she's completely serious.

In the days and weeks after my arrest, as the details about Burke slowly unfolded, and especially as my assets were seized, I came to realize that everything was gone. Our cars were taken away. Our homes were taken away. Every bank account was frozen. And who carries cash these days?

I was left with seventeen US dollars in random bills and coins in my purse, a fifty-Euro note and a handful of pounds in coin from the UK, a Nordstrom's gift card with three hundred and thirty-seven dollars left on it that was given to me by someone at my firm for some reason I don't remember, and that was it.

That was all the money in the world I had access to after the accounts were shut down. Somehow, the Feds let me have $700, which I used to get a secured credit card. That's *it*.

I still have the Nordstrom's gift card and the foreign currency. It's my emergency backup.

A mix-up, I'd assumed at first. Being the victim of a

computer glitch was actually easier to fathom than the truth. Of course, I'd assumed, in a couple of days, I'd have access to all the money I'd carefully accumulated with my husband, right?

My money?

But as interrogators sat across from me in rooms with twitching fluorescent lights that made everything seem so much more gravid, reality intruded. Invaded.

Conquered.

I was a chump. A sucker. A mark.

What I had thought was *my* money was just an illusion.

Here's the issue with being a scandal: No one who has assets wants to talk to you. The only people who call are the gossip mongers. The ones with no real power. I gained the attention of the pettiest people in my social circle, the ones I had only tolerated because they had some connection to the people who actually *do* things.

But when the people who actually do things want nothing to do with *you*, what do you do?

You come home. You stare at your Lisa Frank posters. You run ten miles a day. Sometimes twice a day.

And you cry over a taco while your mother and sister give you pity eyes.

Then you go home and job search.

After eating the perfect ratio, of course.

And letting them group-hug you until the crushing weight of failure is just a tiny bit lighter.

THE LAST TIME I DRAFTED A RESUME FOR MYSELF WAS LAST year, for HR files at the venture capital firm I work for.

Worked for.

Boston is rife with companies I can approach, but here's

the other little problem with having been arrested on RICO charges and being married—but *not* married—to the biggest financial con artist in American history.

No one wants me anywhere near their computer system.

No one wants me in their office.

They don't even want me *applying*.

Funny, that.

I am *persona non grata*. Even when I recreated my phone contacts, they were useless. The only person from my old life who calls me is Ian, and—

Ring

I look at my phone. Speak of the devil.

A very hot devil.

Ignoring the phone, I boot up the desktop computer that my father moved into my bedroom shortly after I arrived. You can do a lot on a smartphone and a tablet, but you can't do *all* of your work from them.

My laptop is still seized.

The mouse, a corded one, is unfamiliar in my hand. I'm so used to trackpads. This is a PC and I use a Mac, so nothing feels quite right, even though I know all the components are there.

It's a metaphor for my life.

I find my way to one of the major jobs sites, a deep curl of rage starting in my belly. This isn't my life, right? Burke turned me into a pariah. I've done nothing wrong. The charges against me are a formality. In exchange for my freedom, I've given investigators every piece of information I can.

I guess it wasn't enough, because they also took a chunk of my soul.

That, and almost all my worldly possessions. And then they informed me that Burke was allegedly hiding out in a country that does not have an extradition agreement with the United States. Nobody is sure which one.

It is also a country where he is, allegedly, *legally* married to a woman.

A woman who is not me.

What is she like?

Stupid question, I know, but it burns the edges of my ragged dignity when I can't sleep at night. Is she clueless? Does Burke control what she sees in the media? Keep her secluded from the truth?

Or is she in on the con, a full partner, his slithering mind working in concert with his feminine equal?

And what am I to her?

That's the point where I usually punch my pillow and go for a three a.m. run.

The search bar for the jobs site sits there, empty, taunting me.

What are you gonna put in there, Hastings? it asks, almost pulsating as I listen to my heart beating slowly.

Venture capital partner, I type in the search bar.

VP of business development.

As I go through each search term, I see that every single one of these jobs is below my pay grade, below my experience grade, below–beneath–*me.*

I have to try, though. I can't live at Mom and Dad's house forever.

I can't stand living *off* them.

After much sorting and sifting, I find five positions that don't make me clench my teeth so hard that I chip a tooth. It takes me nearly two and a half hours to sort through and find these five, because so many of the jobs that I am qualified for are in the divisions of people who won't return my calls.

They're contacts in my phone who never answer.

Why waste more energy on them?

I craft cover letters for each of the five, upload, and send.

This is what I'm reduced to. From a six-figure-a-year (soon to be seven) VC firm associate to someone who applies for jobs with the word *director* in the title.

But you know what? Directors get salaries. Benefits. Staff. They work on a team, and they have purpose.

So director, here I come.

A shower gives me some new perspective. As I head downstairs to grab a cup of coffee before going out for a run, my phone buzzes in my pocket.

My pulse leaps. Already? Someone's read my resume and already they want an interview?

No. It's just Ian.

I have some questions.

That's it? That's all he wrote? *I have some questions?*

That's almost as bad as Burke's *I'm sorry.*

What is it with these men who think I'll jump to answer their cryptic texts? Why haven't I blocked him?

Not Burke, *Ian.*

I'm supposed to keep all lines of communication one hundred percent open when it comes to Burke, so that I can get some information out of him if he ever weasels his way back into my life.

Ian, on the other hand, I can block at will. So why haven't I?

So do I, I type back quickly. *How much did my legal defense cost?*

Three dots appear. *One dinner with me.*

I power my phone off.

Great. What does he want? Sex, in exchange for what he did for me? Is that his price? I knew it would be high, but...

Heat rushes to my face at the thought.

It's not from anger.

And my face isn't the only place where heat pools.

Forget the coffee. I grab my full bottle of water and burst out the front door.

When I run, I'm not Hastings Monahan.

When I run, I'm not Burke's not-wife.

When I run, I am not Ian's project.

I'm not Mom and Dad's pity face, not the sister of the blushing bride who's getting everything she ever dreamed of.

I'm just two legs, two arms, a head, and a torso, moving forward in space.

My ponytail thumps against the back of my neck, a steady presence, a second heartbeat. I know when I get home and turn on my phone, there will be more from Ian.

Do I want more from him?

No. What I want is *less.* Of everything.

Five miles disappear into a flow state, a numbness that isn't about performance. Running used to be performative for me. I chose the best paths, the right clothes, the good form, using Pilates and personal trainers to help me perfect my body in motion.

Isn't that the goal, to perfect ourselves? To reach ever-higher levels of functioning? There must be a peak somewhere. I wouldn't know where it is, but I kept raising the bar, over and over again as I achieved more and more. It felt good. It felt right.

Until... well, until stupid Burke.

Until stupid *me.*

I go for twelve miles. By the time I make it home, there's a note taped to the coffee maker.

Ian called again, Dad's careful handwriting spells out.

I turn on my phone to find the expected text message:

I'm in Boston is all it says.

Good for you, I reply.

It is good, he types back immediately. *This Bruins game is crazy. Too bad you're missing it.*

I don't like hockey.

What do you like? he writes back.

Being left alone.

You wouldn't answer my texts if that were true, Hastings.

Endorphins pump through me, the good kind that running elicits. It's why I push myself so hard, now. Before, in my old life, I did it to relieve stress, to stay slim and toned, to wear the right outfit and run with the right people.

None of that matters here. Now running is an escape.

Ian keeps chasing me, though. Why? And why does the fact that he won't let up thrill me?

That's the part I hate. The thrill. The zing of arousal that shoots through me every time that jerkface–who isn't a jerk–does this. He's pursuing me and I don't understand it, but I do like it.

More than I want to admit.

The fight inside me feels like layers of muscles in my abs are in a tug-of-war. Ian McCrory represents everything I fought to achieve in my old life. Self-made billionaire. Liked by everyone. Admired by even more.

Respected for his hardcore negotiating skills.

And droolingly handsome.

He was my nemesis. My enemy. The guy who sniped deals, and who I sniped *from*. We were adversaries, but he flipped the script, didn't he? Coming to my rescue. Aiding me in a time of need.

I don't want to need him.

And I especially don't need to want him.

I stare at the phone. Just as my finger goes to the Power button to turn it off again, three dots appear.

One dinner. Indulge me?

I go into my contacts, and I block him.

He just proved me right.

Taking help from people means you're obligated.

And no matter how sweet the currency he's dangling, I don't like owing him.

I don't like owing anyone.

Burke turned my entire life into one big debt.

But my body isn't available as collateral.

And neither is my heart.

I t's been two weeks since I applied for those five jobs. Since that first day, I've applied for a grand total of twenty-seven positions. Do you know how many interviews I've had?

Zero.

Do you know how many rejections I've received?

Twenty-seven. Most of them in ten minutes.

Mallory insists that the bridesmaids gather today at Beanerino, the "fancy" coffee shop that Perky's part of. We're planning the bachelorette party.

Please, kill me now.

"Here, honey," Mom calls out as she walks toward me, holding her purse, rummaging through her wallet. She thrusts two twenties at me.

"What's this?" I ask, recoiling from the cash, looking around to make sure no one saw that. The only person who would see it here at home is Dad, but even that's too much for my battered ego to handle.

"So you can go out with the girls. You know, get your coffee at Beanerino, have lunch, plan the bachelorette party...." Her voice trails off as she looks at my hand by my side, the lines between her eyes deepening in confusion.

"You're handing me *cash*."

"Do you want us to add you to our bank account so that you can have a debit card?"

"You're giving me money so I can go out to lunch."

"Well…" Mom reddens. "I thought it would be the nice thing to do. I didn't want you, uh, you know. Stranded."

"Stranded?"

"I wanted to help you save face. I'm sure Mallory could pick up the check for you. Or maybe even Perky."

"*Perky?*"

"Well, she *is* rich. Her parents won all that money in the lottery, all those years ago."

"I don't need other people to—" I cut myself off.

Oh, my God.

I *do* need other people to pay for me, to support me, to help me.

To *pity* me.

I don't need that last one, but it comes right along with needing help.

I have been reduced to a teenager who has to be handed fun money before going out.

Scratch that.

I have been reduced to the equivalent of a *fifteen-year-old*, who can't legally have a job yet, who has to be handed money in order to go out.

Something makes my stomach hurt. If I were a different person, I would call it shame.

"Um, thanks," I say, loathing myself as I reach forward and take the cash, stuffing it in my back pocket as fast as possible, as if hiding it from sight makes this more palatable. "I'll pay you back."

Pity eyes meet mine. "Of course you will, honey."

I decide to run to Beanerino. *Decide* is a bit much, given that I don't have a car. I either have to beg Mom or Dad to use theirs, or call an Uber. Given that I'm at a point where my mother is handing me forty dollars so that I can go have fun with my sister and her friends as we plan her wedding to a guy whose net worth is surely seven–or even eight–figures, I'm going to hide my poverty under the guise of going for a run.

Anderhill has not changed much since I left twelve years ago. Better coffee shops, upgraded traffic lights, and a few new developments, but other than that, it's the same town that I was born and raised in.

Beanerino is an old fast food restaurant turned into a coffee shop and wine bar. I pause before I go in, wiping sweat off my brow, taking a moment to compose myself. Hanging out with Mallory is one thing.

Perky and Fiona are quite another.

As I step inside the coffee shop, the scent of finely roasted beans making me flash back to one of the premier shops in the Bay Area, Mallory calls out my name.

"Hastings!" She's always so damn cheery.

And yet, I smile.

"Did she just smile at you?" Perky asks now.

"Yes, why?" I overhear Mallory answer as I stand at the counter.

"Maybe it was just gas," Fiona says.

Tension forms in my neck. My sister might be perpetually friendly, but her friends are jackals in human form. They're protective of her. I get it.

When we were little, so was I.

"Hey there," says the barista, turning to me. He's got broad shoulders, thick arms, and eyes the color of my favorite whisky. "What can I get for you?"

"Double shot of espresso."

"That's it? Just straight up double shot?"

"That's it."

"Get whatever you want, Hastings," Perky calls out. "It's all on me."

The four other people in the shop turn and look at me.

"I'm fine," I say, holding up a twenty.

She shrugs. I grab a sparkling water and pound it on the counter.

"You know Perky?" the barista says.

"Yeah. She's my sister's best friend."

"Sister? I didn't know Fiona had a sister."

"I'm not Fiona's sister."

"Wait. Mallory's sister? You–*you're* Mallory's sister? Why have I never met you before?"

"Because until last week I didn't live here. I lived in San Francisco."

"So you must be Hastings."

"Yes."

"Hastings Monahan." Lightbulbs turn on in his eyes. "I've heard a lot about you."

"All of it good, too," I say with a smile. "Right?"

"No," he says seriously, either unable to read my social cues or so earnest, he might as well be Mallory's twin brother. "No. Not all of it good. I'm really sorry about what happened to you."

Oh, great. From whisky eyes to pity eyes.

"Uh… thanks. I'm fine."

He slides the twenty back to me over the counter. "I'll just put it on Perky's tab." He leans in. "I heard Burke Oonaj cleaned you out."

"Okay," I choke out, grabbing the double shot and the water, and slinking off to sit with my sister and her friends.

"What did you tell him about me?" I hiss as I slide into the booth next to Perky.

"What?" she asks, eyes a little too wide, a little too innocent.

"He said he'd heard a lot about me, none of it good."

"Raul? *Pfft*. He's a little…" She takes her finger and twists it around her ear. Perky doesn't realize he's right behind her, holding a wine glass, drying it with a white bar towel.

"You told me that Mallory's sister was the biggest bitch you had ever met in your entire life, and that in all of bitch-dom, she was at the top. That her name should be Hastings McBitcherson Monahan. You said that you—"

Perky cuts him off. "Thank you for being my own personal embarrassment curator, Raul."

"It would take a much bigger expert to manage that role, Perky."

The front door opens and a group of eight teenagers walks in, all lining up as Raul makes his escape back to the counter.

I look at her.

With flat eyes, she says, "Bitch? Bitchdom? McBitcherson? Do you deny it?" She's trying to provoke me.

I just smile. "No. Proud of it, actually."

She gives me a lopsided grin.

"Birds of a feather," Fiona says, sipping delicately from her macchiato.

"I'd better be careful what I say to *you,*" I mutter. "You'll pin me to the floor with a victory roar."

"Don't tempt me," Fiona replies.

"Besides, I am nothing like Perky. First of all, my fashion taste is far above hers." I eye her. "Although good job dressing today, Perky. You've upgraded from clothing dona-tion bin in Las Vegas to lost-and-found box in a Unitarian Universalist social hall."

"Hey!"

"And second of all – "

"This is not how I thought we would plan my bachelorette

party," Mallory interjects. "Can you all stop? Stop competing to be the biggest bitch in bitchdom, and let's decide which piano bar we're going to."

"Piano bar!" Perky and I gasp in unison.

"Eww! That's so..." Descriptors defy me.

"So what?"

"So... 2000s."

"Don't even," Perky jokes. "What's your next idea, Mal? Karaoke?"

Perky and I snicker as Fiona turns to Mallory and says, "I think that's a great idea!"

"The only way to do a bachelorette party," I say sarcastically, because it's the last thing I'd choose, "is to go to Vegas for the best spa you can possibly afford."

"Given that *we're* the ones throwing the bachelorette party," Perky says, pointing to me and Fiona, "along with Raye, of course, and Will's sister, Veronica, anything is doable."

Perky has a trust fund, I know, from when her parents won the lottery. Is she planning to bankroll all this?

"It's my treat," she declares, as if reading my mind.

"Perky, you can't!" Fiona gasps.

"Of course I can! I have plenty of money!"

I put my hand on her arm. "We do have to be careful."

"Why?"

"Because of Parker."

"Parker's not invited to the bachelorette party."

"No, but you're with a congressman now. You have to comport yourself with some class."

Fiona and Mallory fold in half laughing, human origami with edges made of giggles.

"I do?" Perky says.

"Of course you do."

"No, I don't."

"Yes, you do. You're planning to marry him, right?"

I look at her finger. No engagement ring.

"Eventually."

"Then what you do is going to be covered by the press."

"Only when I'm in Texas and with him."

"If word gets out that Parker Campbell is a groomsman in a wedding in Boston, among people who matter, the press will cover it."

"'People who matter,'" Fiona repeats, using finger quotes. "What does that mean, Hasty?"

"Hast*ings.*"

"Fine. *Hastings.*"

"You know what it means."

And then it hits me.

I'm no longer a person who matters.

Burke used to be the ultimate person who mattered.

Now he matters, but in an FBI-Most-Wanted kind of way.

The bell on the door jingles as Raul finishes up with the horde of teenagers at the counter. I can't see whoever came in, even though I'm facing the door.

"Let's stop worrying about people who 'matter' and start to worry about the people who *really* matter," Fiona declares, her words carrying the authority of a preschool teacher ending a kids' squabble.

My eyes are on my water bottle, as I unscrew the cap. When I lift it to my mouth to take a sip, my eyes lock on Ian McCrory's.

Ian?

"Speaking of people who matter," Perky says under her breath. "Is that Ian McCrory?

"Dammit," I hiss as he walks toward us. "What is he doing here?"

Perky's eyes cut between me and Ian. "You know him?"

"Hastings," he says, stopping at the table. "You changed your hair. I like it."

"Now it's dark, like her soul," Perky mutters.

His gaze narrows as he looks at Perky. "Persephone Tsongas," he says.

Her eyebrows shoot up. "Do you know me? Have you arrested me before? Maybe we met at that protest in San Diego back in 2015?"

He laughs. "Not quite my line of business. I know you from photos with Parker Campbell."

"You know Parker?"

"We go back a long way."

"See?" I hiss at her. "People who matter."

He looks down at me. "I matter to you?"

I ignore that. "What are you doing here?"

"You're an impossible woman to get a hold of."

"That's the point. That's why I blocked you on my phone."

Perky, Fiona, and Mallory all set their coffees down. They look like they need giant bags of popcorn.

"You blocked me?" he says.

"I did. You were annoying."

"No one's called me annoying in a long time."

"How about condescending? Or egotistical? Or—"

"Your vocabulary is impressive. No need to keep going. I see you scored well on the verbal SAT."

"Actually," Mallory chimes in, "her scores weren't that great. Mom and Dad had to hire tutors for–"

I give her a look designed to set her hair on fire. She shuts up.

"Why are you here?" I demand of him.

"May we talk in private?" he asks.

"No."

"Fine. Then I'll speak in front of everyone here. I want to offer you a job."

"A job?"

"Is the position horizontal, or vertical?" Perky interjects, quirking one eyebrow. Is she coming to my defense? It's hard to tell.

Ian doesn't suffer fools gladly, which is terrible for Perky, but great entertainment for me.

"The position is none of your business," he says to her, turning back to me, big, strong body filling his clothes so nicely, his body language easy to read.

Yes, it says. *Say yes.*

What am I saying yes to, though?

"You came all the way to Anderhill in person to hunt me down so you could offer me a job?"

"Like I said, you're very hard to reach."

"Yes, because I blocked you!"

"We're not getting anywhere. But at least I have an explanation now."

"Why, Ian? Why do you want me to work for you?"

"It's an option," he says to me as Perky whispers in Fiona's ear, the two of them shamelessly gossiping about me to my face.

"I have plenty of options," I huff. That's not a lie. They just aren't *good* options.

"Not good ones," he says.

"How do you do that?"

"Do what?"

"Read my mind."

A slow predator's grin covers his face, lips twitching. "I'll take that as a yes."

"No."

"Why not?"

"I don't do pity fucks, Ian."

"Excuse me?"

"This is the career equivalent, and I won't do it."

I stand to leave. Ian moves to follow me, but Perky, Mallory, and Fiona all rise, making a wall between us.

"Thank you," I call back. "But the answer's no."

His hands go up in the air, like my sister and her friends are shaking him down.

"Good to see you, Hastings."

I look back.

"And for the record, nothing's about pity with you."

His last words carry along through the tears as I make my way home, running. I'm halfway there before I realize I've abandoned the bachelorette planning.

I pause in front of a fire hydrant with doggie-doo bags sprinkled around it, the green plastic tied off neatly at the ends. Yet another metaphor for my life.

I text Mallory.

I'm sorry. I'll help plan later.

We got rid of Ian, she says. *It's safe to come back.*

Sounds lethal. What did Perky do to him?

I wouldn't put it past her to know people who know people who can take care of a body.

Nothing. I talked to him. He listened to reason.

That's it? That's all it took? I type back.

He's a guy. A lot like Will. That's all it took. Turns out they know each other.

Of course they do. Of course.

You told him something you're not telling me, I double-thumb back, a wave of anger rising up inside me, a familiar feeling when it comes to my sister. It's so easy to let the misplaced fury land on her.

I told him you need time. And space. That what Burke did to you was devastating, and that while his offer is nice, it's too much. He's helping you too much. It will overwhelm you and make you say no just to make the issue go away because you hate needing people's help, she types in three different texts.

Gaping, I look at my screen. How the hell does Mallory know me that well?

Every word of that is wrong, I reply.

She sends a laughing emoji.

Come back, she types. *Perky's treating us all to Mongolian.*

When did Anderhill get a good Mongolian restaurant?

I said Mongolian. I never claimed it was good *Mongolian, Hasty.*

OMW, I reply, starting to jog as I hit Send.

On my way.

❦ 6 ❧

Wedding showers are for people who love Instagram.

And, for the record, I'm one of them. I *looove* Instagram. The color palettes. The grids. The razor-sharp alignment. The careful placement of objects with color, with lighting, with balance, that makes everything look optimized and perfect. My shoulders drop when I look at a grid, because the grid looks back at me and says, *beauty*.

Weddings were made for Instagram, and Instagram was made for weddings.

You know what *wasn't* made for weddings? People like me.

People who find out we're not really married and never were, and that it was all a sham. It's a small group, but I'm in it. I'm smack dab in the center of it. Queen of the Suckers.

Mercifully, Mallory's wedding shower is fairly small, at least by Bay Area standards. This one's a Jack-and-Jill. Everyone is a couple.

Except for me, of course.

Will's cousin Chaz, the one who keeps being unable to

attend anything wedding related, isn't here, either. Some guy named Paul, who'll be matched up with me or Raye at the actual wedding ceremony, is also absent. I'm the odd one out. It's Mom and Dad, Will's parents, Will and Mallory, Parker and Perky, Fiona and Fletch, Raye and her wife Sanni, Will's sister Veronica and Justin, her husband.

And… me.

"You okay, honey?" Dad asks, giving me pity eyes. "I know this must be hard on you, with everything with Burke. Watching Mallory move on to a happy phase of her life at the same time that you, you know...."

"Am an abject failure and a laughingstock?"

"What? No!"

"Yeah, Dad. I get it. I get it. I'm fine. It's fine. Every-thing's *fine*." I grab myself a glass of wine from one of the trays. "This makes it finer."

He pats me on the cheek. "I just want to make sure you're okay."

"I'm not okay, Dad. Nothing that's happened to me is okay. But I'm here, I'm happy for Mallory, and I promise I won't make a scene."

As he walks away, Will's sister, Veronica, comes over, a look of not-quite pity flashing through her eyes as she gives me a huge hug.

"Hastings! I haven't seen you in forever!"

"Since high school graduation," I point out.

"No, I think we ran into each other one summer while we were both in college. I kept calling your name, and you just kept walking."

"Oh! Sorry," I whisper, as the hug continues. She's an over-hugger. Mallory's like that, too. Overhuggers have a deep-seated need to inject themselves into other people's space. From a networking standpoint, I see the appeal.

But overhuggers are driven by emotion that is unattached to professional performance.

What a waste of a good hug.

"Oh, it's fine," she says, wiggling our bodies side to side before finally letting me go. "I'm so sorry about what's happened with you and your husband and the whole mess that's all over television."

In San Francisco, if someone said that to me, I would know it was a dig. Here, though, she seems sincere. Who's sincere about someone else's problems?

"Thank you?" I respond, voice tipping up with a question.

"Good for you for getting past it," she says. "Coming back home, hitting the reset button, and seeing what life really means. I admire that. I know what it's like."

"You got screwed over in the biggest financial scandal in American history and found out that you're not really married to the man you thought was your husband?"

"No," she admits. "But I did have to get over the death of my fiancé, ten years ago."

"Oh! I'm so sorry," I say, feeling like an asshole.

"It's okay. Not everyone knows."

"Mallory never mentioned it to me."

"I told her a while ago."

An awkward silence passes between us as it sinks in. The reason Mallory never told me about Veronica's dead fiancé is because Mallory and I don't talk to each other.

Or didn't until I came home.

"So what're you doing with this new chapter of your life?" she asks. "Job hunting?"

"Do you know anyone in the finance industry who's looking for a scandal-ridden person charged with RICO violations whose husband is a fugitive, only it turns out he's not her husband? Because I've cornered the market on being that applicant. I'm one of a kind."

She looks mortified. At least we got this far before that happened.

"Oh, no. I'm really sorry I don't—"

I reach out and touch her wrist. "That was a joke," I whisper. "I know nobody will hire me."

Veronica's pity eyes look just like her brother's. I see the resemblance to Will.

"You do have one job offer," Mallory says as she comes over, Will's arm around her. "Remember?"

"I am *not* taking a job with Ian McCrory."

Veronica looks impressed. "You have a job offer from *him?*"

"Yes."

"You know him?"

"Yes."

Mallory turns to me. "But do you…" she clears her throat "…*know* him?"

"Stop, Mallory! How many glasses of wine have you had?"

Will squeezes her waist and nuzzles her ear. "Yeah, how many *have* you had?" he asks, innuendo radiating off him like aftershave.

Veronica playfully smacks his arm. "The shower hasn't even begun. Keep it in your pants."

He looks like he wants to say more, but doesn't.

This is what the next three hours of my life are going to be. People will tell me how sorry they are for me. They're paired up in cute, affectionate dyads, clearly getting some action tonight.

The only thing that's going to make love to me is a bottle of good pinot grigio.

Which is pretty much what the last year of my life was like anyhow.

Given Burke's nonstop absence as he "built his empire,"

our sex life came to a grinding halt. More like a not-grinding halt.

Even when he was home, he wasn't really there. And he certainly wasn't there in our bed.

Now I know why. Was he saving all his orgasms for his *real* wife?

"Sharon, this manchego is amazing! I don't think I've ever tasted anything like it," Will's mom, Helen, says, startling me out of my pity party.

I overhear the conversation, and before I can turn around and claim credit, Mom does it for me.

"That was Hastings!"

Helen turns to me and asks, "Where did you buy this? At the little fromagerie in Stoneleigh?"

"I made it."

"You *made* the manchego?"

"I did. It's only three months aged, a batch I made around Christmas, but it's one of the few things I was allowed to keep."

"Keep?"

"After losing everything."

"The Feds took *everything* away?" Will asks.

"Except for that sheep's cheese. They said it didn't hold any value."

"They were wrong!" His mother nibbles and sips a glass of red wine. "This is extraordinary! How do you do this? Where do you get sheep's milk?"

"I had to go up to Petaluma to find an organic farmer who had enough to make it worth my while."

"And you just … make cheese?"

"She's done it since middle school," Mom interrupts. "Back then, it wasn't sheep's milk. You mostly did goat's milk, didn't you?"

I shrug. "No one really had much in the way of sheep's milk back then. Now it's gaining some traction here."

"Everyone I know adores manchego, especially the sixth-month aged," Helen says. "It's the perfect blend of creamy and crystallized."

I'm impressed. She knows her cheese.

"Do you have any more? Can I buy some from you?" she asks.

"If I had more I'd give it to you," I say, "but I'm saving some for the wedding." I look at Mom. "She insisted."

"Well, good for you, Sharon! And good for you, Hastings. Find a source of sheep's milk in the area and make some more. I would *certainly* buy it."

"Thank you. But I'm not exactly planning to spend the rest of my life making *cheese*."

"Why not?" Mallory asks.

"Because that's not the kind of thing someone does."

"Of course they do. *Someone* has to make the cheese," Helen says. "Why can't it be you?"

"Because I have an MBA from UC Berkeley. I'm capable of more than making cheese for a living."

"Don't knock it. Seriously." Helen tilts her head, Veronica mirroring her mother's gesture as she joins us. "You're good at this."

"Just because I'm good at something doesn't mean I should do it. People are good at plenty of things that don't matter."

"Maybe you can make manchego matter." Helen pops another bite in her mouth and grins.

She looks just like Will, when he smiles at Mallory and doesn't know anyone else sees.

One of the first genuine laughs out of me in months pours forth at the idea. "Make manchego matter," I repeat, smiling. "I love it. There's my new company motto, Helen."

When Burke and I got married, we didn't do a Jack-and-Jill shower. He thought it was gauche. Even when I tried to convince him that it would be a great opportunity to network, he pointed out the weakness of my local peer group.

Those were his words.

The weakness of your local peer group.

As I look around the room at Mallory's shower, I laugh silently at the irony of his comment. What a difference six years makes. Mallory has a sitting U.S. congressman as part of her wedding party. She's marrying an international real estate investor. Who has the weak network now, Burke?

You know the craziest part about this whole mess? I still worry about him.

Not actively. But you don't spend that many years with someone, no matter how awful they turn out to be, no matter how many secrets they have or lies they tell you, without them becoming a part of you. We intertwine ourselves with the people we fall in love with. You live with another human being, you give pieces of yourself to them.

He's walking around somewhere, in a country that has no extradition treaty with the United States, carrying pieces of me. *Years* of accumulated pieces of me.

And I've got pieces of him.

Given all his lies, probably not as many, and certainly not as high quality, but they're there.

I have to emotionally extradite Burke from my heart, my habits, my psyche. I have to take the holes left over from the pieces I gave him and fill them with something else.

At least I don't have to stare at our mutual possessions or fight with him over money. I literally have none of that left. Until a month or two ago, I would have been at the top of the heap at this wedding shower, right alongside Parker Campbell.

Congressman Campbell.

Now? I objectively have the worst life of anyone in here.

And just when I think that this wedding shower can't get any worse, in walks Dorian Buonacelli. She's wearing a crisp white shirt, black pants, modest heels, and no jewelry of any kind. Her hair is pulled back in a tight, low ponytail. Her face is perfect, brows arched with delicate precision, her makeup something to marvel at.

Her eyes meet mine. They flare, then calm down, her face a mask.

In high school, we were rivals. I was a bigger bitch, but she came damn close.

"Hastings!" she says, in a tone of uncertainty that is completely out of character for her. Her eyes catch Veronica's. Will's sister gives a half shrug and moves on, the movement confusing.

"Dorian!"

Dorian clasps her hands in front of her and approaches me. "I heard about what happened," she says. "I'm so sorry."

There isn't the kind of pity in her voice that I expect. She almost seems genuine.

"Thank you," I say, instantly on the defensive, shifting my stance. My wariness about how I fit into the social hierarchy makes every part of my body feel out of alignment.

"Can I get you a drink?" she asks.

"You don't have to do that."

"Um… actually, I do. It's my job."

"Your job?"

"I'm the caterer."

"You're the caterer?"

"I'm one of them. My partner, Lynn, and I own the company."

"You are a caterer," I repeat, processing.

"Yes." She lets out a little laugh. "I know. It's not the path that I thought I'd be on, either."

"Dorian! You went to Cornell!"

"For two years. Never graduated."

"What happened?"

"Do you really want to know? Or are you just asking so that you can use it against me?" she asks with a tiny smile.

"What?"

"That's what you do, Hasty. That's why I've avoided you since you came home."

"*You've* avoided *me*?"

"Is it true?" she asks, leaning in. "You really got hurt that badly by your ex-husband?"

Her face twists with a perplexed expression. "Your not-husband? Didn't I hear that he was married to, like, five other women?"

My defensive radar is not picking up on disparagement here. Primed to detect insult, I'm confused.

"Whatever you read in the press, believe half of it. Believe the half that makes *him* look bad."

She laughs.

"Catering, huh? What happened to Cornell?"

"That was a long time ago, fourteen years. If you really want to know, let's meet for coffee."

I touch her forearm. "I really do want to know, Dorian."

A blonde woman wearing a white apron waves at Dorian from across the room. She gives me an earnest look, squeezes my hand and says, "Hang on." Fishing in her back pocket, she pulls out a card and hands it to me. "Call me."

"Will do," I say as she walks away, passing the gift table and disappearing into the kitchen. Even that reminds me of my failure. Mom discreetly added my name to their gift to Mal and Will. Said that contributing the manchego was "enough."

Sadness washes over me like I'm floating in the ocean, caught by a swell. Each couple here is a unit, as much a part of that partnership as they are an individual. The grief is a remnant of what almost drowned me when I was released from jail, struggling to comprehend my new reality. The first time a lawyer explained what Burke did–at least, what they knew he'd done, at that point–I was so angry.

Not at Burke.

At the lawyer. The government. The SEC. The financial system. Certain that Burke was unfairly accused, I fought tooth and nail, arguing on his behalf, only backing down when my lawyer and the federal agents explained that Burke left behind a paper trail that made it look like I was the bad guy.

Me.

He set me up.

They knew it wasn't the case. I was legally implicated, though. My only option? To turn against him.

To testify.

When you're bonded to someone, you align pieces of yourself with their pieces, finding ways to make the puzzle hold together in some kind of cohesive whole. To give over information that would ruin Burke's life and leave him behind bars was painful.

Why? Because my edges rubbed against his edges. Our pieces nudged and nestled, prickled and sparred, used friction to smooth out the hard parts and pure grit to get through the discomfort until somehow, they sat next to each other. That's marriage.

To rip that apart? That took effort.

Yes, even when I knew, finally, how screwed I was. How much he'd screwed me over.

And how much every part of our marriage had been a lie.

"Isn't this wonderful?" Mom asks as she puts her arm around me, wistful and assuming my long sigh comes from the same emotion. "Mallory found true love."

"It is."

"I didn't mean to hurt you by saying that."

"You're not. The truth doesn't hurt. I'm genuinely happy for her and Will."

"You are?"

"I'm even happier we're not doing any of those stupid shower games."

"Hasty!"

"Mom!"

"I'm happy you're happy for her. But let's get you settled into a life where you are happy, too."

"I'd settle for a life without pity at this point."

"Pity?"

"Everyone here pities me."

"I don't think it's pity. I think it's compassion."

Maybe I've had too much wine, but her words make the back of my throat sting with the threat of tears. "Mom, you live in a fantasy land."

"I do?"

"You think the best of everyone."

"Of course I do. Except for Burke. He's a raging asshole."

"MOM!"

But we laugh, and then we do what I do best:

Network.

Except this time, I'm not collecting business cards and gossip and insider information to craft deals.

I'm collecting emotional connection.

Which makes me a rank amateur.

"Do something that makes you happy, dear. Make cheese."

"What?"

"Make. Manchego. Matter."

"Hah!"

"Don't dismiss it outright. Helen's onto something. Go back to your roots and do something physical."

"You just want more so you can eat it."

She nods solemnly. "Caught."

Our shared laughter makes me feel lighter than I have in months.

And now I have a plan.

And it isn't half baaaaaaaaad.

7

esserman's Dairy hasn't changed one bit since I was a little kid. They even use the old-fashioned cash registers that *ding* when a transaction is completed, and give you carbon-copy slips for receipts. Frozen in the 1970s, the warehouse-like building attached to the dairy smells exactly the same:

Maple syrup, hay, manure, and coffee.

As I enter the old store, I do detect some small differences. A bank of coolers filled with grab-and-go milk, cheese, butter, eggs, and bacon is the first change. To the right is a series of large bench freezers. Mom told me years ago that Hesserman's started to sell other dairy products besides milk and ice cream, and partners with some local farmers to offer other meats and cheeses, but the core feel of the store isn't different.

And I love it.

"Can I help you?" asks a young tween sitting behind the main desk, the ever-present smartphone next to her.

"I'm looking for Mr. Hesserman," I explain, wondering what in the world I'm doing here.

"Which Mr. Hesserman? There's my dad, my uncles, Grandpa…"

"I have a strange question," I say to her. "So I'm not sure which Mr. Hesserman I need. Maybe you can help. I'm looking for sheep's milk."

"Sheep's milk?"

"Yes."

"We don't milk sheep here. We're a cow dairy farm." She looks like she's desperately holding back the word "duh."

"I know you are. Do you know anyone who sells sheep's milk?"

"Like…wow. I don't know." She gives me a nervous smile, braces gleaming. If this kid is twelve, I'll eat my shoe.

"I mean… I know how to milk a cow, but how do you milk a sheep? Like, do you have to shear it first before you can get to the nipples?"

She's deep in her own thoughts, wondering about the mechanics of it all, when a man walks in through the back door. Thinning light brown hair, darker eyebrows over big eyes, and the look of a man deep in thought. He's wearing dirty jeans, thick work boots, a flannel shirt under a tan Carhartt jacket, and a Red Sox cap on his head.

Which is pretty much the way he dressed in 2003.

"Eric?" I ask, catching his eye.

He gives me the absent glance of someone who is completely focused on something else.

"Uh," he grunts out, and then does a double take. "Hastings?"

Coming back home means running into people I thought I'd run *away* from long ago.

"Like, Dad?" the tween asks. "This woman is looking for sheep's milk. Do you know how to milk a sheep? 'Cuz, like, you've never taught me that before."

"Lori, we don't raise sheep here. That's why I never taught you."

"Yeah, but like, if people want sheep's milk, why don't we start raising sheep?"

Back in high school, Eric Hesserman and I had the strangest friendship I've ever had in my entire life.

First, it was clear he was gay but wasn't out, and I wasn't about to out him.

Second, he was a sixth-generation farmer and knew he wanted to be a farmer. I had no interest in sticking around, so the friendship died out the second I left for college. It wasn't for any bad reason–just lack of proximity.

Some relationships are like that. If you're not around someone every single day, things fade.

He comes at me with his arms spread, a giant hug crushing me. Eric smells like cows and pasture. He's absolutely filthy, but I don't care, laughing in his ear as he says:

"Whatever happened to you must have been really awful if it means you've moved back home."

That's the other thing about people you've been friends with since your youth. They can get away with saying things like that.

"Thanks."

"Listen, I, uh, would love to catch up, but I've got kind of a problem out here. There's a cow that's birthing and we're having some issues. She's posterior. Lori," he says to the girl. "Where's Jackson?"

"Off at the auction to buy the new truck."

"You're it? You're the only one here?"

"Yeah. Grandpa told me to run the store."

Under his breath, Eric mutters profanity.

"What's wrong?" I ask. "Posterior? Is that like breech?"

"Yeah. And I need someone to help with the birthing."

I look at Lori. She shrugs. "I can't. Last time I helped

with the calving, I fainted." Her bright braces reflect the light from behind me as she says the word *faint.*

"We can't afford to lose this one," Eric says. He turns to Lori. "Call around. See if you can get anyone. We're down to a half hour or so."

"I can help!" I pipe up.

"You?" Eric bursts into laughter. His eyes drift down to my feet. "I see nothing's changed."

"What does that mean?"

"In high school, you were wearing four-inch heels most of the time, too, Hastings. Can't go in the barn wearing toothpicks like that."

"I can help birth a calf." I cross my arms over my chest. "Give me boots and you're on."

"You may be my only option."

"Thanks for the vote of confidence."

He hesitates, evaluating.

"Look. Jackson's not around. Everybody else is off at farmer's markets. Make you a deal. You come out and you help me, and you *actually* help–you don't faint on me..." His eyes jump over to Lori, who hunches her shoulders, "... and I'll help you get sheep's milk." He frowns. "Why do you want sheep's milk?"

"To make manchego."

"You still make cheese! I remember that in high school. Used to be goat's milk, though."

"I've evolved. It's nice catching up, but don't you have a calf that's about to die if we don't go out there and do this?"

"Yeah. C'mon. I'll get you some shitkickers."

"Shitkickers?"

"Boots. How're your hands?" He takes my left one in his and examines the nails. "Okay, good. Your fingernails are short enough. I'll give you gloves, but you'll probably destroy your manicure."

"What manicure? This is a five-dollar bottle of polish that I got from CVS."

"You? Buying drugstore nail polish?"

"Don't judge me," I say to him quietly. "My descent is complete. And how are you?"

His shoulders freeze. He knows exactly what I mean. "No time to catch up, so here's the really short version. I married Annabelle. We had Lori. Annabelle turned out to have the BRCA2 gene. She died of breast cancer when Lori was four. Coming up on seven years now."

"Oh, Eric, I'm so sorry. I had no idea."

"I know you didn't. We all kept it quiet. And now I'm partners…" He pauses before saying the words, "…with Jackson."

"So you're out?"

"Mmm." He ponders the use of the word. "It's more that I'm not in the closet anymore, you know? In my line of business, people are enlightened, but they're enlightened *privately*. I don't go to farm auctions, or the fish and game club, and run my mouth about my personal life. It's live and let live."

"This place is so different from the Bay Area," I mutter, as he points to enormous rubber boots that go all the way past my knees. I kick my heels off, set them on a wooden shelf, and shove my feet into the boots.

"You ever help birth a calf before?"

"No."

"First, we pray." He closes his eyes. I join him.

"You pray before every birth?"

"Only the ones where you're helping."

I elbow him and move past him, his laughter like a soundtrack.

The walk to the back barn is nothing but muck. Suddenly, I appreciate the boots, though I could do without the ribbing.

"Normally, cows birth in a field, but something's gone wrong. She won't leave the barn. Bad sign."

I hear the cow before I see it. The poor thing sounds like me after a bad food poisoning incident in Singapore a few years ago. Never trust street vendor sushi, even when a VP for an electronics conglomerate swears it's the best in town.

I expect to see the cow lying on a bed of hay, legs open, a baby coming out, but instead she's standing, tail swishing, with two sharp hooves sticking out of her.

"Ewwwwww! What's wrong with her butthole?" I scream.

"That's her vulva."

"Even worse!"

"You're all I've got, Hastings. I need you to stay calm," Eric says in a voice that doesn't convey a whole lot of confidence in me. He hands me two pieces of suede and burlap. Gloves.

"What is this?" I say, sliding one on. "It goes all the way up to my shoulder. We're not birthing a falcon here."

"No, but if she kicks you, those hooves—"

"*Kicks* me?"

As if on cue, the cow's knee snaps up, the hoof coming within a foot of Eric.

"That wasn't a kick," he chuckles, "but you never know." Suddenly serious, he places his flat palm on her side, along the womb, and rubs. "It's okay, girl. It's fine."

"What's her name?" I ask, struggling to understand which emotion I'm supposed to be feeling right now. I have no framework for feeling compassion toward something that can step on me and kill me.

"Cowtherine." He has a rope in his hand, and he loops it around the cow's head, centering it at her neck, then attaching it to the wall.

"Excuse me?"

"Cowtherine. Like Catherine, only the first syllable is cow."

"You named a cow *Cowtherine*."

"Technically, that's just the first part of her name. It's Cowtherine the Great."

I plant my hands on my hips. "Quit messing with me."

"I'm not messing with you, and I didn't name her. Lori named her. She was in the middle of some World History lesson and thought it would be funny, okay?"

I snort. "I like your daughter."

"I do, too, except for times like this. She faints at the sight of blood, just like her mom." His eyes meet mine as the cow lets out a low, intense moan, legs starting to buckle. "Shit," he says. "Vet's not here. This is bad. We gotta get this puppy out."

"You cross-breed?"

I deserve his glare.

"Why did you tie her head to the wall?"

"Because we don't have someone to hold her nice and steady. She's gonna move a lot, and try to kick. This keeps her in place as best we can."

He grabs the back hooves and tugs with both hands, the cow letting out an unearthly sound, shuffling a bit. Eric leaps back just in time to miss being hit with a stream of poop.

"This is why women have C-sections. *Scheduled* C-sections," I inform him.

"She's not a woman. Not a human one, at least. And if all you're gonna do is stand there and give commentary, you're welcome to go back and hang out with Lori." He eyes me in a funny way. "Or go find a sheep farm and get some milk."

"I'm here to help. What do you need me to do?"

"Hang on. I need some rope." He disappears around a corner, then returns with a thick piece of braided cord. Tying it around the calf's hooves, he takes the long end and tugs gently, increasing the tension, shoulders tight around his ears as he focuses.

"Damn." Releasing the rope's pull, he looks at me, stretching his hand out. "Can you take it?"

"You're stronger than I am. I can't pull as hard."

"I want you to tug gently. Just enough tension to give it some pull. I'll cross her legs and start some rotation."

I obey, giving it enough force to tighten the rope. Eric crosses the calf's hooves, rotating it slowly as Cowtherine groans, but stays upright. The flank ripples as I use my thighs to hold the rope steady.

"Give it a little more power," Eric says, pulling upward on the calf's legs.

The calf doesn't budge. He sighs.

"I'm gonna try to turn the calf from the outside, so I need you to just hold on to the hooves and keep pulling lightly as I work on turning her. Probably won't"

I eye Cowtherine's side. Portions of the calf trapped inside her womb make her flank ripple again. "How're you going to turn a calf?"

"God only knows," he mutters. "But I have to try. Brace yourself," he says.

"On what?" There's nothing around the back of the cow.

"Unlock your knees and hope that all those Pilates classes you do in California come in handy right now."

"How did you know I do Pilates classes?"

He gives me a gimlet eye. "Wild guess."

I reach for the hooves, touching the end of one of them. It twitches. I leap back. "It moved!"

"Of course it moved, Hastings. It's a live calf. We *want* it to move."

"Okay, okay. I'm fine. I'm fine. I'm *fine*," I repeat, moving closer. I close my eyes. I open them. I reach for the hooves. "Got her," I say. "Is it a her, or a him? What sex is the calf?"

"We won't know until it comes out."

"You didn't do an ultrasound?"

He gives me another look that says, *Shut up.*

I press my lips together. I squeeze the hooves and tug gently. Cowtherine bellows as Eric presses on the side of her body, doing something I can't see. At this point, all I can do is close my eyes again and tug gently.

He mutters a curse. "Stop!" he shouts.

I let go and step back.

"Might be a cord problem." He takes one of his gloves off and starts to unbutton his shirt.

"What're you doing?"

"I need my bare arm."

"For what?"

"I gotta go in."

"Go in where?"

He points to Cowtherine's pretty place.

"You're going *in?* Head first?"

"Yes, Hastings, that's exactly what I'm doing. I'm going in head first. Do you suggest breast stroke?"

"Excuse me?"

"Of course I'm not going in head first. Just one arm."

"You're talking about reaching into a *cow's vagina* to pull the baby out."

"That's what we do when it's stuck." He takes a step toward the cow and then pauses, looking back at me. His eyes narrow. He looks at his arm, then at mine, back at his arm and then at mine again.

"Take your shirt off."

"*Excuse me?*"

"I can see you have an undershirt on. Take off the long-sleeved shirt."

"Why?" I realize what he's implying. "I am *not* sticking my arm in a vagina."

"Why not?"

"Because I haven't done that since college."

The words come out of my mouth as Eric turns to the barn door, cocks his head in confusion, and says over my shoulder, "Hello? Can I help you with something?" Eric's eyes are wide with astonishment, his head pulling back in complete surprise.

I turn around to follow his gaze and find Ian McCrory standing there.

"What the hell are *you* doing here?" I scream.

Ian eyes the back of a cow and looks at my now-bare arm. "I could ask the same question."

"I'm helping an old friend with a problem."

"What's your problem?" he asks Eric, who clearly recognizes Ian and is wondering what on Earth one of the richest men in the world is doing in his barn.

"We need someone who knows how to stick their arm in a vagina."

Eric might be impressed, but he's not going to change for *anyone*.

Ian looks at his fingers. He holds up two, then three, then four, kind of frowns, tucks his hand into a pointed fist.

"Oh, stop!" I snap at him. "A *cow's* vagina."

Just then, Cowtherine's back legs buckle and she almost falls to the ground, but rights herself, knees weak. Eric is ignoring us, texting madly, as Ian walks over and starts rolling up his shirtsleeves.

"What're you doing?"

"Helping."

Halfway through one sleeve, he pauses, looks around, and starts unbuttoning his shirt instead.

"What are you *doing*?" I ask again, back to a shriek.

He ignores me, stripping out of his shirt, down to bare chest.

Eric looks up, jaw tightening slightly, eyes all over Ian.

Apparently, Eric and I are *both* appreciating Ian McCrory's personal training sessions.

"Let's do this," Ian says to Eric.

Eric offers his hand. "Let's shake *before* you put it in. I'm Eric."

"Ian."

"I know who you are."

"Good. Now we're even. Let's go."

On the rare occasions that I allowed myself the lascivious fantasy of seeing a shirtless Ian McCrory, I never imagined that it would be in a barn with a steaming pile of cow manure next to us, as Ian, Eric, and I figure out which of our arms to use to enter the vaginal canal of a birthing cow.

Maybe this is a fetish on *YouPorn*? I'll ask Perky next time I see her. If anyone will know, it's her.

Eric looks at Ian. "You've done this before?"

"On my grandfather's farm."

"Dairy farm?"

"Yep."

"Vermont or New Hampshire?"

"Wisconsin." Ian says the word with the flat accent of a cheesehead. "You a Packers fan?"

"No comment." Ian knows damn well we're in Patriots country. "But I don't care at this point. You could be a Jets fan for all I care, if you can get this calf out of there, safe and alive."

"I think we need a smaller arm," Ian says to Eric, looking at both of theirs. They turn to me in unison.

"You two are crazy," I inform them. "I can't stick my arm in there."

"Why not?"

"Because… because…"

Cowtherine lets out a loud sigh, her eyes closing.

Eric's phone buzzes. He looks at it. "The vet is fifteen minutes away."

"See? We're fine," I tell him.

"We don't have fifteen minutes. *She—"* he points at Cowtherine "—doesn't have fifteen minutes. Neither does the calf."

"Let's get her done," Ian says, moving closer to me, standing tall, his hands on my shoulders. Deep brown eyes, edged with gold, meet mine. "You can do this, Hastings. You have to do this."

"I don't *have* to do anything."

"You *want* to do this. You want to do it because it's the right thing to do."

When he looks at me like that, I want to do all kinds of things.

"What do I do?" I ask Eric, who waves for me to come over and bend down.

"Simple. You stick your hand in." Eric pulls the thick leather glove off my hand and replaces it with a pair of latex gloves that go up to the shoulder.

"How far in?"

"As far as you need to go." He sizes up my arm, muttering something about "four feet."

"What exactly am I doing?"

"Something's in there stopping the calf from coming out. You may be able to get a couple of inches in and it'll loosen the poor thing. You may need to go deeper and unloop a cord error."

"A cord error?"

"Umbilical cord around the neck, or around another body part."

"You mean, like a baby?"

"This *is* a baby. It's a cow baby," Eric says.

I snap the glove in place. I stick my fingers on the edge of Cowtherine's labia. I close my eyes. I move forward.

This feels like my first pap smear, first time having sex, and unclogging a toilet, all rolled into one.

In my mind's eye, I imagine the contour of a small cow's body. Knee. Hip. Inch by inch, I move up, fully aware that at any moment, Cowtherine can take me out by kicking or sitting on me, Ian and Eric's presence a relief as they hold her steady.

The calf moves, rotating away from me as I reach a lump I guess might be its hindquarters.

"What am I doing, Eric? I think I feel something. Like a snake along its thigh."

"Cord problem," Eric says tersely.

"It's pulsating."

"Can you wrap your fingers around it? Don't squeeze!" he shouts.

"I can try, but–"

Suddenly, my arm is forced out, hard, shoulder joint compacted like a van slammed into me.

"He's moving! You've got him! Step back, Hastings–NOW!"

Eric's words aren't necessary, because the force of the calf's expulsion doesn't give me a chance to think. The pain in my arm, plus physics, make me pull back, a thick *squinch* sound making it clear I jarred *something* loose.

"MOOOOOOOOOOOOO!" Cowtherine chimes in, grunting as the baby comes out in a gush of red, pink, and yellow slime that smells like all my prison nightmares. Eric guides the calf as Cowtherine's hind legs bend slightly to give her baby a softer landing.

Or maybe she's just *done.*

"You did it!" Ian shouts as I jump up in the air, giddy with excitement. The calf stands on wobbly legs, covered in slick goo, shaking as poor Cowtherine moves to a prone position. Eric grabs the baby's head and uses his fingers to…

"Ewwww!" What're you doing?" I call out, covering my nose. The smell is atrocious.

"The vet'll handle Cowtherine. I gotta check on this calf and clear her nose and mouth of the mucus, but then mostly we need to not touch it," Eric instructs.

"Why not?" I ask.

Ian's arm is around my shoulders, his sweaty, hot, gorgeous chest so close, I could lick it.

"We want the calf to attach to Mama properly. But you did it. The calf's alive. I can't believe the cord was wrapped like that."

"I never even had to move the cord."

"No, but I saw it when it came out. Unlooped it off the neck. You did well, Hastings."

I slap my disgusting, slick, gloved hand flat against Ian's chest. I rub it in circles.

"Thank you," I tell him.

"I'm a human towel now?"

"You're good for wetness." I halt as I realize what the words sounded like.

Ian grins at me. I swear, if Eric weren't here, he'd kiss me. Smiling like a fool, I look up at him. His smile matches mine.

"Why are you here again?"

"I got nostalgic for midwifing farm animals," Ian says.

"That, or you're a creepy stalker who tracked me down and won't leave me alone."

"I like the first one better."

"Hey, Ian!" Eric calls out. "Can you get some water? She'll be thirsty after birthing."

"No problem!" Ian calls out.

Eric appears with clean, dry towels. He points to a big utility sink, over in the corner. "You can get her some water over there, then wash off," he says to both of us, looking at his phone. "I'll go wait for the vet. You two look like you need to talk in private." He tips his head at Ian. "Good to meet you. Never had a billionaire on my farm before, that I know of. Thanks for your help."

"No problem. Anytime."

Eric laughs at him. "I don't think I can afford your hourly rate, dude." His chuckle recedes as Ian and I walk over to the sink and get to work. He takes care of watering Cowtherine, then returns.

We both *reek*.

"Is this your new job?" he asks me as I scrub the hell out of my arms. The clothes are hopeless. Mom's stain remover is going to do double duty on this washload.

"Ha!"

"Gave up on working in finance? Because I know this doesn't pay better than my company."

"More like finance gave up on working with me. I can't get a job anywhere," I tell him as I wash my arm. It throbs from the pressure of being inside Cowtherine so deeply.

Or maybe it's just other parts of me throbbing.

"I email you, I text you, I call and leave messages. How can you say finance has given up on you?"

"I've applied for *seventy-six* different jobs. Do you know what that has done to my ego? Seventy-six rejections!"

"Your ego's big enough to handle that and still remain intact," he says dryly.

I throw a disgusting towel at him.

He laughs. "You forgot about job number seventy-seven."

"That's it. There *is* no job seventy-seven."

"There's the one I've been trying to offer you," he says.

Just then, Cowtherine lets out a loud, disgusting, nasally

snotty snort that is the epitome of my emotional state right now. I do a sad imitation of her.

"You're still offering me a job?"

"Yes. You heard me at the coffee shop."

"I thought that was a bad joke!"

"I never joke with the women I stalk."

"You."

"Yes."

"You want *me—"* I point to myself, "—to work for *you."* I tap my index finger against his chest.

"That's generally how it works when someone offers you a job."

"I can't work for you!"

"Why not?"

"Because we're rivals. We are not on the same team."

"Not anymore."

"That's the other reason I can't work for you. Because you're a jerk."

"I'm not a jerk."

"Yes, you are."

"What did I do that was jerky? I offered you a job."

"You rubbed my face in it."

"We're not going through this again, Hastings."

"Right. Because I'm not working for you." Mallory's words come to mind, sharp and dangerous. Ian's helped me too much. The balance of power is off.

If I accept this job offer, I'm indebted to him even more.

Eric and the vet, a short, squat woman with salt and pepper hair in a messy bun, have come back in and are standing over by Cowtherine and the calf, conferring quietly.

"Look," Ian says, turning us away from Eric, who is eyeing us while the vet gets to work, "I'd be an idiot not to want you."

Eric starts coughing. Ian glares his way.

"You're an asset to any business."

"Are you drunk?"

"Stone-cold sober, Hastings. When you're ready, the offer stands."

And with that, Ian grabs his business shirt, shrugging into it, ignoring the handprint I left on his chest, his back all I see as he leaves abruptly.

"I can't believe you turned him down," Eric says to me as we both stare at the disappearing Ian McCrory.

"It's complicated. You wouldn't understand, Eric."

"You think I don't understand complicated relationships?" He makes a derisive snort. "I may be a farmer, but I'm not stupid."

"I never said you were stupid. I just said that what is going on between Ian and me is complicated."

"So there *is* something going on between you."

"No, not like that." I pause, wondering how to organize my thoughts enough to explain what my life has become in the last month or so.

"I watch the news, you know." He kicks at a thick patch of hay. "I saw you in handcuffs."

"*Everyone's* seen me in handcuffs."

"You know what I thought? When I saw that?"

"What?"

"There's a good woman who needs some help."

If my old friend had gut-punched me, he couldn't have hurt me more.

"And the whisper campaign went from there. Good old Anderhill and gossip."

"You know it did," he says, digging the knife in further. "Your dad told a different version of events."

"*My dad* talked to you about it?"

"Not directly. Small town. Everybody talks to everybody eventually."

"Anderhill isn't *that* small."

He cocks one eyebrow, as if to argue. "You want to hear the story or not?"

"Fine. Go ahead."

"Your dad was mystified, trying to figure out who was bankrolling your defense." Eric looks at the door that Ian just walked out of. "Guess we don't have to wonder now."

"You know who Ian is?"

"*Everyone* knows who Ian is, Hastings. The guy's in the news all the time. You can't scroll twice on Facebook or Instagram without seeing his face somewhere, or an ad for one of his companies. Is he part of the whole fraud thing?"

"No!" I protest. "Absolutely not. That's my ex, my husband, my—I don't know what to call Burke." I laugh at the end, a thin thread of hysteria rising up in me.

"He had more than one wife, didn't he?" Eric says softly.

"*Has*. I wasn't the only one. And I wasn't the first, so I was never really married to him. But I thought I was, so I lived with him all those years. What does that make him? The joke is that he's my 'was-band'."

"It was never a joke to you, was it?" Kind eyes meet mine.

"No. It wasn't a joke. I hate Burke… but I loved him. I loved him as much as I've ever loved anyone. And this is what I got."

"Take the job," Eric says suddenly.

"What?"

"Take the job. McCrory's offering you something."

"I don't want more of his help."

"You took his help before."

"This is different."

"Why? Because you have to work for it?"

"I have no problem with hard work."

"He came all the way to Boston, somehow tracked you

down to this dairy farm, just to talk to you. Meanwhile, your 'was-band' fled the country to hide from you and the authorities, and left you holding the bag. If there was ever a time to take help from somebody, now is it."

"I don't want his help."

"The job he's offering you is an opportunity to prove that you don't need help."

"That makes no sense."

"Earn your salary. Do the work. Prove yourself. You keep applying for jobs and nobody will hire you, but Ian McCrory will. He's giving you a shot at proving to everybody else that you're worth hiring. And besides, you suck at birthing calves. You have no future in farming."

"Hey! I did fine!"

"On a scale of Lori fainting at the sight of blood and a veterinarian delivering a calf, you are closer to my daughter than a trained vet."

I kick him gently with my barn boots. He lunges away, farmer's reflexes better than mine. He grins at me. "Tell you what. I'm offering you a job, too. Now you've got two job offers on the table. I'm offering you minimum wage…"

"Minimum wage!"

"…no benefits, and you will muck stalls eight hours a day."

"That's not a job offer. That's a prison sentence."

"Hey! That's what we all started doing when we were in our teens."

"I'm not a teenager."

"You sure are acting like one."

I laugh. "There's the Eric I know from high school."

"How about you show me the Hastings *I* remember from high school?"

"I'm not that different from who I was back then."

"Yeah, you are."

"How?"

"The Hastings I knew in high school would have said, 'Fuck those fuckers,' pulled herself up by her bootstraps, and gone out and showed the world that she was better than anyone ever expected."

Silence hangs in the air between us as his words sink in.

"I already did that," I say softly. "And look where it got me."

"Maybe mucking stalls for me really is your best shot at greatness."

I glare at him.

"Besides, who would want to work for that Ian McCrory guy? It would be hard to stare at that body all day."

My glare gets stronger, but I can't keep the smile hidden. "If I take his job offer…"

"If?"

I point at him. "It will have nothing to do with this little inspirational speech of yours."

"Of course not."

I lean up against the barn wall, cross my boots at the ankles, and swallow until my throat clicks. "You want to know why I really don't want to take the job working for Ian?"

Eric shrugs.

"I'll take that as a yes. Because it makes me feel even more like a failure. I used to hate the guy. He's really good at what he does. And I was really good at what I did. And when I beat him, it felt amazing. It was better than chocolate. Better than… sex, even."

"You must not have had very good sex, Hastings."

"Why do men keep saying that to me?"

"I'm not the only one? Let me guess. Ian said it, too."

"Eric, stop."

"Sorry. Go on. Do your Hastings-pretending-to-have-emotions bit."

He's joking with me, but in a way he's right. All those pieces inside me are re-organizing themselves, trying to figure out where they live now. How they align. How everything fits together, without Burke, so that Hastings can be Hastings again.

And who the hell *is* Hastings? I don't have a core anymore. I don't have a North Star. There's no defining purpose to my life.

How do you make something of nothing?

"I'll think you're a failure if you *don't* take the job with Ian," Eric announces as he picks up a pitchfork and starts stabbing it into the hay.

"How so?"

"There must be some lesson that you're supposed to learn from all this."

"Don't tell me you've gone religious."

"No. But sometimes life throws us the lessons we're supposed to learn."

"That's awfully close to, 'God doesn't give you more than you can handle'."

I get another shrug from him. "I'm not sure I believe that," he says. "When Annabelle died, I had more than enough to handle. I lost my wife, lost my friend, Lori lost her mother, and suddenly, I was a single dad of a little kid. But I think you should look at the patterns in your life that you keep repeating over and over again. You've always pushed away help, Hastings. Maybe it's time to break the cycle. Maybe when you do that, you'll find out what your purpose is."

"When did you turn into a philosopher-farmer?"

He grins. "Probably right about the same time you made your first million."

"That million's long gone."

I get a third shrug from him, and then he turns his back, starting to clean the stall.

I do the only thing I can think to do: I pick up my phone. I unblock Ian.

Ding ding ding....

Holy textstream. All the texts I didn't see from him while he was blocked come through, more than ten.

All of them in high pursuit of me.

For a moment, I waver. Eric's right, but this hard sell from Ian is confusing. At the same time, Eric's comment about money, and my reply back about losing my first million, is a stark reminder of the very practical fact that I need an income.

Regardless of Ian McCrory's motives.

And as loathe as I am to admit it, it's nice to be wanted, even if I'm wanted by the same guy I schemed to beat for so many years.

I sigh, staring at the screen.

I text Ian. Two words:

I accept.

And then I hit Send.

8

One of the wealthiest guys in the world doesn't even have an office here in Boston.

Ian McCrory's office is a hotel suite. Of course it is.

By the time my smartphone map takes me to the address Ian gave me in his text, and I stare at the fourteen-story hotel in the Seaport District of Boston, I realize I've been had.

My "job"? I'm guessing it involves his pants.

Or lack thereof.

Ian is sorely mistaken if he thinks that he can bring me on the payroll just to be a well-paid bedmate.

Bedmate.

My anger mingles with some misplaced lust I try to shoo away like an annoying mosquito.

I fail.

After a brief series of negotiation texts, we settled on a strong hourly rate and a consultant contract for three months. If this works out, he'll bring me on board as a salaried employee later. Allegedly, my work involves database mining and pattern matching for large-scale, high-tech investment opportunities.

I'm now guessing the data Ian wants me to mine involves his lap and the back of my throat.

I stare at the hotel sign. I look at the address on my phone. The large revolving door mocks me, moving slowly as hotel guests and convention center attendees stream in and out. Eric's comment about making the same mistakes over and over again pings through my mind as I watch the door turn and turn and turn.

Break out of my pattern, huh?

I march toward a regular door, pull the handle, and walk in, ignoring the bellman, who nods at me.

The address says Suite 1401, and as I get on the elevator, I see that's the penthouse. That strange mix of anger and lust begins its slow rise from deep in my core, mirroring the elevator ride to the top. I wonder how many other women he's done this to.

Too many, probably.

Which fills me with a jealousy I have no right to possess.

Over the years, I've been propositioned plenty of times. The wedding ring, the widespread knowledge that I was married to Burke Oonaj, my killer resting bitchface–none of it ever insulated me.

And all I have left now is the bitchface.

It'll have to be enough.

The elevator doors open onto a small foyer. The luxury doesn't impress me; I've seen it all before. Before I can press the bell to the double doors of the penthouse, they open. A woman in a smart suit stares at me with the pleasant but blank expression of a well-trained executive assistant.

"Ms. Monahan. Mr. McCrory is waiting for you."

She guides me into a large living room with four doors off the main area. One is open, and I can see Ian at a desk, talking, one arm motioning. A second door is open. Clearly, it's his assistant's office.

I wonder what's in the other two. A bedroom, I presume.

"Ian is on the phone right now."

"I can see that."

"My name's Irene," she says confidently. "Can I get you some coffee, tea, soda, sparkling water?"

It's like hearing the menu of a trendy hipster restaurant. "No ginger kombucha?" I joke.

She blinks exactly once, then lifts her smartphone. "I'll have some sent up."

"No, no. Coffee would be great. Straight up black. Simple."

She nods. The low rumblings of Ian's voice make their way out to the waiting area.

I sit on the very edge of a stylish chair, smooth, plain wood curved by craftsmanship. Irene returns quickly with coffee in hand and sets it on a table next to me.

"I'm sure he'll just be a few minutes," she says, and then departs for her office. The click-clack of a keyboard, muted but obvious, greets my ears a few seconds later.

The coffee's too hot to drink yet, and there are no magazines here. Nothing to read. No television, and the room is silent, no music. It's me and my thoughts. I could pull out my smartphone, but why? It's time to wait for Ian.

My concerns about this being a sex date have dissolved, unless Irene turns out to be the hired third for a planned threesome, and she doesn't strike me as the type.

Not that I would know what the type is.

"Hastings," he says, walking out of the room, tall and broad and darkly alluring. His eyes comb over my body from top to bottom. "I think I like you better in the barn. How is Cowtherine?"

I laugh. "According to the vet, she's doing fine."

"And the calf? Did they name it?"

"Yes. They named him Peter."

Ian groans. "Peter the Great, I presume, is his full name?"

I nod. The niceties don't really work with him. It feels stiff and strange to make small talk with a man who watched me hauled away in handcuffs, who sent a team of lawyers to help me, who paid for my defense, who stood shirtless in a barn while I fisted a cow–and who is now my saving grace as I stand before him, ready to onboard into some undefined new job.

He gestures to my coffee and then sits across from me, leaning back in the chair, legs stretched out, fingers laced in his lap.

"Let's talk about what you're going to do for me," he says.

My mouth goes dry as a few seconds tick by, our eyes locked.

I finally break the silent gaze and say, "You don't have a big team here. Where will I work?"

He thumbs toward one of the closed doors. "Next to Irene."

"That's it? You, me, and Irene?"

"It's a pilot project. Irene used to go with me wherever I went, but now she's based here. When I'm in town, I'll work from here, too."

"You keep this place even when you're not around?"

He shrugs. "It's easier than dealing with leases and renting office space somewhere downtown." He eyes me critically. "Besides, I'm not convinced you're in this for the long haul."

"You're not wrong."

He nods, chin moving up and down decisively, as if his body knows exactly how to move in ways that complement his internal state. Not many people have mastered that.

"Hence the three-month contract," he says. "I have complete faith in your abilities. I don't have faith in your longevity."

"Why bring me on board?"

"Because it would be a waste not to."

I snort.

"I mean it, Hastings. You've got one of the sharpest minds in finance. Shame to see it go to waste."

"So that's it." I take a sip of coffee and then stare at him. "Three-month contract, work here in your office with you and Irene doing data insights? What's in it for you?"

"I already told you," he says. "Your mind."

But his eyes drift over my body instead. He's not inventorying my *mind*.

"My mind is special. I'll give you that," I tell him. "What's in it for me?"

"A job. A little reputation rehab."

I make a decidedly un-ladylike sound. "There's no hope of that."

"Plenty of people who've committed crimes worse than the ones you—"

I hold one finger up, making him interrupt himself.

"The ones you've been *accused* of," he elaborates carefully.

I back down.

"Plenty of people have pulled themselves up out of the ashes and gone on to a second act."

"Those are the ones who actually committed the crimes, Ian, not the ones who are patsies for the guy who committed the crimes."

"How is Burke, by the way?"

I shrug. "How would I know? I haven't heard from him."

"The SOB didn't even apologize?" Ian grinds out.

"He did. Two words: 'I'm sorry.' You know about that."

He shakes his head. "That text has to be one of the biggest acts of cowardice I've ever seen."

"And you work in finance," I joke. "You've seen more than your share of cowardice."

He bites his lower lip as he smiles, a grin spreading in a boyish manner across his face. "Maybe I'm old fashioned, Hastings. Maybe I just don't like seeing a woman in distress."

"You didn't pay all those legal bills for me because you were worried about my *distress*."

"Did it ever occur to you that maybe I did?" He runs a hand through the hair on the back of his head, absentmindedly rubbing. "There's a point where money doesn't matter."

We both burst into laughter at that statement.

"You know what I mean," he adds. "I couldn't watch you set up as the fall guy and not do something to help."

A prickly sensation begins in the same spot on the back of my head that Ian is rubbing on his. "Are you somehow involved in all of this, Ian?" I ask, the words coming out slowly. I can't believe it's never occurred to me before. "Were you handling all my legal coordination out of a sense of guilt? Is there something you're not telling me?"

"Hastings, the only guilt I feel is the guilt of a man who should have figured it out sooner."

"Technically, you never figured it out at all, not until the zip ties were on my hands."

"Yeah, that was a sight to behold," he says. "When I imagined you in handcuffs, it was never like that."

My skin turns into a blast furnace.

"Like what?"

"In front of other people."

"The other people were *federal agents*, Ian." My breath halts in my chest. "Wait a minute–you imagined me in handcuffs before that?"

Irene happens to walk in at that exact moment. Her face is completely neutral, a testimony to her professionalism.

"Ian, you have—" her eyes flit over to mine "—an advisor on line four."

"It's fine, Irene," he says. "Once Hastings signs the NDA, you can talk openly about our clients."

"But she hasn't signed the NDA yet," Irene points out.

He winks at me. "Let's get that out of the way and get her fully on board and in a position where she can find pleasure in accomplishing her goals."

And with that, Irene takes me to her desk, opens a folder, and shows me a stack of neatly labeled papers awaiting my signature.

Ian closes the door to his office.

I sign forms.

With the stroke of a pen, I am gainfully employed.

And *throbbing*.

9

Mom, Dad, and I are drinking our morning cup of coffee together when the doorbell rings. Confusion bounces between the three of us like a radar signal gone nuts.

"Did you...?"

"Are we expecting...?"

"Kind of early for UPS."

I stand up, staring at my pajama bottoms with bananas and hearts all over them. I'm wearing a black tank top, no shoes, and my hair is in the messiest slipknot you could imagine. It's 6:38 a.m. Who could be ringing the doorbell?

Dad gets up, one knee popping, his groan about getting old an everyday feature of being around him that is *also* getting old. Mom touches her hair with the palms of her hands, fluffing it slightly, smearing the pads of her index fingers under her eyes.

"What're you doing, Mom?" I ask.

"Making myself presentable. What if someone comes in?"

"I'm sure nobody's going to."

"Come on in!" Dad calls out to the doorbell ringer.

I grab a sweatshirt that's hanging off the back of one of the chairs at the kitchen table and throw it on. It's got the logo from Mom and Dad's insurance agency. It was also clearly last worn by Dad.

It smells like Old Spice and grout.

Eric Hesserman appears in the doorway, grinning at me. He's wearing a flannel shirt, a tight gray T-shirt underneath, and is carrying two large containers of something liquid.

"Didn't know Hesserman's delivers!" Dad says heartily.

"What's this?" I ask.

He plunks what appear to be two-gallon containers of a milky substance down on the table in front of me. "Sheep's milk," he declares.

Mom's face lights up.

"Where did you get *that?*" I ask. "I tried everywhere in the eastern half of the state!"

"Didn't come from the eastern half of the state. Came from up north. I found a source right on the New Hampshire/Vermont line."

"You went all the way up *there?*"

"It's not that far. An hour or so." Eric spots the decanter of coffee still in the machine. "Mind if I have some?"

Mom jumps up and gives Eric a big hug. "I haven't seen you in years!"

Eric gives me an eye roll, but it's a happy one, over Mom's shoulder. "How ya doin', Sharon?"

"Does this mean you're making more manchego?" Dad asks me, tilting his head with curiosity. "You used what we had for Mallory's shower." A pouty face emerges. Dad doesn't know the rest is buried in the garage refrigerator. Mom had me hide it in a box marked Vegan Protein Powder, which means Dad will never, *ever* find it.

"I guess so. What else am I going to do with four gallons of sheep's milk?"

"You can make feta," Mom chirps as she gives Eric room to go get his cup of coffee.

Dad gasps in mock horror. "Not when she can make manchego instead!"

It's been years since Eric's sat at our kitchen table. Suddenly I feel like I'm back in high school, only now he's in a committed relationship with a guy named Jackson who I've never even met. He has a daughter, and me?

I'm staring at four gallons of sheep's milk.

"This must have cost an arm and a leg," I marvel, immediately regretting my words because it means I have to ask Mom and Dad for money. Haven't received my first paycheck yet.

"Nah. I bartered for it. Consider it payment for helping me with that cow."

Mom and Dad do a double take. "You helped Eric with a cow?"

"I meant to tell you," I lie.

"Trust me, Sharon," Eric says, leaning across the table resting his fingers on the back of Mom's hand. "Four gallons of sheep's milk doesn't even come close to the payment I owe Hastings for sticking her arm shoulder-deep into a cow's vagina."

Dad starts sputtering his coffee.

Mom stays calm and asks, "Did you do it in your Manolos, dear?"

My turn to sputter.

"Hastings came to the dairy to ask about sheep's milk. We had a cow in bad shape. Between her and this Ian billionaire hot shot CEO guy she's friends with, we managed to save the cow *and* the calf. Mother and baby are doing fine," he says, stopping his explanation to take a long sip of hot coffee.

"Maybe that can be your new job," Mom says to me. "You can work at Hesserman's Dairy."

Eric and Dad laugh. It's a disturbing sound.

"Actually," I say, pulling myself up to full height, stretching the red sweatshirt down as I realize all the coffee's gone and I'm gonna have to brew another pot, "I have a job. I was going to tell you this morning."

All eyes are on me.

"You do?" Dad says. "Who are you working for? Ian McCrory?"

"Good guess. Yes."

"The same guy who paid for your legal defense?"

"That's right."

"Is this some way to pay him back?" Dad inquires.

One of Eric's eyebrows is cocked high.

"No," I say. "Ian refuses to take any money for that. He wants me to do data analysis for him."

"You do data analysis?" Dad asks.

"Of course I do. It's part of finance. Investment, venture capital. You know, all the things that I'm famous for."

"Embezzlement, fraud, money laundering," Eric says under his breath. "Insider trading."

I elbow him. "I may be famous for *those* as well," I inform him, "but I didn't commit any of them."

"Fair enough." Eric smacks the side of one of the milk containers. "How many pounds of cheese will come out of this?"

"You work on a dairy farm, Eric. You should know."

He shakes his head. "Not cheese, and certainly not aged sheep's cheese. I don't know anything about that."

"A gallon makes about a pound. So four pounds or so. When it's done, I'll let you know, and you'll get a cut."

He brightens. "Lori was asking."

"Lori?" Mom looks like a lightbulb turned on behind her

eyes. "That's right! You have a daughter, don't you? I think I saw her working the ice cream van once."

"I do, and it turns out she's a manchego freak."

"I'll be sure to deliver some to her," I tell him. "And if this works out, I would love to know the name of your supplier."

"You really make sheep's cheese for fun?" Eric asks.

"Yeah."

"You're a strange woman, Hastings Monahan."

"Don't look at me like that, Eric."

"Like what?"

"You had your chance in high school."

He's in the middle of finishing his mug of coffee as my words sink in. Deep, wracking coughs make his big chest rumble. Dad has to whack him on the back a few times before Eric can finally speak again. "You were about as likely to date me in high school, Hastings, as you were to watch a botfly video voluntarily."

I shudder. Mom shudders. Even *Dad* shudders, and he has nerves of steel.

Eric walks over to me. I give him a hug. "Thank you," I whisper in his ear.

"No problem. By the way, the woman up at the farm where I got this stuff said that if you're any good, she'd love a sample. I'll hook you and Susan up after you make it."

And with that, Eric leaves.

Mom and Dad run upstairs, separate showers turning on within a minute. I brew another pot of perfectly adequate coffee, sit down, and wait for it to drip.

I stare at four gallons of sheep's milk. Four gallons is thirty-two pounds of milk that will eventually become four pounds of cheese. I just have to figure out how to refrigerate it, because I am due for my first day at work with Ian in an hour and a half, and the train leaves in exactly forty-three minutes.

A frantic shower with what's left of the hot water, Mom's help fitting the milk in the fridge, a travel mug, and a prayer later, and I make it in time. It feels good to be rushed on the way to the office.

Like old times.

The commute into Boston gives me a chance to contemplate the strange thrill of riding a train to work. Last year, the only "public" transportation I took was a private jet that landed in Bedford.

Now I'm using the MBTA app on my phone to buy tickets with my sad little secured credit card.

It sounds silly, but the normalcy of it makes me feel like there's hope.

Like my life has a future.

Like I'm on the right track.

Six months ago, I *never* would have imagined that I'd be *happy* to ride public transit to a job well beneath my abilities, working for my biggest competitor.

And now? The thought excites me.

The reality centers me.

The train sways gently as we make our way toward the center of the city. My travel mug, full of coffee when I left the house, is almost empty. My brief bag rests against my hip, nestled next to me on the seat. I'm in a two-person spot, no one next to me, and the sun is shining straight into my eyes as I look out the window.

Sunrises out here still surprise me. After so many years on the West Coast, I'm accustomed to seeing the sun descend down to the ocean, not peek up from it. You would think being born and raised here would have made me find the sunsets over the water in California the aberration.

When I moved away from home, I reinvented myself. I

sharpened all the edges and left hard granite exposed to the world. Every part of who I was, except for Mom, Dad, and Mallory, relocated itself to my new home.

Only the parts I wanted to take, though.

Now I have holes in me, giant chunks of what makes up a person cut out by Burke. I'm still capable of functioning, but not at my optimal level.

Ian McCrory somehow is helping me fill in the missing pieces of who I am.

Or at least one of them.

The train slows as it makes its entrance into North Station, where the doors open and we pour out like ants released from a jar. My running shoes make no noise as I join the throng and curve to the right, headed to Congress, then Summer Street, where I'll walk the rest of the way. It's a bit of a hike, but I can use the exercise.

Ocean air combined with car exhaust hits me in the face, and then, as I continue to walk, a waft of marijuana joins in. Legalization has changed the terrain for pedestrians in any city. It was true when I lived in the Bay Area, and on frequent business travel to Seattle, actual fresh air was a rarity on some streets.

The fact that I notice it at all says something about my state these days. I'm less in my head and more in my body.

I'm more in the world.

The walk to my office is a good transition from train to Ian. My heart quickens just one beat as I see the hotel and walk through the revolving door.

"Silly," I murmur to myself, knowing that the heart rate change is about Ian. He's getting under my skin. What I want is to have him over my skin.

Over *me*, the rough strength and the sophisticated mind that twist together into the man I see.

When I arrive at the penthouse, I'm greeted by Irene.

And no Ian.

"I'm so sorry, Hastings," she explains as she guides me to my new office. "Ian had to leave the country for an important meeting. He wants me to train you in the basics. He'll be available by teleconference at some point, but not today."

I know a blow-off when I see one.

She looks at her phone, types a quick text, then looks back at me.

Irene's gracious, but I'm now basically the help, and the help never gets the head boss's direct attention.

"It's fine," I lie. "Just direct me to whatever I need to do, and I'll get started."

She pauses, hands clasped in front of her, face impassive. I wait her out.

We sit in silence. It's not tense. There's no conflict here, no rivalry. We don't compete with each other. But her silence and my silence acknowledge each other. She knows exactly what I'm doing, and I know precisely what *she's* doing. There's no need for either of us to have the upper hand, but neither of us are backing down, either.

A phone rings in the distance.

"Don't you need to get that?" I ask her.

Her eyes move, but her body doesn't. "Actually, Hastings, that's *your* phone, in your office."

Curses. I've lost.

I race to the phone, grabbing it just in time. "Hastings Monahan," I say, keeping my voice modulated.

"Welcome. It's Ian. I was hoping I'd catch you."

"I'm at work. At the job you hired me for. Where else would I be?"

He laughs. "You're certainly not in Jakarta."

"How do you know?"

"Because I'm here, Hastings, and you're not."

"How do you know? Maybe I'm VPN-ing from Jakarta."

"Irene told me you're there."

"Maybe I paid Irene off to lie."

"Why would you do that?"

"Because I'm the greatest criminal mastermind in modern history, remember?" I say flatly.

"Look," he says, suddenly all business. "I have a unique opportunity here. I'm sending an encrypted file to you. I want to see if you see what I see in these stats."

"What are you hoping I'll see?"

"That's the beauty of it, Hastings," he says, an intriguing challenge in the tone of his voice. "I'm not going to tell you what to look for. I want to see if *you* find it."

"Day one on the job, and I'm being tested?"

"That's right. That's how it works."

"I thought you hired me because I have one of the best minds in business."

"I did. Prove it."

Click

The call ends before I realize it's ending, leaving me with a bruised ego but a racing mind. Apparently, this isn't going to be some boring job where I check in, sit in front of a bank of terminals, and do the equivalent of maintenance.

Every day I'm going to be on edge.

Every day I'm going to be challenged.

Every day I'm going to walk in the door not knowing what the hours will hold.

And you know what? That makes me smile.

A *real* smile.

The kind I haven't felt on my face in a very long time.

❧ 10 ❧

"W hat're you doing?"

My sister's voice is sharper than normal as I turn and look over my shoulder to find her nose right there, staring at the screen of my phone.

"Avoiding you," I reply as I reach for my coffee and take a sip. I'm at Beanerino with my work spread out before me. Ian gave me permission to do some work from home, and after cashing my first paycheck, I'm joining normal society.

I'm spending my own money, my own *real* money.

I never thought that a four-dollar cup of coffee could taste so good.

"No, I mean what app is on your phone and open?"

"It's a dating app," I tell her as I hide the evidence of my desperation, slipping the phone under a manila folder.

Perky comes on over and plunks herself down on the bench seat next to me. "What's up?"

"She's got the dating app open," Mal says in an arch tone.

"Yeah, so?"

"*The* dating app," Mallory says firmly.

Perky looks as confused as I am. "There's more than one dating app, Mal," she says.

"She's using the one with the conversion consultant."

"Conversion consultant?" I ask as Mallory sits down, too. My nice, quiet work session at a coffee shop is turning into an impromptu social gathering.

Perky's eyes narrow. "Are you talking to a guy on there?" she asks me.

"Yes."

"What kind of date does he want for his first date?"

"Why should I tell you that?"

"Why shouldn't you?" Perky shrugs and takes a sip of some sparkling water in a tiny little bottle. "Unless you're into some kinky sex thing I don't want to know about."

"Fine. His name is Steve."

"Steve. Hmm." Perky and Mal share a look.

"That's not the guy's name, is it?" Mallory says under her breath. "It was David."

"Are you worried we're dating in the same pool? You're almost married, Mallory." I look at her ring, then at my own bare hand. No heirloom engagement ring, no wedding band.

Anyway, it turns out the diamonds Burke bought me were fake. Just like my marriage.

"Of course not! I'm engaged to Will. We're getting married in two months. I don't want to date. I just don't think you should date within *that* app."

"Why not?"

"Has he asked you out to dance?" Perky asks.

I cock one eyebrow. "Why? Spill it!" I insist, looking at the two of them being cagey. "What's going on?"

"Wait a minute," Mallory says, leaning closer to me. "You're ready to *date?*"

"That's really none of your business, but yes."

"Like, really ready? I mean, everything with Burke was so messy."

I don't know why I do it, but I relent and confess something personal to her. "I just need to date, okay?" I take a sip of my coffee just to keep my mouth busy.

"Need to date? Like, *need* needs?" Perky elbows me and winks at Mallory. "Because there are plenty of plastic boyfriends you can use to meet your needs."

"I am *not* answering that," I snap at her.

"But make sure they're BPA-free and slave-labor free," Perky tosses in.

"Then why?" Mal drills down.

"Because I want to. It's good enough to say *because I want to*. In fact, it's good enough to just say *because*. It's even better to ignore you two and pretend you don't exist."

Perky snorts. "Good luck with that."

"My personal life is none of your business. Every single shred of my entire being has been exposed to the world in the media. I have had to talk about things so personal, you can't even begin to fathom it."

Perky leans in. "Like what? You can dish with us. You can tell us anything, Hastings. Burke was a bottom, wasn't he? A toe licker? Did he wear a puppy mask?"

"Stop it!" I throw a napkin at her. "Go away."

"This isn't sixth grade. You can't just throw a flip-flop at my face and make me cry again."

"Try me."

"We just want to warn you," Mallory says sincerely. "When I was dating before I met Will—"

"You met Will in ninth grade."

"Before I *re-met* Will," she clarifies, "there was this guy named David, and he was on the same dating app that you just had open on your screen. He was using women by scheduling these first dates with them at a dance studio–you know, the dance studio–and he came off as this really sweet, nice, charming, smart guy who was offering something unique: a dance lesson for a first date. Cute, huh? All of these women that he was hitting up on the app would show up to the dance class and find out that he not only no-showed, but he was making money if any of the disappointed women turned around and became paid lesson subscribers."

I blink. "This isn't David. This is Steve. And that's the stupidest story I've ever heard," I snap.

"But it's true!" Mallory replies.

"Just because it's true doesn't make it any less stupid."

"She's got a point, Mallory," Perky says under her breath.

"I am not stupid for falling for some con man!"

I laugh in her face. "Anyone who could be snowed by that kind of line is a naïve sucker."

My sister's glare makes me admire her a little. For someone so sunny all the time, the woman can glower.

"I'm *not* a sucker."

"But you don't deny the naïve part."

Perky makes a funny sound.

"Of course she's naïve. She wound up on a porn set because of the word *fluffer*."

"And ended up marrying the best guy in the world!" Mal says hotly. "Yes, I can be overly trusting," she adds, avoiding the word *naïve*.

"Naïve," Perky coughs into her hand. I'm starting to like her.

A little.

"And because I'm trusting, people sometimes take advantage of me. Like David. I'm just trying to protect you, Hastings."

"I don't need to be protected."

"The last thing you need is to be conned again."

"I'm the opposite of naïve, Mallory." My voice fades out

as I realize I *was* snowed by a con man.

People who live in glass houses, and all that.

I look at the app and see the message from Steve, inviting me to meet him for dancing. We've been texting back and forth for the past couple of days, and I like the guy. He's no Ian, of course, who's still in Jakarta and who barely talks to me now that I work for him, but Steve's a guy.

And he's interested.

In *me*.

So I do what any woman would do when confronted by two people trying to tell her that she's wrong.

"Go away," I tell my sister and Perky. I shoo them with the back of my hand, fluttering in the air over my coffee. "I'm a grownup. I can handle myself."

"Fine." Mallory stands up in a snit. "But don't you dare come crying to me when it turns out you've been played by David."

"Why would I come crying to *you*?"

"Because that's what you do when... well, when..." She looks at Perky.

"When someone hurts your feelings," Perky says to me. "And you need a friend to talk it through."

A weird silence hangs in the air between the three of us. I don't do that. I don't have that kind of friend.

I've never had that kind of friend.

Mallory's hand closes over the back of mine as she squeezes gently, then lets go. "I hope Steve is real. But if he's not, at least convince Philippe to give you the first lesson for free."

And with that, I'm alone again.

The app's open, Steve's message stream right there. It starts with:

I'm branching out and trying something new. Would you be interested in a really different first date? A dance lesson?

I'm tired of coffee-shop speed dating and I have two left feet (full disclosure). Want to meet up for some fun? Steve

And ends with:

See you there, Mary.

Mary. I know, right? It's my real middle name. Using Mary is cheating, a little. But Hastings Monahan is so well known, it'll make guys run away if they know I'm me.

Mallory and Perky can't be right. My sister might be gullible enough to get taken in by a conversion consultant, but not me.

In spite of my disbelief, I type Steve a message:

This is going to sound crazy, but this is a real date, right? Not some come-on to convince me to sign up for dance lessons.

Instantly, three dots appear:

Who does that? That's even creepier than guys who send dick pics. He adds an eggplant emoji.

I laugh.

Is that a way to soften me up for an incoming photo? I reply.

No incoming photo from me would involve softening.

The gasp that comes out of me is a mix of amusement and horror. He's not out of line; it's clever and a little seductive, if crude. I started this, and he finished it.

LOL is all I can respond with. Being out of the dating pool for ten years means these particular networking skills are rusty. My wedding ring and marital status shielded me in my line of work, offering a thin veneer of protection against overeager guys ready to put my negotiating skills to the test.

On my knees or on my back.

Nothing about my pics would make you laugh–if I were the kind of creep to send them. But I'm not. Looking forward to meeting you tonight, Mary. Get ready to tango. :)

Crazy. Mal and Perky are crazy.

And Steve is perfect for my first venture back into the meat market from hell we call dating.

❧

I HAVEN'T BEEN ON A DATE WITH ANYONE EXCEPT BURKE IN more than ten years.

There is a portion of the brain that shuts off when you commit to someone. Somewhere deep inside all of us–or at least those of us who are not asexual or aromantic–there's a section of the brain dedicated wholly to tracking and analyzing attractive people.

I'm a heterosexual woman, so for me, that means men.

And a man in a business suit is one of the most attractive creatures on the planet.

These days, I've been combing over my past with Burke, wondering what I found attractive in *him*. It's not hard to understand. Plenty of other women competed with me for his attentions, but I won.

I won.

Lucky me, right?

Even worse, I *thought* I won.

But I didn't.

I'm wearing a short skirt with layers that swirl, but I wonder if I should change into jeans. I contemplate the fact that the last time I had a first date, Facebook didn't run advertisements and Instagram didn't even exist.

Swiping left or right was something you did while reading a print magazine or washing a window.

"Where're *you* going?" Dad asks as I walk down the stairs, headed for the door.

"Out." I halt, swallowing my pride. "Can I, uh, use your car?"

"Of course!" he says, pointing to the keys hanging from a

rack by the door.

"You look really nice, honey," Mom says, popping up behind him. They're going over cookbooks, trying to decide what to make together tonight. "I guess you won't be here for dinner?" Mom asks.

"No. I'm going out on a da—"

Dad smiles. "A date?"

"No. A dance lesson."

"Dance lesson?" Mom says. "Is it Mallory's wedding party?"

"No," I tell her. "I'm just going for an extra one. I missed some of the classes they went to," I choke out, relieved Mom gave me an excuse without realizing it.

Two blank stares greet me.

"Oh," Dad says finally, his voice a bit hollow. "Okay."

The look they give each other tells me that neither of them believes a word out of my mouth, but we're going to play this game of pretend.

By the time I pull into the parking lot at the address Steve gave me, my heart sinks.

Bailargo. Huh.

I'm more nervous than I expected. I decided to go on a date because I need my life to be orderly again. The boxes need to be checked off. Events need to fit into categories. Emotions need to line up in straight lines and right angles–not agitated scribbles.

And this first date needs to be with someone who does not know me. Being Hastings Monahan, that woman from the "guy who ripped off all those people" story, is an identity I want to shed, even if it's just for a few hours.

I need to find a way through the madness of the last few months.

Job? Check.

Money coming in? Check.

Safe place to live? Check.

Touching a man not named Ian McCrory?

Working on it now.

Call it whatever you wish. A booty call. A friend with benefits. A boyfriend. You pick the term–any term but husband. Not going anywhere near that one, ever again.

This time, I need to pick the right guy.

This time, I won't make the same mistake I made with Burke.

This time, I will have con men on my radar.

No one is going to put one over on me, *ever* again.

The parking lot is surprisingly full, about fifteen cars parked randomly. For a dance studio, I assume that's a lot.

I walk up the stairs of the old Victorian house painted in bright red, white, and black. In San Francisco, where the Victorians are so carefully preserved, something like this would be considered a monstrosity.

Here, though, it's quaint.

The smell of linseed oil and lemon assaults me the second I open the door, and as I go down the hallway, wondering exactly where I sign in, I hear people laughing joyfully. It's contagious.

I smile.

This is the life people were living while I was working so hard, 24/7. Meanwhile, these people were coming to dance lessons after finishing a day at the office, standing in groups, munching on cookies, drinking lemonade, waiting to spend an hour just moving their bodies and learning how to do it better.

This is what I was missing when Burke sneered at the idea of doing anything other than networking, keeping his body in peak shape with gym routines–a body he slowly stopped sharing with me.

I've been here before with Mallory, but it was brief and I

didn't stay for the dance lesson, so I'm not sure how this all works. I walk into the ballroom. There's a small table to the left.

"Hello, hello!" says a man with black, slicked-back hair and a Spanish accent. "Are you here for the DANCE?" he shouts, as if the word *dance* is in all capital letters.

"I'm here for the dance lesson, but I'm waiting for my date."

A mask of neutrality falls across the man's otherwise expressive face. "Your date?"

"Yes. His name is Steve."

"Steve." Again, that weird change in tone. "Is this by any chance your *first* date with him?"

I look at the man's name tag. It says Philippe, and then just the word Owner underneath his name. "Yes, Philippe. It *is* my first date with Steve."

A woman behind me taps me on the shoulder. "I'm here for a first date with Steve, too."

"What a coincidence," I say coolly, uncertain why she would care to share that with me, a spike of competition making my blood prickly.

Another woman is on the periphery, to my right. She leans forward and says to Philippe, "She's another one, isn't she?"

"What are you all talking about?"

Philippe's shoulders droop as he stands smoothly, with the muscles of a dancer, preparing for a verbal declaration.

"What is your name, dear? Did you register in advance?" he asks, picking up a clipboard.

"Yes. I registered as Mary Monahan."

"I am sorry, Ms. Monahan. *Monahan?* Are you related to Mallory Monahan?" he asks.

"Yes."

"I do not remember you."

"I'm her sister."

"Oh! You are the bitch!" He claps his hand over his own mouth. "Excuse me, my accent. I meant to say, the beach, the *beach.* You know, the sand? Ocean? The–"

I stop him before he embarrasses himself even further.

"It's fine. I don't consider that word an insult. But what's going on with Steve? Why are three of us on dates with a guy named Steve?" An alarm bell starts in my mind, pinging back to when Perky and Mallory tried to warn me about the conversion consultant.

"There is a man who works for our corporate office. His name is David."

The alarm bell turns into a gong.

"David?" I ask.

"Yes, David, and he uses dating apps to lure innocent women such as yourself—"

I snort.

He corrects himself. *"–sophisticated* women such as yourself to come here for first dates. He thinks that it will increase the number of women who will sign up for paid lessons."

"And does it work?" I ask.

"It does," he admits, studying me nervously, clearly expecting me to fall apart. I'm absolutely mortified, more that Mallory and Perky were right than that I've been taken in by a guy who flirted with me using an eggplant emoji.

Steve is nothing more than a salesperson. I'm a number to hit quota.

But I'm too proud to let my emotional reaction show. The guy who runs this dance studio does not get to pity me, too.

"That's genius!" I say brightly, meaning it, too.

Philippe clearly does not expect *that* response from me, his hand going to the base of his throat, splayed flat, as if he's protecting his heart.

"Excuse me?" he says. "Most women are in tears when they find out."

"I'm not most women, Philippe. I know a good strategic business mind when I see one."

"Of course you do," says a deep voice behind me.

I turn around to stare into the deep brown eyes of Ian McCrory.

"That's what you're known for, Hastings," he adds.

"I am known for a hell of a lot more than that these days. What are *you* doing here?" I ask him, secretly thrilled but trying hard not to show it. If he seemed like a creepy stalker before, when he was trying to get me to work for him, that perspective has shifted in me.

I'm deeply curious about how and why he keeps finding me all over town, but it's exciting, too.

"Why are *you* here?" he counters.

I pause. If I tell him the truth, then he knows that I'm dating, but even worse than that, he knows that I fell for the con.

Again.

I fell for the con.

My blood starts to pound, a ringing in my ears that I know all too well. If I wait much longer, I'm going to faint, so I take a few steps to the refreshment table and pretend that I'm pouring myself a glass of lemonade. I perform the actual action. I just have no intention of drinking it.

A quick sip does the trick in terms of keeping my mouth busy.

"She's taking a DANCE lesson, of course," Philippe says, jumping to my rescue. "Her sister is getting married soon, and Mary is coming here to learn."

And then, damned if Philippe doesn't turn and wink at me. Does he know? Can he tell I'm attracted to Ian? What the hell is going on?

"Mary?"

"My middle name. Hastings Mary Monahan."

"Your initials are 'hmm'?"

Oh, the rumbling sound he makes when he says it that way.

Crossing his arms over his chest, Ian's eyes twinkle with amusement. His beard has about two days' growth, dark and thick, giving his mouth a luscious, rugged look.

"What is your point, Ian?"

"That's why you're here? For a dance lesson?" Ian asks, giving me an annoying yet adorable grin.

"Of course," I say, grateful for Philippe's intervention.

"I thought you were here because Steve lured you, just like the rest of us who got suckered into this ridiculous first-date dance-lesson crap," says the woman to my right.

Ian looks like he's trying to hold back a smile. "Steve did a number on you, too?"

I narrow my eyes. "How do you know about Steve?"

"Because he works for me."

"He works for *you*?"

"My company owns Nationwide Dance Studios. Bailargo is part of it."

Philippe's whole demeanor changes. "Ian... *Ian McCrory*? Oh, Mr. McCrory, it is an honor to have you here!"

Philippe can't see Ian's face from where he's standing, but I can, and Ian rolls his eyes.

"Why don't you stay for my DANCE lesson? You can see exactly what we do here in our beautiful Bailargo."

Ian's eyes don't move. They're focused entirely on me. "Great idea, Philippe. Give me a chance to understand one of my holdings on a deeper level. I'd like to get to know *all* of my employees much better."

His words aren't for Philippe.

"I thought you were out of the country," I venture, still

trying to comprehend the sudden appearance of Ian McCrory at Bailargo, of all places.

"I was. But now I'm here."

Clap, clap!

Philippe calls the class to order. A young woman in an A-line skirt chats with the two other women who were brought here by Steve. I grab Ian's bicep. It's like holding onto a piece of iron.

"You really employ conversion consultants who go on dating apps and lure women into free trials at companies that you own?"

"Yes."

"So you're not even trying to deny it?"

"No."

Could he be any hotter?

"Have you ever thought of doing it with the opposite gender?"

"What?"

"Have women do it?"

"Women setting up fake first dates to lure a guy to a dance studio? That would never work."

"No, Ian. Gyms. Dates at the fitness center. Free weights. Spin centers. Don't you own a chain of gyms?"

"Yeah, but—" The lightbulb goes on in his expression. "Hastings, that's an amazing idea!"

"Of course it is. I came up with it."

His eyes drift to my hand on his arm.

"There's just one problem." I continue, pulling back, folding my arms, and staring at him.

"What's that?"

"It's slimy. You're trifling with people's emotions."

His mouth drops open just slightly, lips parting. He pokes his tongue between them and licks. A flame rises up between my legs, traveling to my eyelids.

"Trifling with people's emotions," he says, echoing my words. "Since when did Hastings Monahan care about *emotions*?"

"Since I was a sucker in one of the biggest cons in U.S. history. Now apparently I'm a sucker in your tiny little con."

"It's not a con."

"Yes, it is, Ian."

"No, it's not."

"Yes, it is."

"No, it's—"

Clap, clap!

The dance lesson is about to begin.

"Partner up!" Philippe says, looking straight at Ian and smiling at me. "You two have already found each other. Good, good. It's very clear that there's a spark between you."

I laugh, but Ian doesn't, instead giving me a smoldering look. One hand reaches out, expecting me to clasp it.

"I guess we're partners, then," he says softly, seriously, broad shoulders creating shadows as the setting sun glints through one of the tall windows.

"I guess we are."

The moment he touches me, everything around us fades. His palm rests lightly on my waist, sending electric shocks all the way into my soul. His hand slides to the small of my back and pulls me in, and my own hands don't know quite what to do.

Obviously, I've danced with men before. I've danced with Burke for countless hours at networking events, weddings, cocktail parties, where the socially appropriate thing to do is to couple off, move onto the dance floor, and pretend that you know what you're doing.

Burke used dancing to read a room.

Ian is reading *me*.

"Have you never danced before, Hastings?" Ian asks, an

amused smile tickling his lips. He's taller than me, even when I'm wearing these heels, and it's nice.

So nice. Burke was about my height.

Awkward, I reach out, my right hand brushing against his hip, resting tentatively above his belt, the weight of his thick muscles pressed against my palm. His hand reaches for mine, and my left hand goes up to his shoulder. There, the connection is done, the circle of our arms making our bodies an endless loop.

I swallow hard, suddenly nervous, as if I'm at an eighth-grade dance again and I don't know what to do with myself. Maybe that's who I am now, someone awkward, someone in transition, desperately hoping that the world really can give me everything I want.

The music starts, and Ian begins to move. The gentle glide of my body being led is a relief. He knows how to do this, his grace so arousing that I have to look away, staring at a distant spot over his shoulder, before my face betrays me.

"Excellent!" Philippe calls out, the only word that I catch because the pounding of my blood in my ears is like the waves of the ocean just after a storm.

"You're good," Ian says. "You know what to do with your body when I touch you."

"Switch partners!" Philippe shouts. But Ian doesn't move, his hands still on me, eyes boring into mine. If we weren't in public, I swear he would lean down and try to kiss me.

Instead, I step back, breaking the connection. A little old man with slumped shoulders and a white beard that reminds me of Santa Claus taps Ian on the shoulder. He moves his hands and turns, staring down at the diminutive gentleman.

"Hey, buddy," the man says in an accent I can't quite pinpoint. "She's my girl now."

Ian laughs, a sound of joy, his hands on his hips as four women all cluster around him, each vying to be the next partner. A soft, dry hand takes mine as I find myself staring directly into the bright blue eyes of—

"Dancy. My name's Dancy," the old man says. "And you are?"

"Hastings."

"Hastings? Anyone ever call you Hasty?" he asks.

"No, never."

Laughter bursts out of him as his palm goes to my back, the other takes my hand, and I do the same. It's jolting, really, to go from Ian to this guy. But as he moves me across the floor, I'm stunned by Dancy's elegance.

"You're a very good dancer," I tell him.

"I know."

"You're also modest."

"That I'm not, my dear Hasty."

For some reason, when he says Hasty, it doesn't bother me at all. I let him get away with it. I have a feeling that Dancy gets away with an awful lot.

"Come here often?" I ask him.

"That's *my* line, young lady. How old are you?" he asks, one eyebrow up.

There's something about him, a bit hollow, a bit familiar. "I'm thirty-four," I inform him.

"Much too old for me," he says. "You're practically one of the blue hairs here."

"Hey!"

Ian and his partner happen to be moving past us just as Dancy says that. Ian makes a sound that's pretty close to a snicker.

"You have no room to talk. How old are you, ninety-five?"

He removes his hand from my waist and clutches his heart. "I'm *half* that!"

"You're half full of it."

His hand goes back to my waist and he dips me. I'm impressed he has the strength, as my loose hair practically touches the ground. I look up at him, neck stretched, as he says, "No, my dear. I am one hundred percent full of it."

Clap, clap!

Philippe shouts, "Change partners!"

The rush of blood as I go upright makes me flushed. Dancy takes a little bow, cackling, as he finds another victim. Soon I'm paired up with a woman named Susan. As you'd expect in any dance class, there are more women than men. She's a good half foot shorter than me, with birdlike bones and bright white hair curled in tight ringlets around her skull. I lead her, clumsily, through the steps.

"Not used to being the man, are you?" she says. "What's your name?"

"Hastings."

She comes to a dead halt. "Hastings Monahan?"

Oh, boy. "Yes."

"You're that girl from the news?"

I don't know what to say to that. I move her to the left, then to the right, my hand on her hip, feeling like I'm turning a doorknob. She's bony, tiny, and this is probably–other than church and the grocery store–her one outing every week.

Face tipped up to me, she waits for a response.

Finally, I confess.

"Yes, that's me."

"Your parents run the insurance agency in Anderhill."

"Um hmm."

She brightens. "I remember you. From farm camp. When you were in middle school."

I pause, unable to continue absorbing the information and instruction from Philippe, move my body in space in concert with hers, and have this conversation.

"How do you remember me?"

"I'm one of the farmers, dear. I taught the alternative dairy portion, remember? I worked with the goats and the sheep."

"You're *that* Susan?" Twenty years melt away, and I'm transported back to the summer of eighth grade, the three weeks I spent at a small farm thirty minutes north of Anderhill, at Mom and Dad's insistence. I'd hated every minute of the first few hours, and then I fell in love with the milking, the cheese making. Susan didn't run the farm camp, but she brought her sheep's milk there and was one of the counselors. "Susan Johnson? You're *Susan*?" I reach for her and give her a gentle hug. "Oh, my goodness. I haven't seen you in—"

"More than twenty years. I know, dear."

Suddenly I want to cry. The bundle of emotions inside is too difficult to describe. It's threads of the past, the present, the me I could have been, the me that I am, the me that I thought I was.

And the me that Burke stole.

She grins up at me. "You were always such a sweet girl, so serious. Do you still make goat's milk cheese?"

Ian happens to dance past us as she asks the question, his face switching to a puzzled look, but then he turns, carrying his partner off to the other side of the room as if sweeping the question away.

"I do," I tell her. "Well, I did. Now it's sheep's milk only. In fact, Eric Hesserman brought me four gallons of sheep's milk last week."

She brightens. "Is *that* what he was doing with it?"

"He got it from you?"

"No, dear, not me. I'm too old now. I don't milk that often. My son runs the dairy."

"But you live so far away. You came and brought your animals to teach us. You're way up in New Hampshire. What're you doing here taking dance lessons?"

"My husband's in a nursing home nearby, a special facility. I come and visit him every other day. My friends—" she gestures to two old women with hair as white as hers, "—insisted that I come to dance. Serendipitous, isn't it?" she says, reaching up to touch my face with a hand so callused, it doesn't reconcile with her fragility.

"Yes, serendipitous," I echo, just as the music stops.

She reaches into her pocket and pulls out a surprisingly modern smartphone. She turns it on and asks, "What's your phone number, Hastings?"

I recite it to her. She enters it into the phone. But before she puts it back in her pocket, she wiggles it in the air. "Handy little thing, isn't it? My grandson taught me all about it. Made me take a class with him."

"Yes, yes it is."

I don't know what to say.

Susan gives me a quick hug and then says, "I'm sorry, dear. I have to go." And with that, she turns away, walking with an economy of movement.

I'm stunned, and because I'm so surprised, I don't realize Ian is at my side until he speaks.

"Hastings, what're you doing after this?"

I look at him, unable to form words, emotion filling up all the corners of my mind that organize speech.

"Hastings? You okay?" He touches my elbow. It zings.

"I'm fine."

"Dinner after this?" He laughs. "You're the local, so you know the best places."

"I'm not local anymore, Ian. I haven't been home and gone out to eat in ages."

"Really? What do you do when you come home?"

"Hide from the media."

"No–I mean, before."

Shorthand between us makes me want to say yes to his

dinner invitation. Ian is the only connection to my old life, my only tether to the Bay Area. It's appealing.

He's appealing.

"I networked. Went to business meetings. Had dinner with my parents and my little sister."

"That's it? Work and family?"

"Sure."

"What about fun?"

He's so appealing, standing before me, offering me the world. Why is he being so kind? Why did he come to my defense and pay all those legal bills? Why did he offer me a job? Why is he here, asking me out for dinner? What's with the pursuit? What's going on?

I want to ask him, and as seconds tick by, the offer hanging in the air between us, I'm tempted, and yet something holds me back.

"No," I say reflexively but with a smile. "I appreciate the offer. I really do. But I don't think it's a good time."

"Why not?"

"Ian, I just got stood up. By someone who works for you, whose entire job was to convince me to come here and then sign up for dance classes, and now you're here and you expect me to go out with you? It's just a little too twisty."

"It doesn't have to be," he says, taking one step forward.

I look around and realize we have an audience. "The answer's no. I need you to respect that."

"That's right," Dancy says. "No means no."

Ian ignores him, his face growing serious. His phone buzzes. He ignores that, too, giving me his full attention.

I touch his hand and give him a grateful look. "I do appreciate it. I do. But we're colleagues. You're my boss now. I can't date you."

"Back in my day, you sure could," Dancy says.

"Fine. Call it a business dinner," Ian counters, upping the

ante. His phone buzzes again.

"Aren't you going to answer that?" I ask.

"No."

"Why not?"

"Because it's less important than you are."

"We're in that territory now, are we?"

"What do I have to say to convince you to go out with me?" he asks, holding his arms over his chest, reveling in the fact that we have an audience.

"This isn't a negotiation. We're not talking about a merger or an investment question, Ian. We're talking about dating. Romance."

"Love!" shouts one of the women in the room.

"Aren't you that woman from the TV?" says one of the older ladies. "The one in that financial scandal. Aren't you married to that guy who took off and left you in trouble with the law?"

My face flushes.

"She's Sharon and Roy's daughter."

"Oh, that's right."

The whispers behind me make me close my eyes.

Pity whispers.

"Poor girl. She really got screwed over by her husband."

Eyebrows shoot up at the word *husband.*

"If she has a husband, why is this man asking her out?"

"Hastings," Ian says, pulling me aside. "You don't have to—"

I cut him off. "I absolutely have to, Ian. The answer's no."

And with that, I walk away, knowing that I'll go into the office tomorrow and see him. And I don't even have it in me to turn around and ask him why in the world he's at a dance studio in small-town Massachusetts.

Asking me out for dinner.

❧ 11 ❧

It's Saturday morning, and now that I'm working a normal job, I've come to appreciate my weekends. For someone who used to happily work ninety or a hundred hours a week, it's official:

I'm a slacker.

But I'm a slacker with an incredibly comfortable childhood bed, now that Mom and Dad bought me a new mattress.

The phone buzzes, then it buzzes again, and finally the damn thing starts to sound like a bee. I groan and roll over, grabbing it.

This is Raul from Beanerino, the text says. *We'd like to place an order for your cheese.*

My cheese? How does he know I'm making cheese?

We know you're making cheese because Perky told us is the next text I get.

Mystery solved.

We like to buy local, keep customers happy with community-minded products. Our wine bar would be a great setting for your sheep's cheese. Are you in?

The next text quotes a price per pound that they're willing to pay.

I reply back with a figure four dollars more per pound. Raul impresses me by coming back, holding steady, and after seventeen or so back and forths, we settle on a decent price. He's only buying ten pounds, so what's my profit going to be? Fifty bucks, if that?

It's more the feel that hooks me, the negotiating.

I have *value*.

I was about to let the words *once again* float through my mind, but something stops me. Burke never valued me. Maybe I never valued myself in the way that I should have.

This feels good. It feels light and happy and pleasant enough, to sell ten pounds of cheese that hasn't finished aging yet.

It's not ready, I tell him.

I know, he writes back. *But when it is, we get those ten pounds.*

Of course. We can do three-month aged. Some people prefer it. It's a bit softer, I write back.

Let's start a pipeline, he replies. *Three-month, six-month, eight-month.*

You know your manchego, I write back.

All I get is a smiley face.

Thanks, I answer, realizing that the nicety needs to be there. This is a client, after all.

No, not a client.

A *customer*.

I'm selling a commodity here. Not a service. Not a financial product. Not my own ability to connect multiple people into a pattern that leads to my benefit.

I'm working with my hands to produce something that people consume and enjoy. This is different.

It feels good, *really* good, in a way that negotiating a deal for someone else never did.

My phone pings with another text.

Hello, you still there? Raul asks.

I shake my head, startled to realize that I've gone off into the deep, winding forest of my own thoughts.

Yes, still here. Pipeline it is, I type back. *Sounds good.*

Now I have to source more sheep's milk. Note to self: Contact Eric immediately to get more.

I look at my phone and pull up Susan's information. Even better. Go direct to the source.

Perfect, Raul writes back. *Come in and sign the contract any time.*

How about today? I write back.

I get a thumbs-up in response.

Falling back against the pillows, I stare dumbly at my own phone. Endorphins race through my bloodstream, making my skin warm, my mouth twisting up into a smile that feels dopey on my face. My shoulders relax. My muscles feel loose.

This is what it's like to feel good, centered and grounded. Like something's going well in my life.

Because it is.

A fifty-dollar profit? I would have spent that on a tip for a good haircut, six months ago.

Now it represents a crowning achievement.

I catch my reflection in the mirror. Half my hair has fallen out of its messy bun, and I'm pretty sure I've had this t-shirt since tenth grade. I look at my toes and try to remember when I last had a pedicure.

It's long past time.

Between my new paycheck and this side business making good cheeses, I'm settling into something close to a life. *My* life.

Defined by me, not Burke.

Not investors.

Not bosses.

Not the social milieu of the Bay Area.

Me. Just *me*.

Instead of letting myself start second guessing, getting caught in a jumble of thoughts that eventually paralyze me, I go straight for the bathroom. I strip down, jump under the hot spray, and think of Ian.

Being naked and hot must be preconditions for thinking about him.

No, that's not true. I think about him even when I'm clothed and cold. I think about him in my dreams. I think about him at the office. I think about him when I watch a movie, when I read an interesting article. I think about him when I'm dragging the trash out to the curb because Dad has asked that I participate more in household chores.

I think about him when I lie in bed at night and cry.

Not because he makes me cry, but because my old life comes flooding in then, and thoughts of Ian are the only thing that gives me hope about the future. Not a future with him; that's a fantasy. I've written it off. I might as well be back in seventh grade, dreaming about Justin Timberlake.

Not a future with Ian, but a future, period. He's helped me so much.

As I soak my long hair, I wonder about him. Where is he right now? He hasn't been in the office lately. Irene has been uncharacteristically quiet about Ian's location. Being secretive doesn't surprise me. What's his day-to-day life like? How can a man who's helped me so much, put himself so much in my life, be so private, so closed off?

Maybe I'm being silly.

After all, *I* rejected his offer of dinner.

Maybe I drove him away.

I rinse the rest of the shampoo out of my hair and pour conditioner in, running my fingers through the tangled strands. I grab the soap, and my hand runs down my belly, stopping just short of places I haven't thought about in a long time.

Except when I think about *him*.

"This is crazy," I whisper aloud, some of the water from the shower spray getting into my mouth. I swallow, exquisitely aware of every movement of my body, the click of my throat as the water goes down, the rivulets as they wind their way along the curves of my back. My skin is on fire, and my heart starts to slam against my ribs, the throbbing between my legs intensifying. That side of myself is supposed to be dead.

Or is it?

The stupid dating app didn't do me any good. I deleted it after the dance fiasco. My entire world is nothing but my job— and now, making cheese.

Too bad there isn't room for Ian McCrory in it.

By the time I'm done showering, drying my hair, and dressing in running clothes, I decide that I might as well run over to Beanerino, sign the paperwork, and get it out of the way. What else am I going to do? Read some of the four hundred letters from creditors that fill my inbox?

Avoidance is a finely honed strategy.

My calves complain bitterly for the first quarter mile of my run. I haven't been going out on these long stretches lately, too busy with work to let myself exercise during the week. After a half mile, though, the rhythm takes over, my ponytail swinging, my long-sleeved shirt warming up under the arms.

It feels good to sweat.

It feels good to move.

It feels good to run toward something and not away from it.

The miles between home and Beanerino melt away as I become nothing but a flow. It's not just the flow of blood and muscle, of sinew and motion. It's bigger than that: It's the flow of escaping the overwhelming tornado inside my head that has stripped everything about who I am down to a foundation littered with debris. Each pounding footstep makes me feel lighter.

By the time I see the small building, I'm absolutely slammed. My skin is bright red, all the blood flowing to the surface, tapping on my pores, so close to being free.

I reach for the door handle, yank it open with arms ready to do some work, and stride into the coffee shop like I own it. Raul looks up from the register and gives me a wave, his big grin evincing a shared friendliness that makes me think coming home with my tail between my legs wasn't the worst thing ever.

"Hastings." Raul's deep voice carries tones that I've never heard before. Because I'm not dead yet, my body takes about three seconds to run its inventory of responses to such a hot guy smiling at me.

"Raul," I reply, marching up to the counter, slapping my palms on the flat, polished oak and leaning forward. "Where's that contract?"

He grins, like a flash of light, as his broad smile captivates me. "Right here." From under the counter, he pulls out a manila folder and flips it open.

"That's quick," I tell him as he hands me a pen.

"I'm working on showing Papá that maybe I'm not a six-year-old with skinned knees anymore." He puffs up a bit. "I'm getting my MBA online, you know."

"Really."

A self-deprecating look crosses his face. "Nothing like what you do, of course, but—"

"Hey," I say, reaching for his hand, pressing mine against the back of his. "Don't do that."

"Don't do what?"

"Don't minimize what you're accomplishing."

My spine tingles, a hot spot between my shoulder blades. Burke did that. Minimized what I did. My deals were never as good as his. My strategy was never as resilient as his. The dollar signs affixed to my deals were never in the same arena as what he was bringing in.

That deal the night I was arrested, the nine-figure deal-of-a-lifetime for me, was the apex. It was the pinnacle of accomplishment. And it was a big middle finger to my own husband.

I can see that now.

I couldn't see it then.

Raul looks at our hands. He makes eye contact, with an expression that says he understands I'm not coming on to him.

"Thank you," he says, glancing over my shoulder. "Why don't you sign? Let's make it official."

"Let's make what official?" says a deep voice behind me.

That prickly feeling in my spine? It intensifies, shooting between my legs, down the backs of my calves to the ends of my toes and up to the crown of my head. My shoulders tighten, the pen gripped hard in my hand as I sign quickly, as if the deal were about to be taken away from me.

I lay the pen down and turn around, placing my hands on the edge of the counter, this time leaning. The small of my back tightens, my legs bracing with bent knees.

"Ian," I say. "Good to see you."

"You're making a deal with Beanerino?"

"I am."

"What's she selling you?" he asks Raul.

Those topaz eyes flecked with dark chocolate meet mine. He gives me a shrug, as if to say, *This is your game.*

I turn to Ian. "Cheese."

"Excuse me?"

"Cheese. I'm selling cheese."

"Cheese?"

"Yes, cheese. It's made from the milk of a mammal."

"I know what cheese is, Hastings. You're brokering a deal? Are you working with the Dairy Association now?"

"Something like that," I reply.

"Either you are or you're not," he says. "There is no 'something like that.' Is this a side deal? Are you consulting now?"

"It's more of a hobby."

"*You* have hobbies?"

"I have hobbies."

"Like what?"

"Like making cheese."

"Making cheese isn't a hobby, Hastings."

"It is for me."

"Macchiato," he says to Raul, who grabs one of the ever-present bar towels near the big espresso machine and wipes something down before a hissing sound cuts through the air.

"Tell me about your other hobbies." Ian crosses his arms and leans his hip against the wide counter. There's a natural indentation in the thick piece of wood that was used to make it, an uneven spot that seems to invite his ass to snuggle in and stay awhile.

"Tell me about *your* hobbies, Ian."

"Is that how this is going to be?"

I stare him down, crossing my arms over my chest. I feel something damp on my forearms, and realize the area under my breasts is soaked with sweat from my run.

I wait him out.

"I like money," he declares.

I snort. "Who doesn't?"

"No. I mean, I literally like money. I collect coins."

"Coins?"

"And bills. It started with my grandfather. I have his collection, inherited it when he died. My dad was into it, too."

"Do you collect stamps, too?" I snark.

"No. Just coins. Want to see my coin collection sometime?"

"Is that like inviting me to check out your etchings in your bedroom?"

Raul slides the macchiato Ian ordered across the thick counter and laughs openly. Ian cuts him a look intended to shut him up, but Raul doesn't care.

I really like Raul.

Sensing an opening, I reach into my bra and pull out my debit card, sliding it to Raul, who quietly takes it.

"What're you doing?" Ian asks.

"I'm paying for your coffee."

"Excuse me?"

"It's on me."

A booming laugh fills the empty coffee shop. "You're buying *my* coffee?"

I bite my lip. "Why not?"

"Does that make this a date?" he challenges as Raul hands my card and the receipt back to me.

"No need for a tip," Raul says, eyes jumping to my bra. "I don't want to know where it's been."

Ian reaches in his pocket, pulls out his wallet, and throws a twenty in the tip jar. Raul's eyebrows shoot up.

"You don't need to do that," I tell him.

"*Shh!*" Raul jumps in, waving me away.

"What other hobbies do you have, Hastings? You never

answered me." Ian takes a sip. His hand goes to that very spot between my shoulder blades that just tingled.

Guiding me over to a table, he gestures for me to sit. Waving at Raul, he gets his attention instantly. "Bring her favorite."

"I think she already has it," Raul says softly.

"Thank you, but I'm good," I say to Raul, shooting him a look designed to kill. I stand and walk over to the small water container filled with slices of cucumber. I pour myself a small cup and turn around to find Ian's eyes exactly where my ass just was.

I tap the table and point to my face. "Eyes up here," I say.

He just grins, charming his way out of it. "Cheese," he says, taking a sip of his coffee. "You make cheese."

"I do."

"How did you get into this cheese-making thing?"

The bell above the door dings. We both look up. It's Perky, although whether she's here to work a shift or just hang out is not clear. She waves at us, walking over behind the counter where the employees enter, huddling with Raul. I can hear them whispering, my name being bandied about.

Perky is about as subtle as a jackhammer.

"I learned in middle school," I tell Ian. "I went to farm camp."

"You went to *farm camp?*"

I nod. "It's a thing around here."

"Is that how you knew what to do with birthing the calf?"

"Hell, no. Eric just needed the right arm for the right vagina."

Out of the corner of my eye, I see Raul's hands halt, mid-swipe on the counter. He winces, then moves as far away from us as possible.

"Who knew? Hastings Monahan does something for fun.

Not for profit, not for the thrill of the hunt, not for the joy of going in for the kill."

"When have I ever been that way?"

One eyebrow goes up, his mouth moving in a tight manner that makes me want to kiss it loose. "When have you ever *not* been that way, Hastings?"

"In the last few months, since I've been working for you. Since my whole life got unraveled by the mess my ex-not-husband created."

He looks at his coffee, running his finger along the rim of the ceramic mug. "Fair enough," he admits, nodding. "I wondered about you."

"Wondered what?"

"I thought I was hiring a barracuda."

"You're not happy with my performance at work?"

"No, no," he says, holding his palms up at me. "It's not that. You've done a fabulous job at work. In fact, as good as I expected."

"Not better?"

He smiles at my words. "I expected you to be phenomenal. You're meeting that expectation."

"I consider that high praise." I take a sip of water before I say anything more.

"But you have changed." The smile drops from his face. "You're more timid."

"Timid!" Perky shouts, sputtering. "Since when is Hasty ever *timid?*" If eavesdropping were a sport, Perky would be regional champ.

"It's *Hastings,"* I hiss through gritted teeth.

Ian and Raul look at each other with delight. I stand, pretending to stretch my legs out.

"What's wrong, Hasty?" Perky calls. "You got a cramp?"

"No," I say, dropping down into a lunge. "Just a pain in the ass."

Raul and Ian chuckle. Perky gives me a look. "Don't be mean to me. And since I ran into you, I'm supposed to tell you you're invited over to my house for a gathering."

"That's how you invite me? No. The answer's no."

"You're really good at turning people down," Ian mutters.

"C'mon," Perky wheedles. "Mallory wanted me to invite you. You and Fiona. We'll have a hot springs gathering."

"What's a 'hot springs gathering'?"

"Where you come over to my house and you soak in the hot spring that my mom made." Her tone makes her sound like a sixth grader.

"You sound like you've been put up to this," I say slowly.

She shrugs. "Mallory wants to talk about the wedding." Exasperation permeates her words. She's as done as I am when it comes to this whole wedding mess.

"Is there free booze? As long as there's plenty of free booze, I'm in."

An extraordinary smile spreads across her face. "Of *course* there's free booze. There has to be free booze when we're trapped with Mallory, talking about her OCD wedding."

"Fine. I'll be there."

She laughs, but turns her back to us, moving down the line toward the area where they store baked goods.

Ian stands, crossing the space between us quickly, his hand going to my lower back as I bend into something close to warrior pose.

"Let's go for a walk," he says. Finishing his macchiato, he puts the cup down on the table.

I look at it. "That goes in the bus bin."

"In the what?"

"The bus bin. You know, bussing tables?" I point to the plastic bin.

A perplexed look furrows his brow. "You are telling me to put my dirty dish away?"

"Yes."

"Since when have you ever cared about anything so menial?"

"If you don't do it, someone who works here has to."

"That's very egalitarian of you."

"No, it's not. It's just…"

A slow dawning spreads over me. He's right. I shake my head. I reach for the cup and my own water glass, walk over to the bin and place them carefully inside. I look at him.

"You're right. I've never cared about anything so menial before. Suddenly I do."

"Why?" he asks.

Hands on his hips, his body relaxes, as if the only thing he needs to do in the world is listen to me talk about dirty cups in a coffee shop.

"Because it turns out, being a human being isn't a competition."

"Since when?" he asks, incredulous.

"Since I've come to realize that kindness is a better barometer of success than being number one."

"Depends on how you define success."

"Semantics matter, Ian. Definitions matter. *People* matter. I think I lost sight of that at some point."

"And now you feel like you found it again?" His hand goes to my shoulder. Intelligent eyes, intense and probing, meeting mine.

"Did you ever lose that feeling?" I ask him suddenly, filled with candor.

"No."

"Is that why you helped me?"

He leans even closer. My toe presses against the soft leather of his shoe. I can smell the lime soap he used under his cologne. His breath brushes a chilled spot on my forehead, and if I stand on tiptoes and he bends one inch closer, we'll kiss.

"I helped you, Hastings, because I could. Because I wanted to. Because you needed someone. Because—"

"Has-teeeee!" Perky calls out, interrupting the moment.

"What?" I scream, shattered by the sudden intrusion.

"Mallory says we're starting in an hour."

"Don't you have to work?" I shout back.

Raul throws his hands up in frustration. "She's just here to manage some musician bookings. You could have done it from home," he says to her with a glare.

I turn back to Ian, but his eyes are on his phone now, which is in his hand as he taps away.

Moment lost.

He gives me a polite smile. "Gotta go. Good to see you."

As he walks out the door with a confident stride, a man intent on going somewhere, to a place where he's considered important, he waves to Raul with a two-finger salute. "Great coffee."

"Thanks."

And as the door jingles with his departure, I wonder exactly how much booze Perky has at her house.

And why Ian McCrory keeps popping up wherever I go.

❦ 12 ❦

Perky has been holding out on me.

Not that we're friends or anything, so there's no reason why I should know about this amazing hot spring that exists in the subterranean wonderland beneath her parents' estate. All I know is, I'm soaking in the water, wearing a bikini, holding a perfect sangria, and wondering if my sister's hair can curl any tighter in this humidity.

"Chris wants me to work with him at the gym part time," Fiona says, making her way through her second large glass of alcohol. She's got sangria in one hand and a huge plastic glass of water in the other as she leans against the jagged rock wall. Steam rises in irregular patterns, blocking faces. I close my eyes and just listen, the lapping of the water against the rock lulling me.

"Do it," Mallory says to Fiona. "Why not?"

"Because I don't have time," Fiona says, as if the question irritates her, like someone's asked it multiple times and she's sick of hearing it.

"You teach four-year-olds during the day. You have your evenings free," Perky says.

I open my eyes, knowing full well I'm going to see Fiona glaring at her friend. The dynamics between the three of them completely escape me. They have been buddies since before they were all in A-cup bras, and the only reason I know that is because I was in a C-cup and they kept stealing mine and stuffing them with balled-up rainbow toe socks whenever there was a sleepover.

Perky ruined my jellies back in the nineties, and even though I wouldn't be caught dead wearing anything like that now, it meant something back then.

It meant she was an annoying little brat.

Still is, even on the cusp of thirty.

"Some of us don't work part time, remember?" Fiona says to Perky. I can hear her teeth grit from across the hot spring.

"Just because I only work twenty hours a week at Beanerino doesn't mean I'm not putting in hours elsewhere," she says in a snappy tone. "I'm plenty busy with Parker and with coffee initiatives, and with fair trade and—"

Fiona cuts her off. Her hand moves like a puppet talking. That just makes Perky's face get redder. Either that, or the sangria is hitting her.

"Ooh, it's getting hot in here," I murmur.

I grab the giant glass of water that Fiona carefully set next to me, and I drink half of it.

As the three of them banter back and forth, the words nothing but a salad of nonsense that flows through my brain, I smile. I never had friends the way that my sister has. Not that I'm jealous. It's more anthropological.

Watching the way they interact makes me see that I don't know their language. I can observe it. I've tried to imitate it, but Mallory's explained that I just come across as bitchy, which I know is wrong.

I'm just in command.

But as I listen to them, something digs at me, a sense of unease. They can talk to each other this way because they've spent almost two decades hanging out together. Other than my mom and dad, I don't have anyone like that.

Or at least I don't anymore.

I spent a decade with Burke, and look where that got me.

I stand, the water stopping dead at my nipple line. The sangria is a more enticing drink than the water, so I finish it first. A giant bubble builds in my chest, pushing hard against my heart, nudging it toward something I can't define.

"What about you?" Perky snaps at me, making me startle and nearly drop the glass of water in my hand.

"What about me?"

"We're talking about business over here."

"We are not talking about business," Fiona says.

"Yes, we are. We're talking about you investing your time and possibly money in Chris's boxing studio, and about me and my business."

"Your business is pulling espresso shots," I say to her.

"My business is advocating for workers' rights and fair trade," she corrects me.

I wave her off. "Oh, right. That thing Parker does for you."

Mal shoots me a look that says, *This is exactly what I was talking about.* Before Perky can answer, I let the alcohol loosen me up enough to be a little vulnerable.

"Did that sound bitchy?" I ask.

Perky narrows her eyes and just stares at me, breathing through long, intense breaths that I don't really care about anymore, because man, this sangria tastes really good.

"You always sound bitchy."

"I do not!"

"You absolutely do," Fiona says slowly, as if the words are on a string that needs to be unraveled.

"I'm being blunt."

"No. Blunt doesn't involve innuendo," Mallory interjects.

"Innuendo?"

"You're implying that Perky doesn't do what she says she does. That she is taking the credit but Parker is doing the work."

"Because Parker is a well-connected U.S. congressman," I elaborate. "Surely, that's obvious?"

"WHOOP! WHOOP! BITCH ALERT!" Perky intones.

"What's bitchy about that?"

"Now you're implying we're all stupid. That 'obvious' comment sealed it."

"How can telling the truth be bitchy? You're being misogynistic," I explain to all of them.

"We're women! We can't be misogynistic!" Mallory counters.

"Maybe you're self-hating women who internalized the patriarchy," I lob back, laughing inside, knowing it'll piss them off.

Wait.

Is *that* what they mean by bitchy?

The chamber we're in goes dead silent, only the lapping of water against the rocks making any sound.

"What about you?" Perky finally says, clearly speaking to me. "How does it feel to lose everything that you sacrificed your personality, soul, morals, and your ethics to achieve?"

"Your idea of small talk really sucks, Perky."

That just gets me the grin I deserve.

Fiona and Mallory cut eyes at each other.

"Pour me another really big sangria, and I'll tell you," I inform Perky, turning her into a servant. She knows the power play I'm using. It doesn't matter.

She's won already.

She's the one who's marrying a congressman. A real one, not a wannabe like Burke.

Parker put in the work. He rose through the ranks. Sure, there was that whole lucky incident where he had to perform CPR on the sitting congressman he was working for, but everyone experiences some kind of luck in their life, right?

Except for me, apparently. Why is Perky taking so long to get me that drink?

She delivers it, moving slowly through the water, holding it up at forehead height, finally handing it over. It's ice cold, condensation all over the outside of the glass, and as I bring the rim to my lips, the cool ice cubes shift, spilling over the edges of my mouth as I take a sip.

"Who made these?" I ask Fiona, who points to Perky. "Good job," I tell her.

"Quit deflecting," she says. She sounds like Ian.

"You want me to open up my heart and tell you what it feels like to be violated emotionally, financially, professionally, and socially," I say between sips.

She shrugs. "You're more entertaining than anything on Netflix right now."

Mallory tries to kick her underwater, but physics slows her down enough that Perky just jumps back and laughs.

"No, really," Fiona says, giving me a serious look. "It has to hurt. I know how hard it was, being the center of a media storm when I took on the attacker in my preschool class."

"That's different," I say, my voice breathy, the bitterness that normally comes out dissipated. I'm loose. I'm relaxed. I'm having actual sincere interactions with my sister and her friends.

This is surreal.

"It's not that different. All of us have had some kind of weird online scandal thing that we've had to deal with.

Mallory was a porn star, Perky's tits were all over the place—"

"Quit saying that word," Perky interjects.

Fiona ignores her. "I had the attack on my preschool class, and now you—"

"No," I say simply. "It's different. Mallory's thing wasn't great, but it was small and local. Perky's thing... I gotta admit, that was big. And embarrassing. Being known as two-dogs-humping girl has to hurt. But you," I say, leaning forward and taking a long, slow drink as I try to figure out what the hell is going to come out of my mouth next. I swallow and finish.

"But you," I continue, looking at Fiona as the steam makes her even more ethereal than she already is. "You were a hero. I'm the opposite."

The stone-cold silence in the hot spring seems to bring the temperature down twenty degrees. I take a big, deep breath, drawing the wet heat inside, feeling like I've just ruined the mood.

"She is a hero," Perky says. "And so are you."

"Me?"

"Yeah. You testified. You gave the Feds everything that they needed to track down all of those other scams that Burke was involved in. You helped them get most of the money that was left before he could transfer it out of the country. Turning on him was the smartest thing you did. If you'd been in on it with him, that would have been different." Her voice fades out as a cold, prickly feeling travels up my back in spite of the hot water.

"Aha. *That's* what this is about. We're not here to talk about Mallory's wedding, are we?" Mal's discomfort drives it all home. "You're here to pump me for information about what I've gone through."

"Not exactly," Mallory says, jumping in, trying to touch

my elbow, but I yank it away before she can succeed. "We *do* want to talk about the wedding. There are all these details, and *some* people," she says in a sing-songy voice, purposefully not looking at her friends, "think that I talk about it too much. But, it's just... Hasty, you don't tell anybody what's going on inside. You work for Ian. You had that horrible experience at Bailargo—"

Perky cuts her off. "That we tried to warn you about."

Fiona stops her. "This isn't about blame, Perk."

"I'm not blaming her. I'm making fun of her for not respecting the fact that we're not idiots. But then again, that's what you do, isn't it?" she says, calmer, more pensive. "You just assume that we're idiots and discount everything we say."

A protest starts deep in my chest. For a moment I think it's reflux, but then it turns into something else: the fast beat of my heart.

"You're right," I tell her, reaching for the glass of water, which Fiona has nicely refilled for all of us. "I do think you're all idiots."

"We think you're bitchy," she shoots back.

"Well, now we're getting somewhere." I look at all three of them.

"We're not ganging up on you," Mallory says, as if I'm thinking that.

"Of course you're not. We're laying our cards on the table. We're being honest and open. And for the record," I say to Mallory, "your hair looks like a copper scrubbie."

"It does not!"

"Yeah, it kinda does," Fiona says, reaching up and pulling one springy curl. "You could really clean a burned pot with that head if we just tipped you upside down, threw a little Dawn dish soap in there—"

"Stop it!"

Perky gazes at me with unwavering penetration. She's trying to figure something out.

"I'm an open book," I tell her, the alcohol sinking in as I pull myself up, palms flat behind me against the edge of the pool. My arms still have the strength to heft me up, wet ass smacking against the stone. My legs are still dangling in the water, calves tickled by the heat. "It sucks," I say quietly to all of them. "I don't even know who I am anymore."

"Sure you do," Fiona says, moving with languid grace through the water, coming toward me.

I drink to hydrate, and then I just listen.

"You do know who you are. You knew it the minute every illusion about who you tried to be was shattered."

"Don't go spiritual on me, kid."

She laughs. "But it's true." Kind eyes meet mine. "You could have kept your mouth shut. You could have only given the prosecutors the specific pieces of information that would make you safe, but no one else. You didn't do that, Hasty."

I bristle.

"Hast*ings,"* she says, correcting herself. "You did more."

"I did more than fuck Burke over. It had nothing to do with morals or being kind to other people. I just… *uh."* I kick my feet, splashing water in anger. "I just want to get back at him. I want him to pay. I want him to experience one sliver of the humiliation that he put me through. So yes, I spilled my guts. I told them everything I knew. I gave them every password. I found every way to reveal whatever I could to help them."

"And you helped other people," she pushes back.

I shrug. "I guess so. A lot of them are just rich assholes who invested in the wrong thing with my hus—my *was*-band, my not-husband–whatever the hell you call Burke."

"Did you know," she says slowly, "that Burke got my parents to invest in one of his schemes?"

All of the numb looseness that the alcohol has given me disappears in a snap.

"No. No, I didn't. Oh, God," I groan, leaning my head forward, raking my fingers through my wet hair. "Oh, Fiona. I'm so sorry."

"Don't be sorry. Because of you, they didn't lose their money. He was about to transfer a huge amount from hundreds of people into some offshore account, but they caught it in time. Mom and Dad won't get *all* their money back, but they'll get most of it. About ninety percent. Because of you."

"No. It was because of *me* they invested in the first place. I remember. Burke wanted me to contact everyone I knew, whenever I was home, to try to push them into investing in something that he was working on. And I did it, because I'm an idiot."

"Join the club," Perky says. "Apparently, we're *all* idiots. The four of us. We're quadridiots."

"I take that back," I say to her. "I used to think you were idiots."

"What do you think we are now?"

"People."

"We're movin' up in the world," she says to Mal, who smiles at me, but her brow is furrowed, pert little nose curled up slightly in a squinch.

"Burke made you do that? He made you get Mom and Dad to invest, to talk to their friends who work on State Street and get them to work the system? Even Will?"

"He made me try. Dad never took the bait, which was a relief. I talked to Will when I was here for your rehearsal rehearsal dinner," I say.

She nods slowly. "He told me."

"He never invested," I tell her, hands up in defense. "I swear, and if I had known—oh God, Mal, if I had known…"

Tears fill my eyes, pressing hard against the back of my throat, turning salty and sickening.

"Oh, Hasty. We know you didn't know. You were doing what you thought was right."

"I was building my husband's business for him. I thought it was part of this grand plan we had, that I would be the venture capital queen and he would be the financial king and we would rule over this kingdom where we were at the top."

"But when you're at the top..." Perky says quietly.

I interrupt her. "'It's lonely at the top'? 'You're all alone'? 'You're only at the—'"

She cuts me off. "There's only one place to go if you're at the top, and that's down."

"That's not how I saw it. Until they hauled me away in handcuffs."

"Then I'm glad they hauled you away in handcuffs," Mallory says, earnest and soft. "Because until you came home, it was like I had a sister who was a placeholder, who fit into a category called sister. But now, it's like I have a friend."

Friend.

The three of them stare at me as if my sister has thrown down an emotional gauntlet I'm expected to pick up and run with. Each heartbeat makes me heavier and lighter, each second that passes without a response from me making it harder to open my mouth and say what I want to say.

What do I want to say?

The light in Mallory's eyes dims, then darkens, her disappointment traveling through the water's waves, soaking into my skin as terror fills me.

Yes, terror.

Being vulnerable is its own kind of torture.

But my lungs feel crushed, pressed down by the fear of rejection.

The only way to have friends like these is to be a friend like them.

"I'm so jealous," I choke out, a part of me screaming to shut up, another one jumping for joy inside. "I never had friends like you do, Mal. You always had buddies. Always. And it was just so easy for you."

"What?" Mal gasps. Perky is uncharacteristically quiet and Fiona watches me with eyes too wise for her years.

"It's true."

"You were friends with Dorian. And Eric. And loads of people from the clubs you were president of. You were symphony chair for clarinet, and student body president, and–"

"Dorian and I were in the same crowd. Eric was, well..." I sigh. "He was my friend. But I didn't have what you three have."

"Maybe it's because you put out vibes," Fiona says.

"Vibes?"

"Stay-away vibes. Don't-fuck-with-me vibes. You have steel in your aura and it's the kind that cuts you if you get too close."

I make a sound I can't stop myself from making. "Auras? Really?"

"See?" Perky interjects. "There you go."

Looking at each of them, one at a time, I slowly force myself to capture their expressions, translate nonverbal facial cues into emotion, and try each one on for size inside me.

This is one outfit I don't like.

"How can correcting people be bad? How can wanting to be correct–to be on top–be a source of bad vibes?" Keeping the acid out of my voice is harder than it should be.

"If you have to put people down, or judge them, then it is," Mallory replies, tilting her head like she's seeing me anew.

"You interpret my words as a put down. I don't mean them that way."

"You don't?" Perky's eyebrows shoot up. Sweat soaks her hairline, the flat outline of her face making her eyes stand out more.

"Judgment isn't a bad thing. It's how we categorize the world. How we protect ourselves from danger. How we analyze and–"

"People aren't facts that fit neatly into boxes, Hasty," Mallory says to me. "We're souls. Not business development projects."

"And this is why I don't have friends like you do," I respond emphatically. "Because my world view doesn't fit into this whole emotional thing."

"What does 'emotional thing' mean?" Fiona's question has no tone to it. She genuinely wants to hear the answer.

"When I talk to someone, I scan their words. Their faces. Their body language. How they carry themselves reveals more than what they tell me. I make snap judgments on the inside. He's in a hurry. She's heartbroken but holding it together. He has a secret agenda about that housing regulation. She wants to screw the guy across the table at a board meeting. That sort of analytical reading of a room has actual monetary value. It's what I'm best at. It's how I excel."

"And it doesn't work on friends," Perky says.

"Right."

All four of us stare at each other. It's clear they are surprised by my answer.

"Was Burke your friend?" Mallory whispers, the words so faint, I almost don't hear them.

"What?"

"Was he your friend?"

"I–"

"Not the object of your scanning," Fiona adds, getting a nod from Mallory in return. "But a friend."

"No."

My answer is immediate and easy.

"No," I repeat. "He never was."

"And do you have any friends?"

Ian.

His name comes to mind immediately, Mallory's next in line.

A smile takes over Fiona's eyes as I blink rapidly.

"You do. There's someone who makes you feel connected. Understood. Someone you can say anything to and you don't have to worry you'll walk away from the conversation feeling worse than before, or defensive–or judged."

She's right. I do.

"Who?" Mallory asks, intrigued.

"You," I inform her. "And Eric."

Perky moves closer to me, catching my eyes. "And Ian McCrory."

I nod.

All three start clapping. Clapping!

"What are you doing?"

"Congratulations, Hastings," Perky says, using my name correctly for once. "Welcome to having a heart. Yours just came online."

❧ 13 ❧

I am missing the rehearsal dinner.

Why? Because I have strep throat.

That's right.

It's been seventy-two hours since I left Ian's office with a painfully sore throat, rode the train home, collapsed in bed, woke up to a fever, and had Mom force me to a local drugstore's clinic for a rapid strep test.

I went to a chain-store clinic. Me.

Six months ago, Burke and I were spending $40,000 a year for concierge primary care. Immediate appointments. Examination rooms with loveseats and ionic foot baths. Easy Botox injections (not that I need them... yet) and prescriptions filled by on-site runners who went for you to a boutique compounding pharmacy three blocks away.

You waited in a lounge with baristas, a light buffet, and a small gym off in one corner. Hand massages, reflexology, you name it.

The chain store clinic had free ennui. You want boredom and tedium? They had it in droves.

Seventy-five minutes later, antibiotics in hand, bill paid

from my own checking account (since I don't have health insurance yet), we left. I dry-swallowed the pills.

Went to bed.

Mallory understands. In fact, Mallory wants Typhoid Hastings to stay far, far away from her wedding party. The rehearsal dinner is a week earlier than usual because of Parker.

A sitting U.S. congressman has limited windows of availability, so Will and Mallory flipped the rehearsal dinner and the bachelor/bachelorette parties.

If I had to miss one, strep picked the right event.

And so here I am, still feverish and sick, with a throat that feels like barbed wire. I'm experiencing a clash of FOMO and JOMO that looks like a Bruce Lee movie, but emotions are sparring instead of bodies.

Sleep is a blissful lover.

Ian McCrory would be even better.

৯৯

HE TASTES LIKE CHERRIES.

Not the kind you find in grocery stores, even high-end places in suburbs where the zip code is a famous year in the country's independence. He tastes like freshly plucked, sun-ripened cherries off a Washington tree, after hiking all day and arriving, sweaty and vibrant, full of pleasure at the simple joy of having made it to your goal.

Ian's mouth makes me think of a future where all I have to do is kiss him like that. No accomplishment is better, more impressive, or more worth my time.

"Hastings," he murmurs against my neck, making my nipples harden under the thin sheet as he slides down, down, down my body, mouth at my breast, big hands moving to my ribs, each finger stroke bringing me closer to him. Long,

massive, with dark hair on his legs and chest, Ian is as glorious naked as he is in a suit.

I'm certain I know which way I prefer him, now that I've had the opportunity to sample him both ways.

The kiss on my navel, tongue flicking out to tease, makes my hips rise up, his next move making me moan, my body a playground for Ian's mouth, ready for serious frolicking.

"Tell me how you like it. How you want it." His grip on my ass lightens as he moves to part my thighs, the anticipation killing me, the pulsing need rising up in me like I'm possessed, part of me foreign and unreal, drawing power from his touch as if he's an angel melting my core with his hot golden light.

Or maybe he's a demon, here to make me sin.

Either one will do, as long as I get to feel it all with him.

"Do you bite your lip when you come, Hastings? Do you clench and writhe? Press your thighs so hard against my ears that you block out eternity?"

"I don't–I don't know," I confess.

One finger strokes the soft, yielding flesh at the swell of my thigh, where I want his mouth, only a few inches up.

"How can you not know?"

Truth burns my cheeks. "It's been a long, long time, Ian. Too long."

"How long?" He shakes me, hands on my shoulders, his question so urgent.

The answer sticks in my throat until all I can do is beg.

"Ian, I–"

"How long?" he demands.

"Please. Please Ian. Use your mouth. Your fingers. Your co–"

. . .

"HASTINGS? HONEY? YOU'VE BEEN ASLEEP FOR A WHILE. How long?"

"COCK!" I scream.

"WHAT?" Mom screams back.

Startled, I jump half a foot in the air in bed, body jolting with such force, I know my jaw will be sore tomorrow. Wildly disoriented, I stare at my mother, wondering how naked Ian turned into *her*.

"Mom?"

"Yes. Honey, were you dreaming about, um, chickens?"

"Yes!" I take the out. "Yes, I was." Nervous laughter is my sister's thing. Not mine. But I use it now, wiping sweat-soaked hair off my face. "I had a crazy dream I was milking a chicken to make chicken cheese out of it."

No self-respecting adult would ever believe that line of crap, but let me introduce you to Sharon Monahan.

"Ahahaha! Chicken cheese. Oh, Hastings, that must have been one hot dream you were having."

"Hot?"

"You know... fevered? Your cheeks are burning red and your hair is a mess."

"Right. Hot dream. Um hmmm." My palm burns like I was holding Ian's, uh, chicken in my hand, before being rudely awakened.

Mom's wearing her special-occasion perfume, a scent that instantly transports me back twenty-five years, to nights she hired Karen Minsky from next door to babysit for Mallory and me.

"Rehearsal dinner. Right. How'd it go?" I ask, laying back on the bed, exhausted by my sickness, my unexpected erotic dream, and the shock of Mom's intrusion.

"It went very well. Helen thanked you for the cheese again, and said she can't believe someone so good at a hobby hasn't turned it into a business. Said that sheep's milk soap is the new thing in boutique retail and you could get ahead of the game."

"Ha! What a hipster statement. Following your bliss is *soooooo* 2009, Mom."

"Is it?"

"It's outdated."

"No, I mean, your bliss. Is making sheep's cheese your bliss?"

"I have bills to pay, Mom. Bliss doesn't pay the bills."

"You're good enough that it could, Hastings. Helen and Larry were raving."

"Raving mad, maybe."

"Why is it so hard to believe that something you take pleasure in and that you're *good* at could be worth pursuing?"

"Because it's too easy!" I clap my hands over my mouth as the words come out, horrified by the emotional storm my words are churning. I must be delirious from the strep.

"Too easy?" She's perplexed, a frown making long vertical lines between her eyes. "What's wrong with easy? It's wonderful to find something that fits in your heart and hands, Hastings. I want that for you. I want you to be happy."

"Happy? *Happy?* Have you seen my life, Mom? Happiness isn't exactly in the top one hundred traits that define me."

"I know, sweetie. That's your problem. If you think being happy is too easy, then ask yourself: Why do you assume that you have to work so hard for happiness? That you have to earn it through struggle or pain?"

"I never said that."

"You just did."

"No, I didn't. I said that–" Abruptly, I snap my jaw shut, the fight in me gone like a thunderclap.

Holy smokes.

She's right.

Her hand reaches up, tentative, the scent of her lemon verbena hand cream another tender reminder of my youth. As she touches my cheek, I sigh, unaware I'm doing it until it's been heard. Felt.

Noticed.

"You, Hastings, have always been a mystery to me. So ambitious. So contemptuous of our life here. You always wanted more. Bigger. Better. Higher. Taller. You wanted to climb to the top and shout it to the world, but..."

"But I failed." I scoff. "I don't need my nose rubbed in it." To my horror, tears fill my eyes.

She frowns again, pulling her hand back. "Oh, dear. You are hot. Still have a fever?"

I nod.

She reaches for my water and hands it to me. "Drink up. I'll refill it in a minute."

"Mom, I'm not eleven. I can–"

Her eyes say *drink*.

So I do.

"You. Did. Not. Fail," she says firmly as I gulp the room-temperature water, avoiding eye contact. It's easier to form a shield around myself if I don't look at her.

Lisa Frank's unicorns are less judgmental, anyhow.

"Hasty," she says in a low voice that's unlike her, the use of my childhood nickname filling me with an awe I don't expect. "You succeeded wildly."

"Now I *know* I'm delirious, Mom, and the strep has invaded my brain, because no rational human being would ever say that to me."

"I don't know if I'm rational, but I do know I'm human, and I'm absolutely certain you're wildly successful at being a good, kind person."

If I hadn't already emptied my water, I'd have sprayed it all over her.

"Good? Kind? Have you met me, Mom? I'm none of those things."

"Of course you are. You just buried it under this mission you had to conquer the world."

"It conquered me, instead."

"You are your own personal Battle of Hastings, sweetie."

I groan. Haven't heard that lame joke since freshman year, European History.

"You're at war with yourself. And you won battle after battle with the outside world, striking deals and being savvy and moving up the ranks in finance, and those battles were important. Your father and I are proud of all you built."

"Whatever I was trying to build, it doesn't even exist anymore! Burke ruined it and I was too stupid to realize what he was doing."

"But you won the war, Hastings. You won in so many other ways. You are finding the center of who you are, unadorned by achievement."

"Achievement *is* who I am! I'm nothing if I'm not an achiever. I'm not like you and Mallory! I'm different!"

Silence ripples out between us, growing in intensity.

Blinking rapidly, she just looks at me.

I close my eyes and whisper, "I don't know how to be like you and Mal. You just naturally have this peace inside you. I used to think you were settling, like you sold yourselves short. Then I realized that wasn't the case. That you were genuinely fulfilled by life itself. And I was so angry."

"Angry?"

"Yes. Angry. Because I don't have that in me, Mom." I look at her, letting my tears spill over. "I'm so jealous."

"Jealous of... me?"

"And Mallory, yes."

"I'm flabbergasted, Hastings."

I don't know what to say. Shame fills my blood, a feeling

I've spent my entire life fighting but didn't know it. This is my worst fear, come to life in my twin bed in my childhood home, where I'm sick as a dog, missing my sister's wedding activities, and confessing my innermost darkness.

To my mom.

"I just thought you were a bitch."

Mom and I turn toward the voice that said that, finding red curls and an arched eyebrow. Mallory walks in like she's the alpha sister, plunks down on my bed, and looks at me with a gimlet eye.

"Mallory, I–"

"Stop." Her palm is out to me, flat and vertical, her jaw tight, shoulders wide. "My turn to speak. You're sick–although non-contagious by now, or I wouldn't be here–so for once, Hastings, let me be in charge of the conversation."

I expect her to add "okay?" but she doesn't.

Because she's not asking my permission.

"All these years, I thought you hated me. That I was beneath you. I never understood it, but it wasn't the same as my friends who had big sisters. Once I met Will and we shared stories, he didn't have the same dynamic with Veronica, but I chalked that up to the fact that he's a guy. I just resigned myself to having a prickly relationship with a sister who decided she was too good to be around me."

Her sad stare elongates, stretching on and on as we sit in discomfort, my fever making my gut clench.

Finally, I have to say it. Have to give her something that was taken from me by Burke: the truth.

"You're right."

Mom gasps, the sound a knife to my heart, but I steel myself.

Mallory's throat spasms as she swallows, the skin around her eyes wrinkling with pain.

"But," I finish, "I don't feel that way now."

"Because of Burke?" Mom rushes in. "He was the one who felt that way, and you were just going along?"

Easy.

It would be so easy to lie and say *yes* to another out Mom has given me.

A shaky sigh comes out of me, like the truth is breaking loose inside, an ice shelf melting in chunks. "No. I can't blame Burke for everything. He made it easy," I say, spitting that word out. "Easy to feel good about myself by ranking the world. Figuring out how to network and leverage people as I moved up. Bigger and better deals, bigger and better contacts, one success on top of another. Until one day, I somehow let him leverage me. No," I add, laughing bitterly, the taste of my own abdication a sour wine on my tongue, "I didn't let him. I begged. I threw myself at his feet and begged him to walk all over me. To use me."

"Oh, Hasty," Mal says. "I remember how you talked to Parker at the rehearsal rehearsal dinner. You kept mentioning Burke running for office in California. It seemed so crass."

"Crass." Sick memories flood me. "That's the word Burke used to describe my life back here. Whenever I told him a story from our childhood, he'd listen, but find some way to undercut it, you know?"

"Like being negged on a date?" Mallory gives me a knowing look.

"What's negging?" Mom asks.

"When a guy says something that's supposed to be a compliment, but it's really a way to make you feel insecure," Mal explains. "Like saying, 'That dress looks good on you. Most women carrying all that weight in their thighs couldn't pull it off.'"

Mom looks at me. "That's–that's how you talk to Mallory."

Bow. Arrow. Release.

"It was. It *was* how I talked to you." Years of being a bitch–Mal's dead right on that one–find their way into my diaphragm, choking me. Breathing through this is an act of heroism on my part.

I have to be my own hero.

And that means facing my hardest battle: fighting through the apologies I owe to the people I love.

"And I'm sorry." Reaching for Mallory's hand is harder than the moment I was zip-tied back at Essentialz. Harder than watching my home raided by the Feds. Harder than the debriefing with the lawyers Ian hired, as they explained Burke's deception.

Harder than coming home with my tail between my legs.

But I can do hard things.

The hug takes me by surprise, my foot going off the edge of the bed to stop myself from sliding off. Mallory's coconut-scented hair is in my face, her arms wrapped around me, her breath hot against my already burning neck.

"I accept," she says. "I always knew that underneath that mean-girl exterior, I had a kind sister. I just didn't know how to get her to come out."

"It was never your job to get that part of me to come out, Mallory. It was mine."

"Make room for me!" Mom sobs, crying with us, the Monahan girls a pile of emotional goo.

"By the way," Mal whispers. "Chaz had to drop out of the wedding. Will's found a replacement, though. He couldn't come to the dinner tonight, but he'll be at the wedding."

"Anyone I know?"

We pull away, Mom and Mal sharing a weird look.

"Yes," Mallory says, eyes gleaming as she wipes tears away and laughs. "It's Ian McCrory."

❧ 14 ☙

Leave it to my sister to choose an activity for her bachelorette party that reminds me more of her birth year than of her wedding.

That's right. We're at a *piano bar*.

A good old-fashioned dueling piano bar. You know why they put pianos in a bar? They do wonders for profits, because you need a *lot* of cocktails to tolerate the sing-along that inevitably comes in a place like this.

If I had been in charge of the bachelorette party activities, I would have rented a tasteful yacht to cruise the harbor islands, capped off with a private meal in a lighthouse. A helicopter would have waited nearby to whisk us all off to somewhere fun and exclusive on the Cape. We'd wake up to cranberry-tinis and stacks of low-carb pancakes, coated in the best maple syrup from a premier shop just outside of Sherbrooke, Quebec.

Or, if Mallory wanted a cookie-cutter, conventional event that screamed cliché, I'd find the best spa in Vegas and we'd do it up.

But no.

Instead, someone who's wearing more flair around her neck than an Olympic medalist places a giant bucket filled with ice and bottled alcoholic monstrosities on the table. There's enough food dye in there to turn a roomful of kids with ADHD into nuclear reactors.

"Hi!" she screams over the raucous cacophony behind us. "I'm Amber. I'll be your server tonight. What can I get you?"

"Ooh! Raspberry lime hard seltzer!" Perky shouts, snatching the glass bottle inches from my face.

I turn to Amber. "Moscow Mule," I inform her.

Fiona bursts out laughing. "You? I never would have taken you for a Mule type."

I shrug. "I'm slumming."

"They don't need to add too much lime, because your face couldn't get any more puckered than it already is, Hasty," Perky says to me.

Mal elbows her. Their friend Raye just blinks, watching all of us. Teetering on heels that are an inch too high, Will's sister, Veronica, comes back to the group, finally closing the circle.

It's me, Perky, Fiona, Mallory, Raye, and Veronica. I don't know what I'm supposed to talk about with these people for the next couple of hours, but I have a feeling it'll involve a lot of screaming.

And Billy Joel lyrics.

The opening notes of Meat Loaf's "Paradise by the Dashboard Light" sound through the open hall. The five of them stand up and start squealing. Amber walks past, snatching the empty bucket off the table. I grab the ribbon on the back of her apron and tug gently.

Or not so gently. I hold up two fingers. "Two."

"Two Moscow Mules?"

"Two of whatever you've got. Mules, bottles, the city of Moscow. Anything to obliterate reality."

She laughs. "I'll bring them out one at a time."

I learn a lot in the next few minutes, as the song infuses every cell of my body. I learn that my little sister and Fiona have perfected the parts of this song all the way down to the baseball announcer in the middle. They know every single word, each nuanced, even as neither one of them comes anywhere close to hitting the right pitch.

Sweaty and giggling as the song ends, they sit down, grabbing their drinks and chugging.

Amber slips by with my first drink and sets a basket filled with fried clams, tartar sauce, and lemons in front of Perky.

She looks at me and points with a pen. I shake my head. She gestures at the charcuterie plate in front of us.

"I can refill anything you need."

We wave her off. A Billy Joel song starts. It's the one about...

A piano bar.

See? I totally called it.

Veronica taps me on the elbow and I startle, realizing she's trying to get my attention. I reach up and pull one earplug out.

"Yes?"

All five of them stare at me, look at the earplug, then back at me.

"Earplugs? Really?" Mallory asks.

"I'm here, aren't I? Don't judge."

"C'mon! There has to be a song that you like," Fiona prods. "Something you'll get up and sing with us."

I stare her down.

Veronica laughs. "You don't know Hastings very well, do you? Nobody changes her mind."

We get a reprieve, thankfully, as the piano shifts to the megahit from *A Star is Born*, two singers moving close to the baby grands, crooning at each other with an intensity that comes surprisingly close to Bradley Cooper and Lady Gaga. I don't know if it's the alcohol, the camaraderie, or the slow release in my muscles as I let go of my own increasingly ridiculous judgment of my sister and her friends, but I'm starting to have fun.

Pure existence has its upside. I don't have to be *on* all the time.

"Hastings?" My name sounds muted, someone behind me asking. I turn around and in an instant, my tranquility disappears, running out of me like I'm a scared kindergartner and I've peed myself.

"Mullins?"

"What are *you* doing in a place like *this?*" we ask each other simultaneously, which would be hilarious under any other circumstances, but this is Mullins Pratt-Janklowski, the great-granddaughter of a famous head of the New York Stock Exchange.

And an all-around predatory bitch.

She's a stereotype of a stereotype, so firmly entrenched in her rich little bubble that she can't see how others perceive her.

And if she could? She wouldn't care.

"Slumming," she says, the slur at the end of the word an obvious clue that she's wasted. If I could rewind the clock to last fall, her current state would be a competitive advantage for me.

Now, though, it's just depressing.

"Mmmm," I say, wondering when I picked up my mother's noncommittal verbal tic.

"And you? Is this where you work, now that no one will hire you? You're a cocktail waitress?"

"Why would you think that?"

Her eyes comb over me with a razor-sharp cattiness. She can be thoroughly drunk and still hold onto every iota of nastiness. "Because the white shirt, the black skirt, the abominable dye job. The de-throning you took for being Burke's scapegoat. You know. Word has it you lost everything, Hastings."

Mullins' voice has risen just as the pianos end their song, so my sister and her friends are suddenly tuned in to us, Mallory's sweet face a study in naïve confusion, Fiona on guard, Raye mirroring Mallory.

But Perky?

She comes right on over, fists clenched, face flushed with some vodka and a whole hell of a lot of street smarts. A magnetic charge connects us instantly, a power I didn't know was in the universe. She can read Mullins in a split second and has become my backup.

Out of nowhere.

"Hi," she says, thrusting her hand at Mullin's waist. "I don't believe we've met. Persephone Tsongas. And you are?"

Disgust radiates from Mullins, but she gives Perky a limp hand. "Mullins. Do I know you?"

"No. Just introducing myself to Hastings's friend."

Mullins looks around. "Where is she?" she asks, descending into snide laughter.

As if they'd coordinated it, Raye, Fiona, and Mallory all raise their hands.

Perky spreads her palm out like she's Vanna White on *Wheel of Fortune*, showing off the missing letters. "We're all Hastings's friends, and we figured we'd meet you. Anyone who comes to a piano bar on a Friday night dressed like you could use a little compassion." One eyebrow juts up on Perky's face like a rocket fired at enemy lines.

"Excuse me?"

"What do you do for a living, Mullins?" Perky persists. I take a single step back and let her run the show, suddenly less triggered by Mullins. The distance from my emotional reactions to my thinking brain is very, very short right now, but it's enough.

She snorts. "If you have to ask, you don't know what I do."

"Gotcha. You're currently unemployed, then."

"What? No! I run an investment bank."

My turn to snort. "No, you don't."

"I'm on the board of directors!"

"Really? Which one are you the chairman of? Maybe my fiancé has heard of it. He's involved with lots of bankers."

Aha. *Now* I see where Perky is taking this. Why did I never like her before? Gratitude washes through me, making my skin ripple and my tongue tingle. The urge to cry horrifies me, and I chug my drink to tamp it down, ears perked to capture their conversation.

"Third State New Trust," Mullins says. "How cute. Who does he work for? I'm sure your fiancé," she says, drawing out the word with a snarky tone, "has heard of my investment bank."

"He works for the government."

"Paper pusher?"

"Something like that."

I try not to laugh. I fail. I reach for Perky's shoulder and say, "Actually, Persephone, Parker is well acquainted with Third State New Trust. Remember the investigations into predatory lending practices that were all over the news last month?"

Mullins stiffens.

"Yes," Perky says with mock thinking, pretending to stroke a beard she doesn't possess, unless she gets fabulous laser treatment.

"Parker's on the oversight committee for banking, isn't he?"

Mullins looks like she's about to puke.

"Parker?" she chokes out. "Who is this Parker you're talking about?"

Perky goes in for the kill. "My fiancé. Parker Campbell." She taps Mullins' wrist gently with two fingers. "Perhaps you do know him after all? His 'cute' job seems to cross paths with your bank."

"Your fiancé is *Congressman* Parker Campbell?"

"Mmmm," Perky says, the understatement so pitch-perfect, I want to give her a standing ovation. A fist bump.

A squee hug.

Who the hell *am* I?

"And any friend of Hastings is a friend of mine," Perky adds in a stone-cold dead voice that makes my opinion of her skyrocket.

"Good," says a deep voice behind me, forcing everyone's eyes up, over my head, astonishment making Mullins' mouth drop.

I close my eyes. I know that voice. The onslaught of arousal makes my body respond to him, like it or not, just as the piano players begin the early notes of a love ballad.

"Ian," I say softly.

"Ian McCrory!" Mullins gasps, mouth closing, lips stretching in a sultry performance. "So good to see you. Last time was San Francisco. Dinner at the Martinelli fundraiser."

"Was it? I don't recall."

Perky just blinks. We all respect a true champion when we're knocked out of first place.

"Hastings," he says warmly, his entire demeanor shifting from cool dismissal to hot and heavy flirtation. His hands go to my shoulders and he bends to kiss my neck in that soft spot right under my earlobe. From the look on Mullins' face, I don't have to guess where his eyes are.

If he's establishing dominance, they're either on her, or–

The kiss he gives me takes all doubt out of my mental equation.

"WILL?" Mallory squeals as my future brother-in-law apparently crashes his future wife's bachelorette party. Not that I care, because Ian is crashing my mouth like he's a professional. Breaking every rule, charming his way in, and leaving the place happier than before.

Ah, that tongue. His hands. He's a roamer. You know the type. The lover whose hands go everywhere, all the time, tracking and touching, consuming and cataloguing, not for data's sake but because they can't get enough. Ian's style demands my full attention, that my body be completely present, because he is.

He's fully here.

And as he presses me even closer to him, his erection makes it clear how full, indeed, he is.

For *me*.

I've dreamt about kissing Ian for longer than I care to admit, and the taste of him is better than I ever imagined. He's charmingly aggressive, until I feel electricity shooting through every nerve system in my body, skin on fire and pulse pounding against my skin, trying to climb into his body and twist into him until we're so tangled, we're hopelessly together.

Forever.

One kiss. It takes one single kiss to do this to me.

"Hi," he says, forehead against mine. Peripheral vision is a blessing and a curse as I see Mullins to my right, eyes narrowed, nostrils flared, mouth pursed.

Why hasn't she left yet?

"Hi," I reply to Ian, reaching up for a lock of his hair, pretending he's mine because hey, why not? Whatever made him kiss me has no basis in reality. Might as well play along with whatever game he's initiated. "What took you so long?"

"Prince Charming needed more prep time than expected," he jokes, but his eyes are serious, hands on my back, still holding me to him tightly.

"PARKER!" Perky shouts, running full blast at him, launching herself into his arms, legs wrapping around the poor guy's waist. Any lesser man would fall back, but not him. He's a rock-solid wall and their kiss mirrors mine and Ian's.

Which makes me feel like part of the group even more.

Fletch is kissing Fiona, and Veronica and Raye commiserate.

Raye pouts. "We're the only ones without a partner."

"Not true," says Sanni, appearing behind her, a sparkling woman with long, dark hair, dark eyes, and a red outfit that shines in the nightclub's lights.

"What are you doing here?"

"Will included me in the bachelor party." They kiss, mutual excitement radiating from them.

"I thought you weren't going?"

Sanni shrugs. "The stripper wasn't half bad. She could have used more up top, though."

"Hey!" Parker said, giving her a shoulder shove, though a gentle one. "I personally chose that stripper."

Perky looked at her own rack. "Guess you wanted variety. And *shhhhh!* Congressmen never admit they pick strippers!"

"Only in closed session."

Sanni, Raye, Parker, and Perky descend into giggles, while Mallory chides Will for crashing her party.

Chide being a relative term. Can you chide someone with your hand on their ass? If so, Mallory is doing it.

"I'll go get another bucket of drinks delivered," Veronica says with a friendly grin, smiling at Mallory and Will as she leaves, the only one of us without a partner.

For once, I'm not the extra wheel.

A million questions race through me, all of them aimed at Ian. He's in the wedding party. I'd expect him to know Parker from working with government officials, but Will? How does he know Will? Why does he keep popping up everywhere in my life, unexpectedly?

Then disappearing when I want him most.

Now's not the time to ask, though. Not with his taste lingering on my buzzing lips.

And not with an audience made up of Mullins.

"Hastings, the car's ready," Ian says, giving her a curt nod, the kind of acknowledgment that's worse than being ignored.

She reddens. Her hair flip is epic, but she stands her ground, grabbing my arm and trying to pull me away from Ian.

He doesn't budge.

"I see what you're doing here," she hisses at me. "We're both stuck in this god-awful place. I'm here because of my cousin's fortieth birthday. You're here because..."

"Because she loves her sister and is celebrating her happy marriage to a great guy," Ian finishes for me.

"Right," I peep, just as Mal and Will walk over, all smiles and, in Mallory's case, a looseness that tells me she's having tipsy fun.

"You two?" She gives Ian a big smile. "I never would have pegged you two as a couple."

"Pegging? We're not into that kind of kink, but thanks," Ian says, pulling me away. He looks at Will, then Mallory. "May I ask your permission to... "

White noise fills my ears, my vision disappearing as he says words that don't make sense in this context. Is he really asking for my–

"...drive Hastings home and spend some time with her? I need more than I've been getting lately."

Mallory cuts me a look that is more than a bit filthy. "Of course. Go get as much of my sister as you want. Fill 'er up," she adds with a giggle, shaking her empty cocktail glass. "And Will needs to fill me up, too."

Ian grabs my hand and looks down at me, bright eyes intense. "Ready to go?"

I shoulder my purse. "Where are we going?"

"I don't know. But I want to go there with you."

A quick kiss on the lips and we wave good-bye, leaving Mullins a bright shade of red and puckered up like a butthole.

"That was amazing. Thank you."

"For what?"

"For pretending like that. Mullins is a–"

The next word out of my mouth is cut off by his, this kiss even better than the first, his tongue running along my teeth, his hands pressing into my waist, my hips, like I'm riding him in bed and he's guiding me. If he keeps this up, I'll slide my thigh between his and move up against him until I come.

Or until we're arrested.

That thought jolts me out of the lust-filled cloud surrounding me, because I've been arrested one too many times already, thank you very much.

"You have no idea how long I've waited to do this," he says, hands pressed hard against my back, my arms moving up until the strong outline of his shoulders gives me a place for my palms. We've made it as far as the edge of the room, still pretty close to Mallory's table, but far enough away that no one can hear, especially with the sound level in here. Ian's body is hot, warmth pouring off him like a furnace, every edge of him hard, big, radiating with power.

"Really?" is all I can think to say.

"Really."

"You've been waiting for a long time to pretend to be my date?"

"No, Hastings. I've been a gentleman for far too long, watching that bastard have you when I couldn't."

"What?"

"You deserved so much more than Burke. It was obvious from the moment I met you at that 3AExpo networking event years ago at. Beni Sandrino's island?"

"You remember the *exact moment* we first met?"

"I do. You wore an ivory cocktail dress that made your hair look like spun silk. Your eyes were filled with an intelligent charm that caught my attention before we even shook hands. The way you talked about private equity and climate change knocked it out of the ballpark. And your husband was a pile of human slime taking credit for half your ideas."

"Ian." His name comes out in a low hush, his words cutting me like a thousand murder hornets have descended on my skin. "What are you saying?"

"I'm saying that Burke fleeing the country and dumping the blame on you for what he did was an act of disgusting cowardice. But the fact that he's not your legal husband any longer means I can do *this* with impunity."

Another kiss slams me, blending his delicious, conflicting words with the feel of his heat, his mouth, his tongue, his body against mine, giving me permission to let go, to let him in, to let myself be touched like I'm wanted. Needed.

Craved.

Years of pent-up frustration pour into that kiss, and not all of it Ian's. I've got plenty of it stored inside me, buried under layers of repressed emotion, stifled irritations, and grieving hope. Burke stole too many pieces of me that mattered.

Every kiss from Ian gives one back.

Suddenly our bodies are shoved to the left, Ian's hand on my hip, then ass, as his arm braces and we break the kiss. Something wet hits my elbow and I look up to find a half-drunk group of women stumbling, a pint glass of beer in a woman's hand now half as full as it was seconds ago.

"Sorry!" she gasps, but Ian pulls me to the main doors before I can answer, my arm wet but the rest of me dry.

Other than my thong, that is.

It feels so good to feel something, to throb, to ache with anticipation, to let myself crack open those emotions and feel them, see them, hear them, to know they have a place within me. Ian moves with determination, but no rush, and a blast of cool outside air makes me feel like I'm on top of the world.

And then the red Lamborghini pulls up.

I look at him. "You are such a cliché."

He grins back. "But I'm a fun cliché." He kisses my temple and murmurs, "And one hell of a ride."

For someone who hasn't had sex well over a year, you'd think I'd jump at the offer.

Jump on *him*.

Instead, I'm jumping out of my skin.

He senses it, turning down the power, dialing back his come on.

"A ride in my car. Topless."

I look at my white shirt.

Low, rumbling laughter makes me smile. "The car, Hastings. Not you. Although you're welcome to change the dress code at will."

I smack his arm and climb in.

But don't climb on.

The car is built to be one with the road, sense every texture of the surface, my senses sharpening as Ian pulls away from the entrance and navigates through the large parking lot, the complex lights receding. I don't know where we're going and I don't care.

I'm with him.

Really with him.

The taste of his lips is on my tongue, the silky memory making my skin tingle. The leather seat welcomes my body, molding to me, reading my signals and doing whatever's needed to carry me through space in luxury and sensual pleasure.

Ian's naked body could do the same in bed, I'm sure.

If that tongue is half as good elsewhere as it is in a kiss...

"Share of stock for your thoughts," he shouts over the car's notoriously loud engine.

"I thought the phrase was 'penny for your thoughts.'"

"Inflation."

"If it's a share of your company's stock, I'll tell you whatever secret you want, Ian."

"Deal. How long have you wanted me, too?"

Seized with surprise, I let my heart gallop off.

And just breathe.

The car is a racehorse. I can feel its incredible power through the floor and the contours of the seat, the engine a contradictory high-pitched roar. It wants to go fast, faster than I've ever been taken anywhere in my life.

Ian has to be even stronger to hold it at bay.

Which he does.

Masterfully.

Ian doesn't ask again, accustomed to using long pauses to his advantage. Like martial arts, he lets the other person show their strengths and weaknesses, then uses those to gain the upper hand.

I want his upper hand on me.

"For a while," I admit, my words slow, my breath shaky as I exhale, the volume hard to shove out, the truth pushing harder. "But I'm married, Ian. *Was* married. Thought I was married. I closed off that part of myself a long time ago."

"What part?"

"The part that let myself be attracted to anyone other than my husband."

He nods, the wind blowing his thick hair off his face, eyes forward, serious. "Which is no less than I would expect from you." He changes lanes, accelerating, as if he's a pace car for my heart.

"What does that mean?"

"You are a deeply moral woman."

We're at a stoplight now, waiting.

Laughter bubbles up from my lowest rib, rising along the ladder of bones and catching in my throat. "I'm *what?*"

"Moral. Ethical. You have a core self that takes your promises very seriously. I knew it the moment I met you, and damn it, that's one reason you were so irresistible. I was deeply attracted to you but had to hold back. And why watching you with Burke was so maddening."

Long red light.

"Why didn't you say anything?"

Cutting his eyes to me for a split second before returning to the road, he says, "It would have just caused us both pain. Plus, I'm a moral person, too. I would never ask someone to break their vows, or break my own sense of decency."

Now I can't breathe at all.

Green light.

He *zooms*.

The leather offers me solace, my neck tipping back, wind whipping my long, brown hair behind in ribbons. Wisps lash at my shoulders and I close my eyes, the vodka I had at the bar loosening its grip on me, the chilled wind sobering me completely.

"Thank you," I finally say, sitting up, my hand going to his knee. He looks down at it, then at me, and finally back to the road.

"For what?"

"For being so decent. Because if you'd said something, I'm not sure I could have resisted."

"You would have. That's why I never did. I don't take rejection well, Hastings. Especially when so much is on the line."

"What would have been on the line?"

He slows the car down, pulling over and decelerating until the crunch of gravel feels like a throat clearing, the engine quieter as he puts the car in park, turns to me, and takes my hand off his knee, moving it to his chest.

"This. *This* would have been on the line," he says fiercely, locking eyes. He laces his fingers with mine, pressing the back of my hand against his heart.

"Ian."

And then he kisses me until I'm free, so free that I can touch him and let him touch me without any decency.

Not one single shred.

My desire is so intense, it pulsates through my body, until bursts of light start to flash inside my closed lids, and I think I might come right there in my Italian leather seat.

Or… wait. Mid-kiss, I open my eyes. The lights are still flashing, but a lot brighter. My thong is somewhere halfway down my thighs, Ian's erection cupped in my hand as we make out on the side of the road, a mile from my parent's house, like horny high schoolers.

And just like in high school, the cops are out, patrolling.

"You have got to be kidding me," he says in a low growl, straightening my skirt like a gentleman, chuckling to himself. "Haven't had this happen since high school," he mutters, echoing my thoughts.

"License and registration, sir," says a female voice, the flashing lights making it hard to see. The throb between my legs wants to anthropomorphize into the Incredible Hulk, picking up the cop and throwing her as far away as possible, so I can get back to being raunchily defiled.

Hold on. I know that voice.

"Karen?" I ask, craning forward and looking past Ian. Karen Minsky is our next door neighbor's daughter, a police officer in Anderhill. She's in uniform, holding a flashlight half the size of a baseball bat, and her eyes are gleaming at me.

Instinct makes me touch my hair, keeping my hands nice and visible, though the idea that Karen would arrest me is about as foreign to me as my father cheating on my mom.

Never gonna happen.

"Hasty?"

I grit my teeth as Ian looks at me and whispers, "Hasty?" Amusement tinges his voice.

"Hi, Karen. Yes, it's Hastings Monahan. How are you doing?"

"Great. Heard you were back in town and living at home again." She eyes the Lamborghini. "What kind of work are you in now?" From the way her gaze settles on my skirt, I can tell what she's thinking.

And that my billable hourly rate involves a motel that rents by the hour, too.

"She works for me," Ian says as Karen looks at his license, eyes widening.

"Ian McCrory? You related to that billionaire guy on the cover of *Time Magazine*?"

"I am."

"How?"

"He's me."

"And what, exactly, do you do for Mr. McCrory, Hast... ings?" she asks me, handing Ian back his license and registration. He sets them in his lap, giving her a patient look. If

Burke were pulled over, he'd try to sweet talk the officer into letting us go, and if that didn't work, he'd pull out a phone and threaten to call the DA's office, using his networking muscle.

Ian's manner is different.

More effective.

He doesn't need to throw his weight around. He could do all that, too, but he doesn't. Respecting Karen is how he gets through this.

"I'm a financial analyst with a specialty in international port issues," I begin to explain, watching the exact moment her eyes glaze over.

"How're your legal problems with that scummy ex of yours?" She leans against the red finish of the car, bent slightly, though the convertible's top is down, so no need to hunch.

"Going well."

"Yeah? Heard through the grapevine someone's paying for all that." She eyes Ian. "Must cost a lot."

"Whatever the expense, Hastings is worth it. When someone like Burke Oonaj scams hundreds – maybe even thousands, as new information comes to light – of investors, violates federal and state laws, and skips out of the country, good people like Hastings need full legal protection. She's cooperated in every way possible with law enforcement and regulatory agencies to make sure people got as much money back as possible, Officer. Hastings Monahan is a hometown hero in this case," Ian says, nodding as if he's using Jedi mind control tricks to get Karen to agree.

"Sounds like your ex is a giant prick," she says to me.

Ian grins. "You are more succinct than I could ever be."

"You two a couple?"

"We work together," Ian says smoothly. She looks to me for a response, but I just smile.

Silence is the bane of small-town existence. The local

gossip mill will be abuzz with the story of disgraced local girl Hasty Monahan tooling around town in a fancy car with billionaire wunderkind Ian McCrory, and found by Karen Minsky, who was worried about her.

If I were a betting woman, I'd lay money down on the majority of folks assuming I'm his escort.

"Why were you two pulled over? Car problems?"

Neither one of us answers. Karen clearly becomes suspicious.

"I'm going back to my cruiser, and I'll follow you home, Hastings. You're going home, right?"

Ian's taken aback. "Officer, I assure you, that won't be necessary. We were just–"

"Mr. McCrory, around here, we take care of our own." She looks past him at me. "After what happened with Mallory a couple years ago, on that porn set, I just want to make sure you're okay."

"Porn set?" Ian chokes out.

"She didn't tell you about her sister becoming a fluffer on a porn set?" Karen says, the words rolling out of her mouth with a satisfaction only a local gossiphound can truly understand, like the first drag on a cigarette for a nicotine addict. "You Monahan girls get yourselves into some interesting situations, don't you?" She smacks the side of the door next to Ian. "How much does one of these cost, anyhow?"

"Karen," I say slowly. "We're fine. Ian can drop me off at home without a police escort. You know my mom and dad will worry if they see you pull up."

She shrugs, giving me a tight smile. "I'm headed to my parents' house anyhow. Mom got a case of Mountain Dew at Costco for me. No bother at all. Just follow the speed limit, Mr. McCrory. Wouldn't want to have to issue you a speeding ticket."

Two smacks of the car later, she walks away.

Ian's eyebrow rises. "What the hell was *that?*"

"Small-town cop. See why I moved away from this place? Small town, small minds."

"No. Not her. She's just doing her job, and I think it's fine for locals to watch out for their own. I mean the porn set. Your sister is a fluffer? Will never mentioned *that*."

I deflect. "How do you and Will know each other, by the way?"

"Real estate deal from a couple of years ago. Helen and Larry are really nice people. Will, too. It's the kind of friendship where you go long stretches with no contact, but when you connect, it's like you're picking up a conversation from the day before."

"Low maintenance."

"Exactly."

Honk!

Karen flashes her lights at us. Ian starts the car and pulls out.

"Turn left here," I explain, realizing we'll be at my house in under three minutes.

"Hastings? I mean, *Hasty*." He laughs. "I'm learning so much about you."

"Is that why you keep appearing everywhere?"

His hand goes to my knee and squeezes. "Yes."

"Turn right," I tell him, suddenly overwhelmed. We abandoned my sister's bachelorette party and Mom will have a million questions.

Especially when I arrive home in a red Lamborghini, followed by a police car.

"Here." I point to the house. He parks in front of it. Karen pulls past us, turning into her parents' driveway, waving as she walks in.

"So weird," he says.

"Small towns."

"No, I understand small towns. I was brought up in one, in Wisconsin."

"Then what's weird?"

"You won't answer my fluffer question."

"You don't know what that is?"

"I know what a fluffer does, Hastings." He moves in for a kiss, nuzzling my neck.

"You watch porn?"

"Is this really the conversation you want to have right now?"

"No. But I can't exactly invite you in, so I have to deflect somehow."

"Why can't you invite me in?"

"I live with my parents, sleep on a twin bed, and a Lisa Frank poster bears witness to my poor taste in the 1990s."

"I have a hotel room in Boston–"

Blue and red lights flash three times in quick succession.

"Public indecency is still a crime in Anderhill," Karen says from a loudspeaker attached to her cruiser.

Porch lights pop on like fireworks all over the neighborhood, including my house. Instantly, Dad opens the door and looks out.

I kiss Ian on the cheek and open the car door.

"You're really not going to invite me in? Meet your parents?" he asks.

"Not yet."

"So there's a *yet?*"

Bzzzzz

Ian's phone lights up. He ignores it. Three times in a row, it buzzes. Mom, in her bathrobe, is now on the porch with Dad.

"Sounds urgent." I point to the phone in his lap.

"It is." He moves the phone to reveal something even more urgent.

"I meant your phone call."

"You're my priority."

"This is not how I want you to meet my parents."

"Then how?"

My mind races to find something, anything, that will make this better.

"Be my date."

"Date?"

"For Mallory's wedding."

Bzzzzz

Ring!

His phone is going insane.

"I'm already in the wedding, Hastings. We're paired together."

"I know. But that's not the same as being someone's date. Being public."

"You want to be public about this?"

"Yes. Whatever 'this' is."

"You need a definition?"

"Just say yes, Ian!"

"I need to think for a minute. Usually I'm the one asking women out. This is quite the role reversal."

"Welcome to the twenty-first century. We have horseless carriages and everything here. Pocket phones with more power than a 1970s supercomputer that we use to order four-dollar coffees."

He just stares at me as the neighborhood chatter grows.

"Are you begging?" he finally asks, stretching back in his seat.

"What? No! Why does that matter?"

He just grins, ignoring his crazy phone.

"If you don't want to go as my date, just–"

He grabs my wrist, pulling me to him, our lips brushing together with a wild frenzy that makes my knees weak. Then he finally looks down at his phone, his entire demeanor going cold.

"Please," I whisper. "Please come with me to the wedding. Be my date."

"I will."

And with that, he starts the car and disappears into the night, taillights two small red pinpoints, leaving more questions than answers.

And a big, red throb between my legs.

Always a bridesmaid, never a bride is a phrase I thought I'd escaped years ago, when I married Burke.

But now that I know we were never truly married, was I ever truly a bride?

The dress Mallory settled on long ago is from Ahern's, the "fancy" wedding and formal gown shop in town. For three years in high school, this was where I came for my home-coming and prom dresses, and now they've delivered the bride's and bridesmaids' dresses to the wedding and reception location.

Mallory and Will decided to get married in the place where the word *twee* was invented.

My back teeth ache just from being here, the castle part of a larger farm that's been preserved as conservation land, registered as a historic place here in Massachusetts. Once land and buildings get that designation, two things happen: The price of repairs goes up astronomically, and you instantly have a photogenic venue.

Castle Celtic is on a cliff overlooking the ocean, and that is wedding crack for people like Mallory and my mom.

It's an outdoor wedding, but the eccentric person who owned this place and shipped an entire small castle over here from Ireland also left an obscene amount of money in a trust for ongoing maintenance. Some smart trustees built a large, open-air barn that easily seats two hundred people, the wooden folding chairs now adorned with bows and fresh flowers that match Mallory's colors.

My contribution?

Cheese, of course.

"Hastings? Have you been in a wedding before? You were sick for the rehearsal," Dancy asks. Mallory told me a while ago that the little gnome-like man from the dance studio was the officiant, but I didn't quite believe her.

"Hi, Dancy. Yes, I have. I know the drill. Smile until your face feels like it'll crack in half and drink loads of cocktails so you can make it through the best man's toast without dissociating."

He pats my hand with sympathy. "You're a pro."

"That was the most jaded description of a bridesmaid's role I've ever heard," Perky says, offering me a bottled water. I accept it gratefully.

"But I'm not wrong."

"No," she says with a smile. "You're not."

"Am I finally going to meet Paul?" I ask her as I look behind the final row of chairs to see Parker and Fletch chatting with my dad. Ian isn't here yet. Maybe he's with Will?

"He's on his way. You heard about Chaz? He had to pull out at the last minute. His wife had an ovarian cyst? Something like that. Surgery back in St. Louis."

"I heard. That doesn't sound good." Mom's talking with Dad now, whispering in his ear. Both of them look behind me, at the long rows of chairs.

"And you know about his replacement?" Perky winks.

"Of course. It's Ian."

Her eye flit over my shoulder, halt, then widen.

Parker, Dad, and Fletch all turn and look the same way.

A warm hand surprises me on my shoulder, the very familiar scent of a man's custom-blend aftershave tickling my nose.

"Hi, there," he says, right by my ear, making it impossible to hold back a delicious shiver.

A man in a tuxedo is always a sight to behold, but Ian McCrory in a bespoke tux is a *god*. The colors white and black bow before him in supplication, grateful for the opportunity to be draped along the lines of his body. The cloth *worships* him.

His hair is newly cut, face covered with three day's growth but carefully trimmed, and he smells like Ian, a crisp scent of fine wool, pressed cotton, cherry, burnt oak, and spices too mysterious to name.

If wide-open spaces had a scent, it would be Ian.

"You're not dressed yet," he says. "And I normally pick up my date at her home." A gentle, obviously public kiss on my lips makes Mom's eyebrows shoot up.

Dad grins.

"This isn't a normal date."

"No." Something in him flickers. "And I need to talk to you in private."

"What about? Personal or business?"

"Both."

"Are you going to introduce us?" Dad interrupts, still smiling. "Unless my daughter has suddenly developed a habit of letting strange men in tuxedos kiss her?"

"I hope not, sir. I'm Ian McCrory. Nice to meet you," he says, pivoting to do the manly handshake thing with Dad.

"Roy Monahan."

Ian studies Dad for a moment. "I see the resemblance." He looks at me, smiling through his eyes.

"And I'm Sharon," Mom pipes up, offering her hand. "Thank you so much for everything you've done for our daughter. The legal bills, the consultants, her job..."

Now I feel like a charity case. Not his date.

"My pleasure, Mrs. Monahan."

"Oh, please. It's Sharon." But his politeness pleases her.

"Sharon."

"Yes," Dad says, stepping next to Mom, putting his hand on her shoulder. They share a glance, the kind of look you can only have with someone you're entwined with. "We really appreciate it."

"It's the least I could do."

I can't thank him yet again. I just can't. It feels weird now, awkward and unclear, the fuzzy line between our last kiss in his car and this moment too blurred for me to know what to say.

Or feel.

"And now the focus is on Mallory and Will," Ian says fluidly, with confidence. He's obviously accustomed to using charm to transition away from tension and awkwardness.

Which he senses in *me*.

"Absolutely. It's my sister's special day," I say, standing. "And it's time for me to change out of yoga pants and into my dress."

Ian leans in, hand on my hip. "I like you in whatever you're wearing. Or nothing at all."

Thankfully, Mom and Dad have started to move away, so the comment goes unheard.

"Are you hitting on me, Mr. McCrory?"

"If you have to ask, I clearly didn't do it well, so let me try again. This time, I won't fail to communicate *exactly* what I mean."

"I like the sound of that."

That vaguely troubled look comes over him. "But I do need a few minutes to talk about–"

Before he can finish, Perky comes running over, a huge Vuitton bag over her shoulder, a dashing Parker Campbell behind her, on his phone as she drags him by the hand.

"HASTY!" she calls out. "We have an emergency!"

"What's that?"

"Mallory's mascara is the wrong shade. It was supposed to be Burnished Mink and they sent Polished Bronze instead."

"*That's* an emergency?" Ian asks Parker over our heads.

Parker shrugs. "I guess?"

"How bad is the freak out?" Walking away from the men, we head for the dressing area as I try to let the wave of arousal inside me abate.

"She's sobbing. Something about the mascara shade matching the brown ring around Will's blue-green irises?"

"Oh, boy. Anyone give her a Xanax yet? Some CBD?"

"She refuses. Fiona's feeding her four-basil tea and rubbing a crystal on geopathic lines in the dressing room to help."

"Is it?"

"Is it what?"

"Helping?"

"God, no. But the dressing room smells like caprese and Fiona found a lost quarter under a radiator."

"Good for her. That probably doubles the net worth of a nursery school teacher."

"Meow. Good to see the old Hasty's back."

A genuine laugh rolls out of me. "Was I that bad?"

"Yes. But I like you better now."

"Who knew being ruined would make me likeable?"

"Do you care about being liked?"

"It's better to be respected than liked." The old canard comes out of my mouth before I can stop it, but I don't agree with it anymore.

"HASTY! Give me all your mascaras. I need to find the best match," Mallory snaps as we enter the dressing room. I'll give this event center its due: The building is designed for bridal parties. One big room with ten smaller rooms, like a dressing area at a bridal boutique, is the perfect layout. We have three private bathrooms, each with a shower, but ventilation prevents steam from leaking into this big prep area. There are water dispensers, plenty of coffee and tea, and a buffet set up on a side table.

Bottles of ibuprofen, acetaminophen, and boxes of tissues are on a tray. Tampons and pads are in a discreet covered basket, too.

"The photographer is coming for the pre-wedding pictures in twenty minutes," Mom says. We've all gone to our various hairdressers already, and our pedicures and manicures perfectly complement our outfits, so I find my dress and head for a room.

Dressing is easy, though I need a zip up. I pad out to the main area in bare feet and turn, Mom reading my nonverbal signal and coming over to help.

"This reminds me of your wedding," she whispers. "Oh," she adds. "I'm sorry. Maybe I shouldn't–"

"It's fine. It's natural to compare."

"He took so much from you."

"Just ten years and all my money, Mom."

"What do you have left?" Perky asks, the flat sarcasm making me laugh.

"Cheese. I have cheese."

"Sounds like he got the short end of the stick then, because your cheese is awesome."

"Burnished Mink to the rescue!" Raye calls out, entering

with her hand held high, a slim rectangular box in her hand. Her hair's in a gorgeous updo, much like mine, and following on her heels is her wife, Sanni.

Mallory halts mid-sob. "What?"

"Sanni found it! She had to go to three different malls, but she finally found it at the makeup store."

Mallory tackles Sanni like she's JJ Watt. "Ahhhhh! You are my guardian angel!"

"Over mascara?" But Sanni takes the hug and the designation in stride.

"I know it's silly. I just–everything's color coded. Spreadsheets, rooms, décor, my clothes, everything. And if it all doesn't line up just so, the energy's off. And if the energy is off, the comfort won't be there. And if the comfort's not there–"

"If you give a mouse a cookie," I whisper to Fiona, who brightens with laughter.

Mom holds a steaming cup of tea in front of Mal. "Drink."

"What's this?"

"More of Fiona's four-basil tea."

She takes a sip and makes a face. "Who put *whisky* in this?"

"Me," Fiona declares. "There is no amount of woo that can unwind you now. We've moved from herbal to distilled relaxation."

"I can't be drunk at my own wedding!"

"Not drunk. Just a little less tense," Mom soothes.

Red-rimmed eyes meet mine. "Were you this nervous when you married–" Mallory's hands clap over her mouth.

I roll my eyes. "You can say Burke's name. He isn't Voldemort."

"He's close."

"I had a life with him. We were together for eight years.

My wedding was part of that. All the things you're experiencing marrying Will, I experienced with Burke. Maybe the emotional stuff's not the same," I say, waving as if that's trivial. "But the rest? Sure. We did the wedding shower and the bachelorette party and the rehearsal dinner. Remember?"

"All of your events were carefully planned for maximum corporate networking. Who has a bachelorette party at a *regional bank*?"

"It was their private events center, and it's very exclusive, and..." I hear the defensive tone in my voice.

Then I start to laugh.

"That was Burke's idea."

Before anyone can comment, the photographer appears, all smiles and buried in equipment, a young assistant trailing behind with a rolling case and an eager expression.

"And away we go," Mom says under her breath, tears in her tone.

"Don't cry, Mom. Remember your mascara. No one likes a raccoon in wedding pictures."

"Where's Veronica?" Mallory asks, frantically looking around.

"She texted me," Raye says. "She's on her way. Said there was an accident on I-95, but no worries. Just stuck in traffic."

"There's always someone who's late," Mom says reassuringly. "It's almost a requirement. A good luck omen, even. It'll be fine."

Weddings are assembly lines.

No one will admit it, because we all like to think our wedding is unique, but the rituals are pre-determined in our little corner of New England culture. There's a proposal. The wedding shower. The bachelor and bachelorette parties. The rehearsal dinner. The ceremony and reception, the guest book and presents, the seating arrangements, the honeymoon–a series of checklists that vary something like birth plans.

They may be individual, but there's a certain inevitability to it all.

And at the end of a big wedding, everyone's exhausted, there's a big mess left behind, and a new life is forged.

See? Just like giving birth.

(Minus the pain).

Since Chaz isn't here, Veronica's husband, Justin, is paired with her. I've got Ian, and Paul is matched with Raye. Fiona has Fletch, of course, and Perky has Parker.

Five bridesmaids, five groomsmen.

And a glowing bride marrying her Prince Charming.

"I am so, so sorry!" gasps Veronica, who rushes in, hair perfect, face completely devoid of makeup. "Horrible accident. Everyone was rubbernecking. They had it cleared by the time we got to it, but it was on the other side of the highway, so there was no reason for people to drive so slowly except morbid curiosity."

"It's fine," Helen soothes her. "Let's get you into your dress and get some makeup on you." While the two of them scurry off to a private dressing room, Mom comes up to me with a bottled water and a plate of my own cheese, some olives, and a couple of grapes.

"What's this?"

"I gave some to Mallory, too. We need to eat. Once the ceremony starts, it'll be a blur. You'll forget to eat or pee, and after a hundred handshakes your arm will go numb. You'll forget your own name, dear," she says pleasantly.

"Mom! You almost sound cynical!" I take the plate, though, and sample my own cheese. The crystallization hasn't set in quite yet, but the taste is smooth, creamy, and has the hint of musk that gives it depth.

"Pragmatic," she corrects me. Her eyes get misty. "I'm marrying off my second daughter. I want everyone to be well."

Second daughter.

Marrying off.

"But I'm not married off. I had a wedding, but I'm not married," I mutter. Mom hears it and sighs. She holds my left hand as I pop the rest of the cheese in my mouth with the other.

"Your wedding was beautiful. And who knows? Perhaps you'll have another one someday."

"A real one."

"Hastings, your wedding to Burke was real. The marriage was real. *You* made it real. Not him. Don't diminish your own authenticity just because some prick conned you."

"Mom!"

Clap clap!

The photographer draws everyone's attention. "Pictures. Five minutes. Let's get everyone ready for the bridal prep set."

We rush to finish makeup, the pictures taking exactly as long as Sarah-the-wedding-photographer says they will, her schedule as precise as a Swiss train. She's confident, firm, and has the kind of voice that projects, an artifact of years of doing this for a living.

"Mallory? One more shot with your besties!"

Fiona and Perky go straight to Mal's sides, Raye standing back with a serene smile. Veronica and Helen hover near Mom, chatting away, and then Helen walks out discreetly, grinning.

We know what "besties" means. I've been in enough weddings to know that exclusion is part of the deal.

I'm never in these shots.

Ever.

"Hey! Come here," Mallory says to Raye, who steps forward, shy but moving to Fiona's side.

I turn away, reaching for a white paper cup to fill with coffee.

"Hasty?"

My shoulders tighten at the name.

"Get over here."

It should not matter.

It.

Should.

Not.

Matter.

But it does.

A tingling covers my entire back, mid-calf all the way to neckline, the rush of blood and relief and–gratitude?–filling me with a warmth that comes out in a smile as I make eye contact with Mallory.

I take my place.

We pose.

And then I go to her, reaching out for a hug.

"Damn it, Hasty," she laughs in my ear. "I'm going to cry!"

"Too late for me," Mom says from behind me. "I already am."

"No raccoons!" I shout, which makes Mal laugh harder, and soon the room is a series of sniffles and giggles.

Which is what Helen Lotham finds when she walks back in, carrying a huge wheel of cheese on a platter.

My cheese.

"Oh, Mallory. Will is going to be completely speechless when he sees you."

"Because of my raccoon eyes?" Mal jokes, as Mom carefully wipes her makeup.

"Because you are stunning. Absolutely stunning. I cannot believe how lucky my son is to have you as his lifelong partner," she says, setting down the cheese, her hands over her heart as she chokes up. "And how lucky we are to have you as our daughter-in-law."

Mom breaks in half. The sobs are seismic.

I don't have in-laws. Not just because Burke never legally married me, but because he told me his parents died years ago in a train accident in France.

That was a lie, too. Pritha and Thomas Janoo live in Taos, New Mexico, a fact I learned from the Feds while being grilled. They, too, were the victims of Burke's massive identity theft–he took out $175,000 in credit card debt using their social security numbers.

And yes, Burke flipped his real last name backwards.

Fitting for a guy who turned my world inside out.

Helen, Mom, and Mallory become a puddle of tears as Dad appears, tapping on the door.

"Ten minutes, everyone." He beams at Mallory. "You're gorgeous, kiddo." His eyes jump to Mom, and he frowns. "Oh, Sharon. You're crying again?" Fishing in his pocket, he pulls out a tube of mascara. "Here you go."

Mal takes it. "Burnished Mink!"

Raye gasps. Sanni, who is on the sidelines, starts to snicker.

"What?" Dad asks, clearly innocent. "Mom asked me to hold it for her as we were leaving the house this morning. Said she didn't want it to get lost."

CLAP, CLAP!

The room turns to find Dancy standing outside, peeking in, his hand covering his eyes. "Sorry to intrude, folks, but it's time to line up. We've got a bride and a groom to join in holy matrimony."

"Holy shit," Perky says to Mal. "You're really marrying Will Lotham."

"OMIGOD!" Fiona screams. "Mallory is marrying *Will Lotham!*"

"Is this news to them? I mean..." I mutter to Veronica, who smiles.

"I think they're channeling their ninth-grade selves."

"And that's different from..?"

"Didn't you ever have a crush? Imagine marrying him."

Ian comes to mind. Instantly, like a magician's flash of smoke, conjured by her words.

"Who knew Little Miss Perfect would end up marrying the asshole quarterback?" Perky says, making Veronica go tense.

Before I can ask who Little Miss Perfect is, Helen starts to line us up, shooing Veronica to her place. We are, in order:

Raye.

Veronica.

Me.

Perky.

Fiona.

Mallory has no maid or matron of honor. Said she couldn't pick just one.

Indecision was always one of her most annoying traits.

This time, it's endearing.

Besides, this isn't a competition.

Life doesn't have to be one.

I'm more nervous than I should be. I'm not the bride. In truth, I'm just a decoration. All five of us are, just as the groomsmen in tuxes are there to make Will stand out. Look good. Uniformed men, like soldiers who have his back.

That's how this works.

As we turn, I see Dancy's already at the altar, Will looking proud, not a hint of anxiety about him.

Mallory's idea that the groomsmen and bridesmaids walk down the aisle together is egalitarian. It also gives me a chance to hold Ian's arm, and as Raye goes first with Paul, then Veronica with Justin, I'm suddenly holding Ian's elbow, the fine weave of his jacket like heaven against my fingertips, his tall grace matching my rhythm as we walk down the aisle, all eyes on us for few moments.

Well, not all. A few widen, then disappear as heads huddle. I don't know if they're gossiping about me or the famous Ian McCrory, but I don't care.

Imperceptibly, Ian turns his head toward me and whispers, "You look extraordinary."

I smile and glance up at him, my whole soul glowing.

Because he makes me *feel* extraordinary.

We part at the altar, followed by Perky and Parker, Fiona and Fletch, the crowd's murmurs growing as people start to cry happy tears. I look out upon the one hundred fifty or so people and marvel at how tiny our side of the family is.

There's me, Mallory, Dad, and Mom. Aunt Trish and Uncle John from upstate New York. Phoebe is Mom's cousin who flew in from Tennessee. Mom is an only child, and our last living grandparent, Mom's dad, is in an Alzheimer's facility two hours away, unable to recognize Mom anymore.

I'm sure Mom told him about the wedding, even though he wouldn't really understand.

So this is it.

Mallory has some local friends, and her former employers, the Tollesons, are here. All the people from the Habitat for Humanity table Mal volunteers at during the Dance and Dairy festival sit in a small cluster in the middle, Mrs. Kormatillo in an aisle seat, wearing an enormous hat. The Hessermans are here, Eric and Jackson with Lori, his dad somewhere in the back, and I see Philippe with a young guy who could be his son or his lover.

Hard to tell which.

Raul and his dad, Thiago, are sitting next to Karen Minsky, who looks really different out of uniform.

Almost *friendly*.

Will and Veronica are Helen and Larry's only kids, but they obviously come from large families. Aunts and uncles, cousins and cousins' kids abound, the Lotham side of the open-air barn bursting with toddlers and tweens, two babies in arms, and the low-level rustling and murmurs that come from active people at a ritual designed around happiness.

Sheer joy.

And also?

Will's family is way more connected. Bigger, stronger, socially and financially. An old analytical piece of my mind kicks in, computing and calculating, wondering if–

"Dearly beloved," Dancy begins as the crowd hushes.

And I point a firehose at that part of me.

It needs to be snuffed out.

During the next half hour, my little sister will make a vow to marry the man who will be my brother-in-law forever. He isn't a con man, and he has actual, living parents who are here to support him. A sister I know. A family business.

Roots.

Will is real.

A quick glance across to the groomsmen makes me think again of my own wedding. All of Burke's groomsmen were well-connected finance guys he schmoozed with, but they weren't his *friends.*

Will's guys are people from high school. College. Grad school. A slow-rolling timeline of connection and friendship, of deep meaning and value.

Mallory found her soulmate right here in Anderhill.

Right where she's known she belonged, her whole life.

And while I'm insanely jealous of that, I'm also insanely happy.

For her.

The rest of the ceremony is a blur.

It has to be.

I'm not sure I can compare my life to hers anymore. I'm feeling two different layers of emotion, and they're at odds with each other, so the easiest way to manage is to just do what I'm told, and think later.

Act now.

Think later.

Feel it all *much* later.

&

"HERE," IAN SAYS, STRETCHING ACROSS ME TO FILL MY GLASS with Champagne. We're at the wedding party table, all twelve of us stretched across, paired off. He's to my left, Fletch to my right, and I feel like I'm in my element, performing for an audience.

That, or the third glass of wine is kicking in.

"Are you trying to get me drunk?"

"I'm facilitating your experience."

"You are too smooth."

"Au contraire, madame. My smoothness is finely calibrated."

"Like your Lamborghini engine?"

"Exactly." He squeezes my hand under the table, then moves his palm to my thigh. Champagne bubbles float up my nose, making me sneeze.

The hand doesn't move.

"You realize the third glass of Champagne is the 'come fuck me' glass, right?"

He endearingly leans on his hand, elbow on the table, smiling at me.

"Do tell."

"Glass number one is a social convention. Number two is the 'tell all the true stories about the bride' glass. But number three is what you give someone when you want them naked, in bed, writhing in good fun."

Expansive, confident, and so, *so* suave, Ian picks up the green bottle and tops me off.

"Here you go," he says.

"Mr. McCrory," I whisper.

"Mmm?"

"What are you implying?"

"Implying? Nothing."

"Your hand begs to differ."

"My hand would like to make you beg."

Before I can answer, Fletch stands. Dinner's over, though we barely ate any of it, too consumed with pictures and wedding formalities. The alcohol is rushing straight to my head, so I reach for my bread plate and hope the carbs soak up enough that I don't make a fool of myself.

One more glass and I'll find myself humping Ian in a coat closet.

"Best man speech," Ian whispers.

"But we didn't have a best man or a maid of honor?"

"I think Will put him up to it."

Clink clink

Fletch, a guy who is a paramedic and owns a boxing studio a few towns over, doesn't strike me as the eloquent-writer type, so my expectations for this speech are low.

Fiona beams at him, the two a couple now. Mal, Fiona, and Perky all found their partners.

Ian squeezes my thigh.

Maybe I have, too.

"So," Fletch begins. "First of all, I'm not a public speaker. At all. I'm more of a doer. This'll be short."

Cheers erupt, especially from a table full of guys who seem vaguely familiar. Will's football buddies from high school?

"I've known Will my whole life. I'm an Anderhill guy,

born and raised here. He was always way cooler than me, which meant he left the second we graduated high school."

Polite laughs abound.

"But we reconnected when he came back to work for the family business. Not the way he reconnected with Mallory, though. I don't work on porn sets."

He went there.

Mallory turns red.

"I spent plenty of time in football locker rooms, though."

"SAME THING!" one of the beefier guys at the table shouts.

Those are *definitely* Will's football buddies.

Fletch fumbles with his piece of paper, reading the words carefully. "So Will and I go way back, and his life is really different from mine. While he was out in the world, going to grad school in England, winning awards, putting together real estate deals, I was here rescuing cats from trees. Opening a tiny gym. Living a small life. Will's was bigger. Wider. More sophisticated."

A perplexed look covers Will's face.

"But he came back, ran into Mallory, and learned that no matter how big your life is, what matters is meeting someone who makes your heart even bigger. There's no small town too small for that."

Mallory presses her palms together and brings her fingers over her lips, like she's praying.

"We were jerks to you in high school, Mal," Fletch continues.

"And middle school," Perky mutters under her breath, but loud enough for me to hear from three seats away.

Fletch takes a deep breath. "And I hope you forgive us. Because now we're all part of the same community, and we love you. We love both of you. You couldn't find better soulmates for each other. If she put up with you through the urine perimeter incident, then–"

"Did he say *urine* perimeter?" Ian asks me in a strangled voice.

"–then she's your forever gal. To Mallory and Will: Thank you for showing us all that love is about growing together."

Kisses, claps, the *ding ding ding* of spoons on wine glasses–it all erupts as applause grows, Ian kissing my cheek. Music begins, the Daddy/Daughter dance about to start.

I excuse myself to go to the ladies' room.

By the time I come back, Mal and Will are on the floor, the song one I don't recognize, a slow, beautiful tune that feels custom made for this. The bridal party is herded to the edge of the dance floor, and then we pair off, Ian masterful in guiding me, Dancy offering his hand to Mom, who accepts with grace.

"You are radiant," Ian whispers.

"That's what you say to the bride."

"I'm saying it to you."

"Thank you."

"You seem happy."

"It's the Champagne. Three glasses, you know. You could be a cad."

"It's more than that."

"Maybe it's you." I squeeze his shoulder. He tightens his grip on my hip.

"Me?"

"What're we doing, Ian?" The words come with a smile, a vulnerability, a wistful hope.

"We're dancing."

"Dancing around our feelings."

"I'm not. Come with me."

"To your hotel room?"

"To Australia."

"What? An entire continent? That's way bigger than a king-sized bed!"

"I have to spend four months there. I leave in a few hours. I have the jet lined up. We can work together there."

"Four months! You're going away for four *months?*"

"Yes."

"Why didn't you tell me before?"

"I tried to."

"Earlier today? When you wanted a few minutes to talk?"

"Yes. I just found out this morning."

"Does this mean I'm fired?"

"What? Why would I fire you? You're the best analyst I have."

"But what happens when I need to consult with you?"

"If you're next to me in Australia, you can just ask."

"I can't just move halfway around the world, Ian!"

"Sure you can. Don't you want to?"

"Of course I do!" Hysteria tinges my voice. "I mean, I literally *can't.* I'm not allowed to leave the country. My passport has been confiscated."

Pain tightens the skin around his eyes. "Damn it. I forgot that part of your file."

"File? My file?"

Guarded calculation fills his eyes. "From the lawyers. The consultants. It was mentioned in the reports, but I'd forgotten until now."

"So had I. Not that I was planning any glamorous out-of-country trips, but still."

"I'm sure I can pull strings. Find a way to get you out of here. Surely we can–"

"Ian. Stop." His heart hammers against my palm, as if it wants to be pulled out, cradled, held. "You can't insert yourself into a global financial scandal. Not one with the Feds looking into every little detail."

He stiffens. "Why not?"

"Because no one who reaches your level of success is a Boy Scout."

His face remains impassive.

"And because I don't want you smeared with the taint of Burke. It's bad enough I reek of it, but it was my own stupidity that got me here. I won't have it touch you. Don't interfere, Ian."

The tone of his skin goes pallid, face slackening with each word I say, a strange sadness filling his eyes.

"Right. Of course," he says softly, kissing my temple. "I won't try to get permission for you to leave the country."

I work to lighten the mood. "It's not as if you have that kind of pull, anyhow. Even the great Ian McCrory can't bend the federal government to his will."

Shoulders expanding with a deep breath, Ian gives me an unreadable smile, the light on the dance floor flickering with shadows, making his eyes hard to see.

"But I can bend you."

And then he dips me, the crowd whooping, applause crackling at the edges around us, my eyes catching an upside-down Dancy, who winks at me before I'm whisked upright into a kiss that dissolves the world, turning liquid and hot.

Until people begin clanging spoons on wine goblets and Will and Mallory take center stage.

As it should be.

Breaking away, Ian takes my hand and walks me toward the edge of the open-air barn. When we reach a small stone bench, patterned pebbles at our feet making a large Celtic knot, he sits me down, so serious.

"Hastings, I have to go."

"I know. You just said so."

"I have to go *now*."

"Now? Why?"

A kiss on the forehead makes me feel a spike of fear. "It's time."

"We can FaceTime. We can have video chats and text. I'm sure you'll be back at least once in those four months, right?"

His smile doesn't commit.

And it doesn't reach his eyes.

"Ian?"

"It'll all be fine, Hastings. I know you're fine. I don't expect to be back before October, though. But maybe this is for the best."

"For the best?"

"I'm pushing you. I can feel it."

Bzzzz

His phone lights up, putting pressure on the moment, lending a sense of desperate urgency.

All the certainty I was beginning to gather in the space between us crumbles at his words, plates shifting deep in the Earth.

"You're not pushing! It's just that I can't–they have my passport!"

"I know you can't. I understand why you can't. And maybe some time away from each other is what we both need."

"Oh, God, not that line, Ian. Come on. You're more original than that. What's next? 'It's not you, it's me?'"

Finally, I see a flash of something in his flat eyes that hurts more than contempt. It's confusing, and I can't define it. When I can't define something, it's a threat.

Unsafe.

My heart is open to him. I can't live with the duality of being open and feeling unsafe.

And then his hands are on my waist, lips hard against mine, his body pulling me to him to answer the unfathomable, to shift the plates back to where they belong, to do the impossible and bend reality to his will. Our will.

Our *desire*.

The kiss is easy. So easy and true and rough and intense.

And then he breaks away, phone buzzing as he walks into the night, the dark air swallowing his tuxedo-framed body, and says over his shoulder:

"It's me."

❧ 16 ❧

The first email is from Helen.

I have to tell you that I mentioned your cheese to a friend who owns a wine shop in Stow, just inside of I-495. She's interested in buying from you. What you served at the wedding yesterday was divine. Yes, I'm meddling, mothers can't help themselves. I'm so glad we're family now!

THE SECOND EMAIL IS FROM... HELEN.

Oh! And now a friend of mine who owns an inn in York Harbor wants to know about steady orders, too. They have a weekend winery package and she's very interested in working with a local provider.

THE THIRD EMAIL IS FROM RAUL.

Don't forget our deal. I hear your cheese is becoming popular and we want to be sure people know Beanerino is the only place in Anderhill to find it.

. . .

THE FOURTH EMAIL IS FROM CASTLE CELTIC.

We made an exception and allowed Mr. Lotham and Ms. Monahan to self-cater the manchego for their wedding, and many guests have asked us where it's from. Mr. Lotham's mother informed us it was you, and we're sending this note to ask if you take wholesale orders?

THE FIFTH EMAIL IS FROM DORIAN.

Hey, Hastings. I heard all about your sister's wedding, and congratulations to her, but among caterers, the buzz is all about your cheese. I know this is awkward, but I'd love to ask you more about it. Over coffee? We could catch up and do some business networking LOL.

AND THAT'S ALL BEFORE NOON, THE DAY AFTER MY SISTER'S wedding, when I'm hung over from too much Champagne, way too many feelings, and not enough Ian.

Because he's gone.

I grab my phone, the impulse too hard to resist. Ian's number is right there, but I hold back, not texting. Anyway, he's still airborne, so it doesn't matter.

Instead, I pull up Eric Hesserman's info and type:

How do I buy sheep's milk at wholesale?

I hit send, put down the phone, and stare at the ceiling, head throbbing, heart trying to figure out how it feels. Ian is gone. Gone to Australia for four months.

And I can't go with him.

Our conversation last night, before he left, runs on an endless loop in my mind. Where did it go wrong? He changed, his body and tone shifting into a disengagement that was worse than any other emotion.

When I mentioned the Feds, my passport being confiscated—that was the pivot point.

Shame rushes through me like a mountain melt in spring.

I can't be what he wants me to be.

I'll always be tainted by Burke's scandal.

"*It's me,*" Ian said last night, but he's lying. I know he is.

It's not him. He helped me. Pursued me. Kissed me and lit me up, but once he got close enough to see who I really am, my baggage, the stain of scandal, he backed off.

I can respect that.

I don't like it, but I respect it.

Okay, fine—I don't.

I don't respect one damn thing about it.

But what choice do I have?

A notification on my phone makes me look:

Let's go up to Susan's farm together. She'd be happy to make a deal with you, Eric replies.

When? I ask.

I'm free at 2.

Today?

I'm so accustomed to my old life, where putting an event on the calendar eight weeks in advance was necessary to pin it in time. People who can do something at the drop of a hat used to be objects of ridicule for me. How important can you be if you're not scheduled into the next quarter?

Sure. 2 sounds good, I answer.

It's a relief not to be too "important" to go on a field trip with Eric.

Great. I'll drive. Need a 4x4 for this trip. Bring shitkickers, he says.

?? I reply.

I get an eye roll emoji. *Boots*, he answers. *I'll bring a pair of Lori's, but you need to get your own if you're planning to make this trip on a regular basis.*

I'll order some on Amazon, I reply.

Another eye roll.

Pack some cheese and good coffee for the trip. Susan needs to know what you're making these days.

By the time he arrives, I'm more than ready, cooler in hand, two thermoses ready. It's less than an hour to her farm, but as Eric turns along my neighborhood's side roads to get to I-95, I settle in, ready to just hang out.

Until he asks: "Are you and Ian McCrory a thing?"

"What?"

"You know." He makes a weird noise with his mouth that I think is meant to imply having sex.

Or a dog's squeaky chew toy.

"What does–" I imitate the sound, "–mean?"

"Are you sleeping with him?"

"Why is that any of your business? Besides, he's gone to Australia for months."

"You were seen leaving a piano bar with him in a Lamborghini. Then you got pulled over by the cops. Then you were dancing with him at Mallory's wedding. Word gets around."

"We did not get pulled over. We already *were* pulled over. Small towns are the worst."

"For secrets? Yes. Did you know Chris Fletcher eats peanut butter on his tacos at Taco Cubed?"

"With a memory for detail like that, you'd make a fine analyst."

"I do fine analysis of crop failure rates and nematode eradication."

I drink some of my coffee to avoid talking.

"Well? Ian McCrory?"

I drink some more.

"He clearly likes to go Down Under." The sideways glance makes the double entendre clear.

"STOP IT! When did you get so vulgar, Eric?"

"*This* from the girl who papier-machéd a penis head and swapped it for the Trojans's mascot before the rivalry game in 2004?"

"No, I'm not sleeping with Ian. There. Happy?"

"Not really. I was hoping for some juicy details I could live through vicariously."

"Ew!"

But we laugh. Being grilled like this makes me realize I do have friends like Mallory's. Or, at least, I did. One. I had one.

Eric.

And he counts.

The teasing makes me relax enough to take a tentative step forward. "He asked me to go with him. To Australia."

"Why didn't you?"

"The Feds confiscated my passport."

"That excuse beats 'I need to wash my hair.'"

"Right. And then he said he could pull strings, but I didn't want that."

"Why not? The guy offered."

"Sticking his neck out for me in that way brings him into the mess. I don't want that."

"The guy's a grown up, Hastings. He can make his own choices."

"He backed off quickly. Got cold. Kissed me goodbye, shut down, and left."

"Maybe his ego was hurt."

"It didn't seem like that."

"Maybe he's human."

"Huh?"

"No one likes to be rejected."

"I had a really good reason!"

"But he offered to remove the obstacle and you said no."

"For his own good!"

"And... we're back to the fact that he's a grown up and can make his own decisions."

"His choice wasn't logical!"

"It's not a chess game, Hastings. It's an emotional landscape. That's how relationships work. Nothing is really about logic when it comes to feelings."

"You are so wrong!"

"Let me guess–you've already created a seventeen-point list of all the reasons why."

"With sub-headings and color-coded categories." I smile a little.

"Ian was probably stung. Shut down to avoid being hurt further."

"Hurt?"

"Guy offers to take you to Australia? Wants to live with you there and you say no? Offers to fix it for you so you can go, and even then, you turn him down? Yes, hurt. I'd be hurt. Plus, the whole billionaire thing."

"I don't like Ian for his money!"

"Never said you did."

"Then what's the 'billionaire thing'?"

"Billionaires aren't used to being rejected. Bet it hurts more than for us average schlumps."

"You're not average!"

"Thanks for arguing on the schlump part."

We're exiting the highway, turning onto state routes that will wind along the growing hills that eventually lead up to the White Mountains.

"So he shut down and closed off, told me 'it's not you, it's me,' because–"

Eric's eyes pop. "He said that?"

"Mmm hmm."

"That changes everything."

"Why?"

"Because guys never admit that. Ever. If he's saying that, it's totally you."

"Hey!"

But Eric's smiling, teasing me. "What were his last words to you?"

"'It's me.'"

"Huh. Then he's hiding something."

"Hiding something?"

"Yeah. A guy like Ian is smart, and he's powerful. He says what he means, right? He's direct."

"Which means he's nothing like my ex."

"I never did understand Burke."

"Why do people say things like that *now?* You were at my wedding, Eric. You could have spoken up then! People are crawling out of the woodwork now to tell me how much they didn't like Burke."

"If we'd said something back then, you would have sharpened your claws and shredded us. No one could ever talk you out of anything, Hastings. You figure out what you want and build a world that reinforces every decision."

"I don't understand what you mean."

"You create a filter. Anything that doesn't line up with your decisions is irrelevant."

"You're dangerously close to saying I 'create my own reality.' That's the kind of bullshit Burke peddled."

"You lived with the guy for years. Maybe some of him rubbed off on you."

"Of course it did. Just like you're gay, but you married a woman and built a family with her."

"Right. I created a reality that I desperately needed to be true."

"That doesn't mean you didn't love her."

He grips the steering wheel like he's holding back emotion with his hands. "Of course I loved Annabelle. And you loved Burke. But you let whatever you wanted from your life with him blind you a bit. You didn't want to see that other people didn't like him. Didn't like him for you. Wanted you to find someone better."

Old Me would have yelled at him.

Who am I kidding? Old Me wouldn't have come within ten cheese wheels of this conversation.

Bzzzz

"That's yours," he says, coming to a stop at a four-way, where a red covered bridge makes me wonder if we accidentally crossed the border into Vermont.

I look at the notification. Another email.

About my cheese.

"Will's mother has a serious hard-on for my manchego."

Eric shifts uncomfortably in his seat. "That is not a good mixed metaphor."

"She's sending all these different potential customers my way. A high-end inn in Maine. The Castle Celtic catering services. Her friend with a wine shop."

"You're well connected on your own, Hastings. Go for it."

"Go for what?"

"Make the cheese."

"I am! That's why we're visiting Susan."

"You're a businesswoman. Make a business plan. Treat this the way you'd treat any other project. Instead of working for someone else, though, *you're* the investment."

"Me? I can't make a living doing this."

"Sure you can! Plenty of people do."

"Like who? How? Anderhill doesn't have a big enough market for sheep's milk cheese."

"You're thinking too small."

"I'm being pragmatic."

"Web sales. You can ship. Makes your business global. Institutional and restaurant sales, too."

"The return on investment and time isn't there."

"You know how much Hesserman's Dairy makes off web sales?" He names a figure.

I drop my (thankfully closed) thermos of coffee. "*That much?*"

He nods.

"But you're a dairy… you can't sell milk and ice cream online..?"

"No, but we sell maple syrup, and honey, and we can even ship some of the perishable stuff, like bacon. Your product has the same profit margin. Artisanal is the new black."

"Oooooh. I like that. Can I steal it for a tagline?"

"Too late. Lori uses it on our website."

"Your daughter? Isn't she eleven?"

"Almost twelve. She's our webmaster. Says farming is great and all, but code is the twenty-first-century cash crop."

"Smart kid."

"Nah. She just hates mucking stalls."

The roads get progressively narrower, last winter's frost heaves breaking up the tar. Finally, we come to a farmstand, one big enough to be fully enclosed with ten parking spaces in front. On the other side of it, Eric turns onto a gravel road, the ascent up a mountain pass making my ears pop. Finally, we turn a corner, and an enormous farm appears, as if it had been cloaked by an invisibility spell and magically revealed to us.

A big farmhouse with three wings, newer additions, is at the peak of the hill, flanked on the right by an enormous red barn, and on the left by another, smaller metal building that has farm equipment in front of it.

Susan is sitting on the front porch at a small wicker table, a pitcher of lemonade and a pile of poop on a plate next to her.

Wait. It can't be.

"Remember Dung Donuts?" she asks when Eric and I have ascended the stairs, Susan rising slightly in her chair and dropping back. Never big on hugs, she was always a quiet doer, a woman who followed the rhythm and flow of a skilled task, pivoting as needed to make sure the outcome was optimal.

And she wasn't afraid to get dirty.

"I forgot until now! I wondered why you had a plate of poop," I say, taking one when she offers the plate. The scent of chocolate, cinnamon, and maple overwhelms me.

Eric looks at us like we're loons.

"You never went to farm camp, did you?" I ask.

He snorts. "My entire life was farm camp, Hastings."

"Susan," I explain around a mouthful of yummy dung, "made sheep-poop donuts. Have one."

A hairy eyeball is my only acknowledgment from him.

Susan laughs. "It's just a goofy thing I did for the kids."

Within five minutes, Eric's eaten three dung donuts, we're well into our lemonade, and laughter fills the porch.

"When I found out you were an MBA-toting, financial industry person, Hastings, I was shocked. You always struck me as a farm girl born into an insurance agent's family."

I look at my manicure and hold up my hands. "I think I'm a hybrid." I show her my boots.

"Let's put those to good use," she says. "We don't make cheese here, but we make sheep, and sheep make milk, and that's close enough." As she stands, Susan winces. It's clear her bones are getting old.

But within ten strides, she's walking faster than me, Eric between us as I bring up the rear. The scent of dung hits me hard as we enter the huge barn, some sheep behind a small gate, the buzzing sound of clippers nearby.

I groan. "I think I still have lanolin in places from twenty years ago."

Susan's laughter is contagious as she props one foot up on a gate slat and leans toward the animals. "You sucked at shearing."

"Hey!"

"We can't all be gifted at every single thing we try," she says sagely, making Eric bite his lower lip.

"Do you know how painful those words are to someone like me?" I ask her.

"Truth often hurts," she comments.

Through the other door of the barn and down a small slope, Susan leads us to a pasture where hundreds of sheep graze.

"No worries about having enough milk," I say, eyeing the greenery, wondering if someday, maybe, I could own a place like this.

Someday.

After I get my passport and my dignity back.

And a whole lot more capital.

Two goats spar on top of a tractor with a crooked seat. I start laughing at myself. Who knew I'd reach a point like this, wishing for a farm of my own?

A year ago, I wanted a penthouse condo in the Marina district of San Francisco.

My, how times have changed.

"I have plenty for you, Hastings. But what're you gonna do with it?"

"I'm starting to get demand for my manchego. My mom and Eric think I should turn my hobby into a business."

"Do *you* think that?"

"I don't think the market's there."

"That's not the question I asked." Her hard stare is judgmental but also revealing. I feel like I'm prying open a closed door inside myself.

"Should I turn my hobby into a business? I think it's cloyingly Millennial of me."

Hard stare.

"Um, I, uh–I don't know," I clarify.

"Why don't you know?"

"Because it seems... foolish."

"Do you produce an inferior product?"

"What? No! Of course not."

"And would you line your manchego up against the finest cheeses in the world?"

"Well, maybe not yet, but someday. Someday soon. Hell, yes!"

"Then get out of your own way."

"Excuse me?"

"You don't have any reason you can't open a cheese business other than yourself, Hastings. This is about you. This isn't about the market, the customers–they're out there. It's not them, it's–"

"Me. It's *me*."

"The Cortlands are renting out their old farmstand," Eric says suddenly, a gleam in his eye. "Bet you could get it for cheap. The estate is tied up in some legal mess, and they're desperate for some cash. I've heard their hands are tied about commercial use for the space, but artisanal cheese won't have huge foot traffic."

"Then why would I want to do it? The more foot traffic, the better."

"You want some, sure. But web sales, Hastings. That'll be where you build your business."

"Do both," Susan urges. "Help your community, feed

your soul, and provide an outstanding product to a global audience. Do what makes you feel good. "

Ian makes me feel good.

But I can't do *him*.

"I don't have the capital I need to get started. I'm still being investigated. I can't even leave the country because the Feds have my passport."

"What capital do you need?" Susan asks, eyebrow up.

"Oh, no. No, no, no. No way do I want your money."

"Who said anything about money?" Susan waves in the direction of the land behind her. "I'm talking about milk. I have plenty of milk. You use old-fashioned methods, so the equipment is cheap. You won't be able to scale up for a while."

"And I'm sure Edina Cortland will cut you a rent deal. It's not like the big leagues here, Hastings. You could get this up and running for a few grand."

"I have a job. I don't have time for this."

"Your job means you must have some money coming in, right? Plenty of small businesses do it on a shoestring budget."

"Five months ago, I was negotiating nine-figure deals. Now I can't even swing three-figure rent."

"But maybe you can." Susan frowns at Eric. "What about your old sugar house?"

"Huh?"

"The old one, from when your dad and I were kids."

"We put a fence up around it twenty years ago. Dad uses it for cold storage now."

"It has electric, right? And water?"

"Sure. The guys use it to wash off after really heavy work days."

Susan's eyes cut over to me. "Does it have a place for parking?"

"It did. Hasn't been maintained. Needs a new layer of stone."

"Why not rent it to Hastings?"

"What?" Eric and I blurt out together.

"Dairy farm. Foot traffic. People accustomed to buying local. Add something new. Give Hesserman's some buzz."

"It's the size of a large garden shed, with an attached bathroom. You can't run a retail shop out of there."

"A non-farm one, no. But you're already zoned for limited retail, if Anderhill is anything like most small towns in Mass..." Susan argues, voice fading out to make a point.

"True," he says, eyes narrowing as he looks at me. "Let me ask Dad."

"You're both crazy," I inform them.

"Sure," Susan replies. "But that doesn't mean it's a bad idea."

And then she winks.

Bzzz

"It's me," I tell them, looking at my phone, shocked to find a text from Ian.

My heart soars.

Just landed in Hawaii. Missing you already. Sorry for leaving like that. About to board for Oz. Would love a video call after I kick jetlag.

Smiling, I reply: *Glad to hear you're safe. Video call tomorrow? At business meeting now.*

Why are you in the office on a Sunday? he quickly answers.

Different business. Not yours.

You're job hunting? Whatever they're offering, I'll double it to keep you.

"Susan," I call out. "How many gallons a week can you produce?"

"A few hundred," she answers. "Why?"

Can you produce a few hundred gallons a week of warm, white fluid? I throw back at him.

I'm pretty sure I will while we're apart, he types back.

"Geez, Hastings, you're blushing. That must be Ian." Eric's teasing makes me smile even more.

"It is."

"Well?" Susan asks. "Are we in business? I'll front you the milk, you pay me as you can, and Eric'll see if he can get the sugar house for you."

"I am good at massaging zoning and planning boards to get business regulations in alignment," I murmur, thinking it through.

"What'd she say?" Susan asks Eric.

"She's good at sucking up," he translates.

She snorts. "About all that MBA is good for."

I'm still working for you, I inform Ian. *But I'm exploring my options.*

I wish I'd explored you more, he replies. Then I get a heart.

And a peach. And a...

Hot dog?

You are terrible at emoji sexting.

But I'm great at it in person. I can double-thumb like you wouldn't believe.

Try to sleep on the plane. Get the jet lag out of your system, I answer, turning my phone off entirely, the Power button my only shield to keep me from embarrassing myself any further.

"Let's do it," I say, Eric and Susan erupting into applause. "What do I have to lose? My reputation? My money? My dignity?"

And then I laugh into the wind, so loud that the sheep *baaaaaaa* back, like they're happy for me.

🦋 17 🦋

T hree months later

"WE HAVE A PROBLEM," MALLORY SAYS, NEAR TEARS.

"What's that?"

"The bunnies are blocking the refrigerator vent."

"Could you repeat that?" I ask, sure I've heard her wrong.

"The bunnies are blocking the refrigerator vent."

"*Bunnies?*"

"Yes. A mama must have given birth to a bunch, and her little warren is a hole right where the HVAC guy needs to dig to make sure the fridge air system has plenty of room."

"So?"

"We can't hurt the bunnies!"

"I don't want to hurt the bunnies, but every day I'm not open yet is another day in the red!"

"Susan's fronting you the sheep's milk. You already had

most of the equipment for processing. Eric's dad cut you a sweet deal on rent. How in the red are you?"

"Two-days-behind-schedule in the red."

"So the only red is on your color-coded Excel spreadsheet?"

"It still counts!"

"Hastings, you haven't even picked a grand opening date. And you have three more months to go before the cheeses are completely ready. You can't open with a few pounds of eight-month-aged manchego and hundreds of three-month cheeses. You need the time. Literally."

"But that doesn't mean I can't optimize, and following a damn schedule is part of that."

"Bunnies don't know how Excel spreadsheets and schedules work."

"Then *you* tell them. You seem to be able to speak to the animals. Maybe whistle a bit and they'll do some housework for us? You've got the red hair. You'd make a good Ariel or Merida."

"Ha ha. And besides, Fiona's the one who talks to animals. Not me."

"But do they talk back to her?"

"Only when Perky brings out the ouzo."

Eric taps lightly on the main door, frowning. "You've got a bunny problem."

"I know!" Mal says, hands going up in the air.

"Gotta re-route the vent pipe."

"What? That'll cost more money!" I argue.

"You have no choice. No one wants to buy cheese from a bunny killer," Mal says emphatically.

"I'm not saying I want to kill them!" Her comment bugs me more than it should. "Can't we relocate them?"

"To where? A nice condo in Back Bay?"

"Mal, just glove up and pick them up and move them," I insist.

Eric snorts. "You know nothing about bunnies."

Mallory crosses her arms over her chest and gives Eric a look like he's her new bestie.

"You're right! I don't!" I retort, blowing a long piece of stray hair off my brow. "Do I really have to pay more to change the pipe?"

"Yeah. But think of it this way: If the bunnies stay, you have something fun for kids to look at. Blog about it on social media. Make it a thing."

"Can you make rabbit's milk cheese?" Mallory wonders aloud, looking to Eric for the answer.

"I mean... I guess? Rabbits have teats. Their babies drink their milk."

As Eric responds, Mallory whips out her phone, typing rapidly. "AHA!" she exclaims. "Rabbit's milk cheese. It's a thing!"

Eric and I make sounds that resemble a dying zombie.

Or... can zombies die? They're already dead, right?

"And how, exactly, do you milk a rabbit?" I ask.

Eric holds his hands up and pinches his index fingers and thumbs rhythmically. "Like this?"

"Ewww, gross."

"How is it gross? It's mammal milk."

Mallory looks down at her breasts. "Right. We'll make milk one day when we have kids."

"Don't compare that to rabbit's milk cheese. No one makes cheese out of human breast milk," I say, regretting it instantly.

Mal Googles. I groan.

She holds up the screen. "Actually, Hastings, that's a thing, too."

"It's not *my* thing!"

The *beep-beep-beep* of a delivery truck backing up catches Mal's attention, and she mercifully scurries off. I walk outside to look at the bunnies, adjusting the strap of my overalls, then pulling the hair tie out of my messy bun, combing my fingers through my hair and re-doing it. Over time, I've softened the dark chestnut to a light ash brown, moving from Mom's Madison Reed color suggestions to a good local stylist.

I like being brunette. It's like I'm reinvented.

Outside first.

Inside second.

"How much milk does a mother bunny make, anyhow?" I call out to Eric, whose shoulder and leg come into my peripheral vision as I bend down to peer into the rabbit hole.

"I leave for three months and this is what I come back to. Hastings Monahan, bunny milker."

Ian's voice is absolutely the *last* thing I expect to hear, the shock of it pitching me forward, flat on my face in the grass, a dandelion head brushing against my lips. Scrambling up, I throw myself into his arms, his embrace picking me up off the ground, the scent of him so good, so exciting.

So *real*.

"What are you *doing* here?"

"Learning new details about you. Your fine motor skills must be exceptional if you can milk rabbits. What else can you milk with those fingers?"

"Ian!"

Before I can ask another question, his mouth is on mine for a kiss I've dreamt about for months, full and rich, extraordinary and filled with questions.

"I missed you," he says. "And wanted to see you, so I came back early. FaceTime and texting is no replacement for the real thing."

"I missed you, too."

He looks around, then down at the hole in the ground, face softening as a tiny bunny head pokes out, then retreats. "And you have been keeping a secret."

"I didn't want to tell you until the store was ready."

"When does it open?"

"Another month or two. Okay, probably three, because of the six-month aged cheese. Depends on... a lot of factors." I was about to say *money*, but stop myself.

Because I do not want Ian McCrory swooping in and rescuing me.

Again.

"Show me around. I'm intrigued. This is what you do when you're not in the office?"

"It is."

"Turning a hobby into a business? How–"

I kiss him before he can say *hipster*.

Then I give him the full tour. Which takes exactly ninety seconds. It's not a big space. We basically stand in the middle of the former sugar house and spin in a circle while I point.

"And you've done the analysis? You can turn a profit here?"

"This is more of a community-based retail site. Most of my profit will come from institutional contracts and online sales."

"You've done your research, of course. Can you make a living doing this full time?"

"Not until year three, according to my business plan. I'm assuming I can continue to consult for you, just on a more limited basis."

"Of course. I know Irene had you sign a six-month contract after your initial three-month contract was up, but I was planning to offer you a higher position. Full time. Better salary, benefits, the whole deal."

"Corner office?" I joke. "My own barista?"

"If you want that."

He's serious.

"You know, part of me does want what you're offering. But it's like an echo. I love consulting, but this..." I gesture to the giant pots, the cut oak logs, the cheesecloth, the five-gallon buckets lined up neatly, the bottles of rennet, the bags of lavender. "This is mine."

He takes a deep breath, clearly inhaling a scent, searching for something in the air. "It is yours. And it reminds me of home, my grandfather's farm in Wisconsin."

A small frown develops between his eyes, then fades quickly. If I weren't intently studying him, I wouldn't have noticed.

"How much capital do you need?" he asks abruptly.

"What?"

"I'd like to do a private equity deal with you. I'll invest in your business."

My laugh isn't nervous. Not tentative. No giggle emerges. Instead, a full-throated, mature sound of deep amusement rises up.

When I stop, the answer is easy:

"No."

"No? Who is funding you?"

"Me. A break on rent from Eric's dad. Susan's helping with milk. And my father."

"You'll take money from your dad but won't let me invest?"

"Dad filed a theft claim on the insurance policy he had for the family engagement ring Burke stole. It came through. So he's helping fund some of this."

"That's great. I want to as well."

"No, thank you."

"I don't handle rejection well."

"I'm not rejecting you."

"*No* is the very definition of rejection."

"Think of it as the opposite of yes."

"And your point is...?"

"I'm saying yes to me when I say no to you."

"You want to do it on your own."

"I do."

"*That* I understand." His arm goes around my shoulders, sliding down my arm to land on my hip. "When you do it yourself, you calibrate. You decide. You control. And the victories are all on you."

"Exactly. But that doesn't mean I won't need team members."

"You'll let me help?"

"Of course. We need someone to clean the bathroom."

His face opens up with a smile of surprise and delight. "Do I have to do it in a French maid's costume?"

"Ew!"

"You seem to enjoy telling me what to do, Hastings." His grip tightens and he kisses me, tongue caressing my teeth, pulling in my lower lip, the taste of him sweet and simple and groaningly perfect.

"If anyone's wearing a French maid's costume in this relationship, it's me."

"I'll take that as a promise."

Eric walks in, head down, reading a manifest. When he looks up, he says, "Ian! Good to see you with a shirt on."

Mallory gives Eric a raised eyebrow, then looks at me. "Is something going on between the three of you I should know about?"

"Ian tried to get his arm in the vagina, but it was too big," Eric elaborates.

Mal gives me moon eyes. "That really doesn't clarify," she says in a whisper-thin voice.

"Good to see you too, Eric," Ian says. "You clearly got to work with Hastings while I was gone."

Eric shrugs. "I just hooked her up with some old friends, and we had this sugar house sitting empty. Hastings took the opportunities and made this all come together."

"We're calling the company Anderhill Cheese," I tell him. "I grabbed the domain name and we're getting online commerce established. Susan, my old farm-camp teacher, is fronting me the milk in bulk." I walk over to one cooler and slap the door. "Sixty pounds in here, aging, and everyone I know is storing a wheel or three in their fridge until we can get the big cooler in place. The bunnies are causing a snag."

"Bunnies?"

"Long story." My stomach growls. He notices.

"Let me take you somewhere for a hot shower, a good meal, and fabulous company," Ian says as Eric and Mal suddenly find something to do.

"You know a place where I can get all that?"

"I do. About a mile from here, in a rented house."

"What?"

"I'm here in town. Got a small house. Irene had it stocked with food. Do you like steak? Or salmon? I'm pretty good at a grill, especially after all this time in Australia."

"You want to take me back to your house and cook me dinner?"

"And take you to bed."

"That's very direct of you."

"I'm a direct kind of guy."

"I like direct."

"Good. Because I like *you*." He kisses me again.

Mallory clears her throat. We look up.

"You want Eric and me to handle the rest, Hastings? There isn't much left, except giving the HVAC guy the info on the bunnies."

"Save the bunnies, Mallory. Make a little bunny garden. A shrine. Whatever you want. Add some gnomes and geopathically sensitive crystals for all I care. Let Fiona go wild."

Her eyes light up. "Really? Because she has *ideas*. Says this place is perfect for a gnome village."

As Ian guides me to his car, I shout over my shoulder, "Go for it."

"Same to you!" she calls back.

Yet another delivery truck has arrived, the ubiquitous brown box blocking Ian's car. A guy in uniform trots over to us, looks at an address label, and says, "Hastings Monahan?"

"That's me."

He asks for a signature, then hands me a thick envelope. I tear it open.

My passport falls out.

"What the heck?"

Ian nods. "Look at the letter."

"'Charges dropped in full… no further review… ask for future cooperation should Mr. Oonaj contact you…'" I frown. "The lawyers you hired for me never said a word."

"They may not have been notified yet," he offers. "Congratulations."

"Dropped? The charges are really dropped? I'm *free?*"

"You are." He kisses my temple. We watch the dust as the truck pulls away.

"I can go anywhere now!"

"I can think of one place I want to go with you."

The kiss he gives me tells me where, without words.

It's a place where clothing is optional.

And I'm exploring all my options now.

❧ 18 ❧

"This is Marvelle Johnston's old house!" I exclaim as Ian pulls up to the English Tudor, the ivy crawling up the walls like it's Spiderman.

"Who is Marvelle Johnston?"

"Car dealer in the area. He had the craziest jingles on the radio and television." I pause, letting the memory hit me. Then I sing, "When you gotta go, you gotta go, so get one of ours and hit the road."

"That is the worst jingle I've ever heard."

I gesture at the house. "It worked on someone. He sold a lot of cars."

"Let me guess. Nineteen seventies and eighties?"

"And into the early nineties. I was really little when his commercials were everywhere. His tagline was 'At my lot, you won't pay a lot.'"

"You're killing me. Those are terrible advertising choices."

"He knew how to appeal to a certain market niche. Is it worse than some of the social media marketing videos you see?"

"Good point." We climb out of the Lamborghini and head to the front door, where Ian punches in a code.

"After you," he says, hand on the small of my back as I enter first. It's tastefully appointed–whoever owns the place now is going for an upscale rental look. Nothing really personal in sight, but it hits all the "English Tudor" notes, with plaids and velvet and some muted flowered chintz for good measure. Wide oak floors gleam under the glow of iron and glass lanterns.

"Not my style, but it's private. We have a hot tub and pool outside, too."

At the words "hot tub," my aching muscles cheer.

"Let's have a drink. You hungry?" he asks, moving into the kitchen, the entire first floor an unexpected open-concept space. Someone must have remodeled, but the wide-open rooms don't detract from the style. Exposed antique brick in the kitchen and leaded glass windows that flank the double doors keep the continuity. An English garden is off to the left of a small pool, a hot tub flowing over into it.

Back in the Bay Area, a house like this would be snickered at, made fun of, considered kitschy and quaint in a condescending way.

Here, it's just nice.

The company, though, makes it exceptional.

"I'd love a drink."

Ian pulls a small cheese board covered in plastic wrap from the fridge, the wooden surface spread with an assortment of cheeses, cured meats, and olives, with fig cake and Marcona almonds.

My stomach roars.

He grins. "Eat. I'll find some wine. You like a good Sancerre, right?"

"How did you know?"

"I've been to enough networking events with you over the years, Hastings. I paid attention."

"I feel like a jerk, then, because I have no idea what your favorite drink is."

"Lemonade."

"With what?"

"Lemon juice. Sugar. Sometimes with honey. My grandmother used to make lemonade with fresh honey from their hives, and she'd ask me to clip some mint from the overgrown plants around the foundation at their farm."

"So just straight-up lemonade? That's your favorite? What about alcoholic drinks?"

"Vodka and soda with a pickle."

"A pickle?"

"Your face is judging me."

"My face is trying to imagine what that tastes like."

He searches the cabinets, returning empty-handed. "No vodka. Just wine and some pale ale in the fridge. I'll have to take you out tomorrow and order you one."

"Tomorrow?"

I pop a piece of fig cake in my mouth after asking the question, afraid to chew in case I don't hear his answer fully. Searching the drawers, he finds what he seeks–a bottle opener–and swiftly gets the cork moving.

"Yes, tomorrow. You're spending the night, right?"

"I... am?"

Our eyes meet, his wide and hard to read, sharp and attuned.

"Let me formally invite you. Hastings, will you stay the night?"

"Is this a sleepover?"

One corner of his mouth curls up as the cork pops and he pours a glass of liquid goodness.

"If you want to call it that, yes."

"Can we watch horror movies and eat popcorn and braid each other's hair?"

"That's not quite what I had in mind." He slides the glass to me, then holds his own aloft.

"A toast?" I ask.

"To sleepovers," he says, our glasses clinking.

"To sleepovers."

The wine is cold and delicious, with crisp notes of oak and apple. "I can't believe you're here," I finally say.

"I can."

"Aren't you jetlagged?"

"I arrived a few days ago. I've adjusted already."

"A few days?"

"I wanted to see you first, but there were other pressing matters to deal with."

"Of course."

"And I needed to think."

"Think? About what?"

A slight pause.

"What am I to you, Hastings?"

White wine hurts when it becomes a sinus rinse.

But he waits until I can breathe again. Just... waits.

"Are we having this kind of conversation? I don't think I've ever had one before."

"What kind?"

"Most guys dance around definitions of relationships and expressions of emotion. They're not usually the ones asking that kind of question."

"I'm not most guys."

I gulp the rest of my wine, placing my empty glass on the granite counter.

"I'm also very, very out of practice with this kind of talk. I spent eight years with Burke."

"I'm well aware of that." His jaw clenches.

"Why don't you go first? What am I to you, Ian?"

"In negotiations, the person who speaks first, loses. I'm not falling for that."

"This is a negotiation?"

"In a sense."

"You want terms?"

"I want to know how far you're willing to go here."

"In bed?"

That earns me a chuckle. He drinks half his wine, then watches me.

"No. In here." Fingertips brush his chest, over his heart.

Warm eyes meet mine. This isn't a grilling. There is no hot seat here.

Ian's opening his heart to me, and asking where mine is.

"I don't know," I answer honestly. "And this is definitely a two-glass conversation."

His hand goes to my wrist, stopping me. "Let me get the steaks on the grill first. Or salmon? I have both."

"How about half and half? A small piece of each."

His head tilts. "That's exactly what I wanted."

"Then we're a perfect match."

I get a quick kiss on the lips before he steps out on the terrace, turns on the grill, and comes back into the kitchen, searching the fridge, pulling out plates.

"Come outside with me. There's a table and chairs and I want your company." Reaching for his cuffs, he unbuttons one, curling the white cloth, making me pause as I stand. I stare at him.

There is something *so* sexy about watching a man roll up his shirt sleeves.

By the time he starts his second cuff, he realizes I'm gawking.

"Like what you see?"

"It's a cuff thing."

"Cuff?"

"You look really good when you do that."

"Do what?"

"Roll up your sleeves."

Hand in mid-roll, he pauses, giving me a confused look. "You... like that?"

"Mmm hmm."

"Why?"

"I don't know. It's not a conscious choice."

"Some primal need to watch a man prepare to get dirty, perhaps?"

I gasp. "I think you're onto something!"

He reaches for his collar and loosens his tie.

I bite my lower lip.

One eyebrow goes up. "I'm sensing a pattern here."

I flutter my eyelashes.

"Why don't you slip into the hot tub while I cook?" he asks, eyeing my overalls.

"I don't have a suit."

"Do you need one?"

"You tell me."

"I'm a man who finds you incredibly attractive, Hastings. As far as I'm concerned, you don't need to wear clothes, ever."

"That would make working with you and Irene very awkward. Plus, how would I make cheese? Hot milk scalds."

He unbuttons his top button.

I moan.

A quick slap on my ass from him makes me smile as he says, "Actually, I asked Irene to send swimsuits, in case you were modest. They're in the second bedroom, the one without my things. If you want, go put one on." He runs a free hand through his hair before turning around to carefully lay a steak on the grill.

I have a very fine view of his very fine ass.

"Ian?"

"Yeah?"

"What am I supposed to do here?"

"What do you mean?"

"We've kissed. That's it."

"And...?"

"And now you're inviting me to get naked in a hot tub."

"I am."

"Do you always go from zero to sixty in 1.3 seconds?"

"Have you seen my car, Hastings? Yes."

Maybe it's the wine. Maybe it's the surprise of seeing him. Maybe I'm half addled by sheep's milk fumes. But I walk up behind him, caress his ass, and kiss him as he turns.

"If I'm going to be naked in a hot tub, you have to be the one who undresses me."

"Is that how it goes?"

My answer is another kiss.

Guys like Ian are rare. Self-made billionaires are rare by definition. Rugged and hard, laser-focused and never afraid of being disagreeable, they are also fiercely single-minded in getting what they want.

That's me. *I'm* what he wants.

Right *now*.

Lost completely in the kiss, I don't even realize he's deftly unfastened the overall clasps until denim pools at my feet, warm air turning my thighs to gooseflesh as his hands caress my breasts, each cupping me, thumbs at the nipples, his intent strong and unequivocal.

The shirt I'm wearing under the overalls has buttons that he releases one by one as we kiss, eyes closed, the synchrony of his hands and my body a mystical phenomenon. Being led like this is a joy, no pretense or tentative elements to make it awkward. I'm free to want him right back, and I take his movements as license to match whatever he offers.

So my hands roam to his waist, slipping under the thick belt, finding a man who is commando.

"Mmmmm," he groans in my mouth, my shirt peeled off me. I'm standing before him in bra and panties...

And socks and shoes.

I kick the shoes off, peeling my socks into balls that fall at my feet as Ian undoes his belt and unzips his pants. He undresses completely as I stand before him and just watch.

Oh, how I watch.

And then the fear hits me.

I haven't had sex in *over a year and a half.*

And I haven't had *good* sex in a whole lot longer than that.

Even if my marriage was a sham, the vows–for me–were very real. Letting go of the vestigial shreds of it is so much easier as a very naked, immodest Ian McCrory reaches for me, kissing my neck as he undoes the clasp of my bra, pulling it off me like it's three feathers he strokes across my skin.

"You're beautiful," he murmurs, eyes combing over me with a reverence and lust that make me believe him.

Fully.

"So are you," I reply, eyes doing the same.

"Let's get in the hot tub."

My pulse is thrumming through my entire body, the searing of the steaks and salmon and the scent of cooking herbs adding to the wine buzz.

"Hang on," he says, reading my mind, walking over to the grill and very carefully leaning over it with a spatula, removing the food and turning it off. Such a practical, domestic act from a man who has all the money and power in the world.

Taking thirty seconds to manage such a tiny detail somehow adds to the thrill of this.

By the time he's done, I'm out of my panties and lowering my thighs into the steaming water, the normal relaxation that comes from this kind of soak most certainly *not* kicking in.

"Tell me about Australia," I say as I watch his thick legs climb in, his muscles grabbing my attention as each one moves under the skin, tendons popping out. His hands go behind him for the slow descent into the water, eight-pack of abs curling in, shivering just once before sinking down and sliding over to me.

"It's Australia. What do you want to know? Or are you trying to make small talk because you're nervous?"

"Nervous? *Pffft.* Why would I be nervous?"

"Because I'm about to make love to you and until about eight months ago, you thought you were a committed married woman and I was a complete asshole."

"Just because both of those statements are true doesn't mean I'm nervous."

Pure delight fills his dark eyes. "That is why I like you so much, Hastings. You have no fear. You say what you're think-ing, and it's always smart."

"I'm not so unique."

"That you assume the world holds more people like you makes you naïve." His kiss is deeper, more intense, and defi-nitely more intimate as we explore each other's bodies, completely bare before each other, wet and enticing.

"You have been worth the wait," he says. "I never thought I had a chance. But fate gave me one." He pulls back, eyes intent, hands cradling my jaw. "And I'm not a man who squanders chances."

Permission to let another person touch you is conveyed in verbal and non-verbal cues, my moan making it non-verbally clear exactly how much I like what he's doing and please do more more more.

But his words give me permission, too.

Worth the wait.

"I really like you, too, Ian. You meet me at a level of being that I always felt I could see, but couldn't experience."

"Let's experience it together." His hand dips between my legs, careful in the hot water. My muscles are loose now, blood racing, body on fire, and all I want to do is straddle Ian in bed and writhe above him as I make him explode.

In me.

And then it hits me.

"Um, do you have something?"

"Something?"

I look down between us. "Do you have condoms? I'm not on birth control."

"I do."

My sigh of relief makes him laugh.

He looks like he wants to ask me a million questions, so I tip my face up to him, the setting sun casting long shadows, the privacy of this unfamiliar backyard oasis making me feel like we're in a different world.

"Is it really this easy?" he finally asks.

"There's that word again," I say with a smile. "Easy."

"I feel so relaxed with you. You let me let my guard down. Not many people can do that."

"Like who?"

An expression of contemplation takes over his face, sweat breaking out along his hairline, making me tune in to my own body, which is overheating in the water.

And from the naked proximity to him.

"You. Irene. My grandparents, when they were alive. My mother."

"Not your dad?"

"No. He was a hard man to be easy around."

"Gotcha."

"Your dad seems friendly. Relaxed. Not a go-getter."

With any other guy, being naked in a hot tub and talking about my *dad* would feel like a bizarre experience, but with Ian it feels natural. We're going deep.

Which means talking about all the ways we are complex human beings, with pasts, families, fears, friends–

And inner demons.

"Roy is his own breed. I used to think the insurance agency was just some generic business he ran on human automation–it wasn't until I got my MBA that I realized my dad is a salesman. And a financial planner. And a psychologist. And a community development team. And a business development department. He's all those, in a tiny local business, with Mom as his partner. So, Dad? He has ambitions. Just not–"

"Not like you and me." Ian stretches back and watches me as if we have all the time in the world to talk.

Naked.

In a hot tub.

"Right."

Suddenly, he stands, giving me a full sense of how complete he is. "We're in the danger zone here."

"I like the danger zone. Might buy a condo here."

His laughter is infectious as he reaches for my hand. "Stand up, Hastings. We don't want to ruin the night by passing out in the hot tub."

"I'd rather pass out in bed."

"Great minds think alike."

"You're right," I say as we grab towels, Ian checking on the steak and salmon he left to keep warm on the grill. "This *is* easy."

He kisses the tip of my nose.

"Shower? Bed? Food? Which comes first?"

My stomach votes. Loudly.

"Let's eat."

Without a stitch on, he goes to the fridge, pulling out a bowl of shrimp and two small salads. I go searching through cupboards for dishes. This is surreal, making me laugh at times, but it's also... cute.

Endearing.

The big, bad billionaire is naked and waiting on me.

I kinda like this.

Scratch that.

I *really* like this.

"Simple food. Easy and good," he declares as we go back outside and sit at the small table next to the pool.

For the next five minutes, we just eat. Flavors are enhanced when all the senses are engaged, or at least they are when I'm with Ian. The shrimp tastes like the Gulf of Mexico. The salmon reminds me of Pike Place Market. The steak is juicy and melts like butter in my mouth, the flavor triggering a good memory of my father's father, grilling at a tailgate party before a Pats game.

"You are a fabulous cook."

"I turned on the grill. Others made my success possible, in the culinary sense."

"Then compliments to them all."

"Wine?"

He stands, disappearing into the house, coming back with a bottle of Brunello and a wicked grin.

"Stop," I order him.

He does, shifting his weight onto one hip, left hand holding two wine glasses upside down by the stems, right hand grasping the neck of the wine bottle.

"I cannot believe you're the same Ian McCrory I've been butting heads with for all these years."

"You like my butt?"

"Ian!"

"What? It's a nice ass. Better be. I bust it at the gym enough."

Playful is the last word I'd ever have used to describe Ian. But here we are.

As he pours me a glass, I reach over to test the merchandise. He jolts, then laughs, never breaking the flow of wine into the goblet.

"I can believe you're the same Hastings Monahan, though."

"What do you mean?"

"I always knew there was a more earthy woman under that bitchy exterior."

I smack his ass.

"Huh."

"What?"

"That was a compliment, and I got spanked. How far can I go before crossing a line with you?"

I roll my eyes while I sip the wine.

"And does it go the other way? Do I get to spank you every time you cross a line, babe?"

The *babe* does me in.

No one has ever called me *babe*.

Suddenly, Ian is smacking his own ass.

"Now *that's* a turn I didn't see coming," I say as he stands and looks up.

"Dusk. Bugs are coming out. Let's head inside." He grabs the wine bottle and ushers me ahead of him, whistling appreciatively as we walk into the house.

I feel every part of my skin turn red.

"Look at you," he croons as he sets the wine down, pulling me into his arms. "You're a blusher. I had no idea."

"I'm not normally a blusher. I guess I am with you."

"You know what's so special about blushing?"

"Mmm?"

"Blood flow increases *everywhere*." He nestles the top of his thigh between my legs, pressing up enough to make me gasp, proving he's right. What had been an acute sensitivity, an aching craving, now becomes a pulsing searchlight, seeking his...

Lighthouse.

I'm still holding my glass, mouth half full of wine, so I force myself to sequence, swallowing first, then setting the glass on the counter, body completely humming under his attentions. Ian's hands go to my ass, pulling me to him, hips moving in a light rhythm that quickly brings me to an unfamiliar place, an exquisite sense of pleasure rippling through me, my skin turning warm and liquid at the same time, his mouth finding mine, our bellies touching.

He nips my ear, then licks the edge, my breath quickening as he brings me up, up, up, hands and tongue and the scent of him mingling with sensation until I'm gasping for air. My body is aglow with the rush of adrenaline as I come against his leg, in his arms, my mouth fighting for more of him as we kiss again, all wrapped up in one hell of an orgasm.

And we haven't even made love yet.

Instantly, I unravel myself and move down his body, long, powerful torso painted with thick, dark hair, a delight to behold–and hold.

He stops me.

I freeze, suddenly uncertain and shy.

"How about we move to the bedroom?" he says as he pulls me back up to him, every inch of skin that can possibly touch pressing together as he kisses me again, hands roaming. Being appreciated like this, with a warm touch and a wanting hand, is filling a hollow inside me I didn't realize was there.

"Of course," I reply as he takes the lead, holding my

hand, turning left at the first door down the hallway. An enormous king-sized bed awaits us, a single long bolster pillow stretching across it. The room is neat as a pin, just one of Ian's bespoke cashmere jackets draped over a chair.

His navy blue pinstripe.

My favorite.

I expect him to pull back the covers, or that I'll do it, but instead he just kisses me. It's a slow, sensual, reality-bending stretch of time that makes all my edges blur until I'm nothing and everything, his body meshing with mine, our hands learning each other's body, and making sure we feel known.

It's such a good feeling.

Being explored means the other person wants you. Wants to know you. Sees you. Touch like this is so gratifying, soul-filling and worshipful. Ian's kisses tell me he's right where he wants to be, giving me pleasure, taking my own offerings, and giving us both a chance to make something greater than ourselves.

"Lie down. On your back," he whispers in my ear, making me shiver, his hands on my shoulders, my hips, guiding me until he's on the ground, hands parting my legs, lips soft on my inner thighs and I gasp as I realize where he's going.

"But I already–"

"*Shhhh*." He stops, but doesn't look up. "Unless you really *don't* want this?"

The blush takes over my whole body again.

I breathe. I breathe again. By my third breath, he moves up to look at me.

"Hastings?"

"I'm not used to this."

"It's okay. We can–"

"Don't stop. I just… it's been a while."

"Right. The arrest wasn't that long ago, and–"

"No. It's been a long time, Ian. A long, *long* time."

He blinks rapidly, processing what I'm saying. One eyebrow goes up, obviously judging someone, and it's not me.

"How long?"

"More than a year." I don't even want to admit exactly how long.

"That bastard."

"I do not want to talk about him."

"Hell, no. Neither do I. But clearly, I have to make up for lost time. Lost time *with* you, and lost time *for* you. Because you deserve to be worshipped, Hastings. And I can't change the past, but I damn well can make sure you're treated the way you should be, now and in the future."

The future.

"Do we have a future?" I ask. Hey, if the gloves are off, I'm going for bold.

"I want one with you."

"You do?"

"Do you want one with me?"

"Yes."

"Then it's settled." He kisses me, inhaling deeply, breathing in my scent.

"It's that easy?"

"There's that word again. Yes, it's that easy. Quit fighting *easy*."

The words *I love you* are right there, ready to be said, but it would be verbal premature ejaculation to say them, so I hold back.

Guys recite baseball statistics to keep from coming. I recite kinds of cheese you make from sheep's milk.

"Let me show you how easy another orgasm is with me, Hastings. And then another. And another. And..."

His mouth moves down the hollow of my belly, pausing

to tickle my navel, reaching my second pulse as his firm hands slide under me and cup my ass. Within a minute, I'm arching up for more.

Two minutes, I'm pulling at the bedsheets.

Three minutes later, I'm smothering myself with a pillow, because who knew I could scream like that?

The racing thoughts that normally fill my mind during sex are gone with Ian, the sense of his full presence eliciting my own. We're in a bubble of our own making, and he's crawling up my body now, his lips tasting like wine and me, his powerful body hard and tight, erection thick and in need of attention.

"I want you, Hastings," he says as he kisses me. "Do you want me, too?"

Being asked like this feels sweet and sultry at the same time, his words commanding and respectful, finding sensual balance.

"Yes, Ian. Yes."

Turning to the bedside table, he finds a condom and does the necessary with it, moving back for a kiss, my legs falling open with eager anticipation. I want him in me, my legs around him, our bodies joined so I can know him better.

And be known.

Me. The real me. Not the me I had to construct for reasons I still don't understand.

Oh, no.

This me.

The me who meets him in the middle and who gives as much as she gets.

As he enters me, a wholly new sensation, emotional and physical all at once, grips my heart, my breasts, my mouth—every piece of me that tingles and every part of me that feels. He moves inside me, thrusting slowly, our mouths joined as he goes deeper, then impossibly further, my body opening for him, heart along for the ride.

As his strokes quicken, I feel the long muscles of his shoulders, his biceps tight as he braces himself on his arms. We're swimming in each other's embrace, then moving like athletes, choreographers, in graceful synchronicity as we crest.

His climax comes first, mine finding a wave to ride on, brought forth by the power of his reaction, Ian's groan in my ear turning me on with white hot heat. Our bodies move together in a first for me, the simultaneous orgasm no longer the myth I derided, my words dissolving as sensation takes over and this is all I am.

Naked with Ian, coming and coming, being well sated.

And deeply wanted.

I have no idea how much time passes before I open my eyes and find him stroking my hair, one of my knees up over his thigh, the evening light turning to a sliver through a slit in the curtains.

"Hastings?"

"Mmmm?"

"You were worth flying half a world to see."

"I know."

The rumble of laughter from his chest makes me grin.

"Ian?"

"Yeah?"

"I didn't know two people could be like this."

"Neither did I."

"You feel it, too?"

"Yes."

"What do we do now?"

"More of it."

"Oh. Okay."

And so we do.

❧ 19 ❧

I *need you, Hastings.*

The words make me smile, Ian's text a lovely mid-day break from–

Hold on.

This text isn't from Ian.

It's from *Burke*.

"What the hell?" I squeal, dropping the old wooden paddle I'm using to stir the boiling milk, the big drum steaming as the glowing embers from the carefully built wood fire burn like witnesses. I'm in Mom and Dad's backyard, making a small, experimental batch of feta, four gallons of milk ready for rennet.

My phone is a snake, ready to strike, the bite venomous.

Burke is finally talking to me.

And these are his first words?

New phone who dis, I type back, hitting send before I can change my mind.

I'm sure it's being tapped, but I don't care. Plus, no one can trace me. I need help, Hastings. Please, he replies, leaving me speechless, the glass screen reflecting my dropped jaw.

What could I possibly do to help you, Burke? I write back, the high-pitched ringing in my head getting louder. *You stole every resource from me.*

"Including my pride, you asshole," I say aloud, needing the solidity of words not double-thumbed on a screen.

I can explain everything, are the next words he types out, like he's following a worksheet from *The Narcissistic Sociopath's Guide to Gaslighting Your Wife and Other Ways to Kill Time.*

Except I'm not his wife.

Never was.

You could have explained. Had plenty of time. Why didn't you?

I would have, but you told the Feds everything and I had to scramble. You slowed me down.

GFY, I reply, using an acronym he knows all too well.

Because he taught it to me.

Ring!

I look down. Unknown Caller.

My heart is beating like all four of Burke's wives are living in my chest, working on a jailbreak.

I kill the call.

Within seconds, the house phone rings. Of course, he's calling my parents' phone.

Of course.

"Don't answer that!" I scream, racing through the slider, thumping across the carpeted floor like I'm fifteen again and waiting for a guy I like to call me. Mom looks at me like I'm crazy as I whiz past her, desperate to get to the phone before she does.

"Hastings, what is going on?"

In my hurry, I grab the phone and press End.

Hah.

"Um, nothing," I say. "Aggressive telemarketer."

"That makes no sense."

My phone is in my hand. It rings again.

She looks at the screen.

"Unknown Caller. These telemarketers have all kinds of ways to mask–"

"It's Burke," I blurt out.

"What?"

"Burke. He's texting and calling."

"After all this time?"

I nod.

The house phone rings again.

She reddens. Guess I know where I got my blushing. "That slimy little douchebag."

"Mom!"

"Answer it! Let's call the police."

"No. The police aren't the right people. We need–"

The ringing is driving me crazy. It alternates between the two phones, my cell buzzing, too, with a barrage of texts.

Why now?

"Honey, answer the phone. Consider this an information gathering session," she says calmly, over the cacophony. "I'm texting Perky right now. We'll get Parker on this."

"What does a congressman from Texas have to do with Burke?"

"He's all we've got. It's not like Karen Minsky can help with international financial crime," Mom says, poking her phone screen like she's killing ants. "There. Now answer the damned phone, Hastings!"

I do. And not just because Mom's cursing makes the urgency feel even greater.

And then I just... breathe.

"Hastings?" Burke snaps, his voice triggering eight months' worth of resentment in me.

Who am I kidding?

Eight years' worth.

"Who else would this be?" I reply, matching his tone.

"What's wrong with you? Why didn't you say something when you answered?"

Silence.

I give him more of what bothered him. The worst thing you can do to a sociopathic narcissist is to ignore them, right?

"I don't–I don't have time for this," he says, exhaling a puff of irritated breath. My mind's eye takes what he's saying over the phone, the sounds he makes, the tone he uses, and creates a FaceTime of him in my imagination. I know him so well, I can track his facial expressions. Imagine what he'll do next. My shoulders hunch in anticipation of how he'll–

Wait.

No.

NO!

I don't have to hold my breath and be worried about pleasing him. Calming him. Helping him.

He subtracted himself from my emotional equation a long time ago.

He should be begging *me*.

"If you don't have time for this, then goodbye."

I hang up on him.

Heart racing, I stare at the phone as Mom walks back in.

"Parker's texting with me. Says you should keep Burke on the line for as long as possible."

My phone buzzes three times in a row, three texts.

WTF? says Burke's.

Agents will be over shortly, says Parker's.

On my way, Ian's says.

"Ian? How would *Ian* know about Burke's call?" I mutter. "Why is he texting me?"

"Parker must have told him," Mom suggests.

"Right. Makes sense."

Ring!

"Keep him on the line this time. Draw it out!" Mom says, miming taffy with her fingers.

I accept the call.

"Ha ha, very funny, Hastings," Burke says with a carefully calibrated self-deprecating chuckle. "I deserved that. Bad boy. Whap me on the nose with a newspaper. And I'm sorry. I really am."

His attempt to imitate a jocular person with an actual conscience is suddenly clinical. I can view him as a specimen, noting behaviors, putting them in context, rather than reacting to them.

"You lied to me, Burke." Guys like him love to get away with something.

"It was a lie of omission."

"Thank you for apologizing. Now what do you want?"

"Want? Can't I just call to reconnect?"

No.

I want so badly to say *no*.

But I can't.

"Of course. I've been really worried about you," I lie, knowing the longer I draw this out, the more info the Feds can get, and if they can track his location, they can catch the son of a bitch. Nothing about my life would materially change if Burke were caught, tried, convicted, and imprisoned. The damage to me has been done.

But revenge is the flip side of justice.

And I can fake it with the best of them if it means Burke gets what he deserves.

As long as I use a steel wool pad and exfoliant cream by the bucket to take a shower after this call.

"Thank you. I heard you turned on me, though."

"Have they caught you yet?" I ask with a laugh. "I convinced them they got the real info. Just enough to send them on a few wild goose chases."

"That's my girl," he says, buttering me up. "You always were smarter than you looked."

Mom is at the front door, quietly letting someone in. Out of the corner of my eye, I see Ian, followed by a woman in a dark pantsuit, blonde hair in a bun, and a guy in a similar dark suit, a little shorter than she is, tight curls of salt and pepper against his scalp.

Feds.

Ian's hand goes to my shoulder in a gesture of comfort, while the two agents flash badges, the guy frowning as he spins his wrist in a gesture of "keep him going."

"I try. Never as smart as you, Burke. You know there's a term for being attracted to guys like you?" I croon into the phone. Ian's entire body tenses.

"Yeah? What's that?"

Sucker, I want to say.

"Sapiosexual," I drawl instead. "It means when someone is sexually aroused by intelligence."

He laughs. "Then you must have been horny *allllll* the time around me, Hastings."

A tinny laugh comes out of me, suddenly full and as fakely real as can be.

Everyone seems to disappear for me, Ian, Mom, and the agents, too. I turn away, Ian's hand falling off my shoulder.

"Two more minutes," the female agent whispers, pulling out a laptop, the keys quiet on a silicone board.

"Of course," I lie to Burke. "I always knew you had some higher plan. You didn't just disappear on me and leave me holding the bag like the Feds said. I knew you would come back to me when the time was right." My mouth fills with a bitter, sick taste. I hold down my gag reflex, but the words come out like caramel. "And now here you are."

"Here I am. And I forgive you."

"You–you do?"

Real emotion doesn't matter. I have to suppress my actual reaction and override it with the obsequious response that makes Burke happiest.

"I do. You really fucked up talking to the Feds, though. Should have kept your mouth shut. You were never good about that, though. Always a talker. Sure, it helped grease the wheels. We're a good team, Hastings. You schmooze the crowd and I close the deals."

"Right. We're a good team. So why don't you come home? Or I could come to you."

"How? Didn't they seize your passport?"

Ian takes a piece of paper and scribbles, *Be careful. He must have someone on the inside feeding him info.*

"They did. But you know there are ways around that," I say, playing along, nodding at Ian. "Maybe I could use one of those services where you get one from another country."

"Those are for people who don't know what they're doing." A bird call in the background, loud and sharp, interrupts the call, the sound fading but still audible. The second it happens, the male agent perks up, typing furiously on his laptop.

"Oh. Okay," I say in a breathy, stupid voice.

"Listen–I need you to make up for what you did to me."

"How?"

"I'll work on getting you here, Hastings. I will. But it'll take time and money."

Here we go. The real reason he called.

One of the agents shoves a note at me:

He routed the call through the darknet. We can't trace it. Get as much info as you can.

I nod.

"Money? I–I have a little, but–"

"I know you're dating Ian McCrory. He's your new sugar daddy. Smart cover."

"Dating?" Ian's eyes catch mine. "No, I just work for him," I lie.

"The guy's a snake. Don't trust him. But you can use him."

"Use him? How?"

"Get some money from him. Give him a sob story. Create some fake company and get him to invest."

Ian's eyes go dark. If he could murder my phone, he would.

"How can I do that? I just work for him. I needed money after you left."

"You wouldn't have needed money if you'd handled the Feds right. And your mistakes led me to this point. You owe me, Hastings. I need you to wire me $700,000."

I choke, the cough coming on involuntarily. *"How much?"*

"Just seven hundred. It's a start."

"I don't have that kind of money, Burke! I don't even have *seven* thousand."

"McCrory does. It's easy to get it if he won't offer it. You work for him, right? Just move some money around in his business accounts."

"That's–that's not what I do for him."

"Then get down on your knees and do something else for him."

"Excuse me?"

"Sex, Hastings. Give him sex to get money out of him. That's how this works. You always were a prude."

Disgust and rage combine in Ian's dark eyes.

Shame fills the air around me, making it hard to breathe.

Because for years, Burke told me I was wasting my looks by being too "prudish" to sleep my way to better and better deals. I thought he was *joking*.

"Ha ha, yeah," I say, going along, the weird bird call in the background followed by a ship's horn, then another. "I just don't have it in me. You always said that opening my legs would get investors to open their checkbooks."

Ian's eyeballs are about to pop out of his head, get on a plane, fly to Burke's location, and pummel him to death.

"Look," Burke says, suddenly flattering again. "You are gorgeous. Beautiful. Mesmerizing and, man, you can network like no one's business. You're the perfect assistant."

"Right," I say weakly. "Thank you."

"And now I need you to assist me. You're going to wire the money to these three accounts. Got a pen?"

"Mmm hmm." I don't need to write the numbers, knowing the agents are recording everything.

Burke recites a series of numbers.

"Don't get cute and tell the Feds. Those accounts can't be traced to me. But you have to get the money, Hastings. Start with the seven grand you already have, if it takes longer than it should to pry money out of McCrory. What about your parents?"

"My parents?"

"Roy and Sharon have a 401k, right? Or they could take out a loan on their house."

"Why would they do that?"

"BECAUSE I TOLD YOU TO!" Burke screams into the phone, temper triggered.

And away we go.

"You are INSANE," I scream back, "if you think I'm

gutting my parents' assets for YOU, you festering bag of bunghole juice!"

So much for keeping my cool.

I see an entire stadium crowd applauding in Ian's eyes.

"They are going to BREAK MY LEGS, you BITCH!" he screams back, suddenly speaking to someone else in rapid Spanish. Then: "GET ME THE MONEY!"

Mom comes running into the kitchen, skittering on her heels as Ian stops her, everyone as quiet as possible.

"GET YOUR OWN FUCKING MONEY, BURKE!" I scream. "Your other WIVES can HELP YOU!"

"THEY DON'T HAVE THE CONNECTIONS YOU HAVE!" he screams, the sound of that strange bird in the background. "DO IT OR YOU'RE DEAD!"

A calm, cold feeling envelops me. "If you were going to have me killed, you'd have done it by now. No one is going to hurt me, but it sounds like you need to beg me for help."

"Jesus, Hastings, I mean it! They're, I–I borrowed some money from some guys down here. These drug lords don't fuck around."

"You borrowed *money* from *narco-traffickers?*"

The female agent mouths, *Keep him talking*.

"It's the only option around here. And I had a solid lead on a deal, but it fell through because some guy screwed up. It was a sure thing."

"Where are you, Burke?"

Dead silence.

Call ended.

"Great work, Hastings," the male agent says, extending a hand. "I'm Carlos Medina and this is Felicia Morrison. You kept him talking long enough to get significant identifiers."

I can't speak. Can't shake his hand, can't think, can't feel, can't *anything*.

"Hastings, sit," Ian orders. Mom bustles behind me, the

distinct sound of coffee being brewed floating into my awareness.

"That bastard. That manipulative, slimy, self-righteous, egotistical bastard! How *dare* he call me up and make demands? And *threaten* me! You caught that, right?"

"Sure did," Agent Morrison says. "Ups the ante." She holds out her hand. "I have to ask for your phone."

I hand it to Ian, who transfers it to her.

"Those account numbers are probably the first in a line of shell accounts. And he knows chances are slim you'll actually send money, but he's going to try," she adds.

"I don't think he 'knows' chances are slim. In his mind, I should do what he says. Period. He was like this in the marriage, over time." Mom catches my eye. "Not in the beginning."

Ian makes a low sound, primal and protective.

"Toward the end. The last year or so it got really bad," I admit. "He alternated between ignoring me and pushing me to do increasingly edgy deals for him."

"Edgy?"

"I–he never outright asked me to do anything illegal."

Ian snorts.

"But he wanted to leverage loans. Do short sales that didn't make sense. Create shell companies to transfer money to other shell companies, and then to offshore accounts in the Caymans. He was gone a lot, so I just didn't follow up. It was easier to get into an argument over not doing something than to take the ego hit and approach someone about a weird deal. Our last fight before he disappeared was about using my corporate credit card to buy a bunch of plywood from China and float it for a month. His desperation was really intense."

"Now we know why," Agent Medina says, looking at Ian. "He got in debt with the wrong people. Just like two years ago."

"What do you mean, two years ago? Burke was charged the day they arrested and charged me, too, eight months ago," I ask Agent Medina, who twitches, eyes darting to Ian, whose own lids close in anguish.

Caught.

That's the look of a man who's been *caught*.

❧ 20 ❧

"I should have told you. I couldn't, Hastings," he begins, the two agents cutting glances at each other, faces slack, revealing nothing.

"Wait. Hold on. You've been working with the Feds for *two years*? Against Burke?"

"I couldn't tell you."

"Wouldn't."

"No. *Couldn't.* I didn't have a choice."

"We always have choices, Ian."

He looks at Morrison and Medina, who give him curt nods. "We can follow up later."

Mom's phone buzzes. "Oh, dear. It's your father. He wants me to bring him lunch. I think I'll go to Taco Cubed and–"

"Thanks, Sharon. See you later." Ian's firm voice leaves no room not to be obeyed.

She leaves. I start to go with her. He grabs my arm. I freeze, still facing away from him, watching Mom pick up her purse from the table in the foyer and look back at me, both her hands going to her heart, her wince palpable.

"Hastings." Hearing my name from his mouth is a new kind of pain.

"Let me guess. It's not me–it's *you*."

"My work with the Feds was how you were protected. If I told you the truth, you'd have faced worse. Much worse."

"But you were part of the investigation that led to it all in the first place! Long before I was arrested. You knew what was coming before I–oh, my God... That's why you were at Essentialz that night, wasn't it? You knew. You knew? That wasn't a coincidence. And you came in and paid for the bill and–you *bastard*."

All the anger that Burke deserves has lived unexpressed inside me. It's finding a handy target.

Ian.

"All those 'coincidences,' the job offers, the relentless pursuit. Showing up in Anderhill all the damn time, in the exact place I was. Oh, God, Ian, the kisses? Making out in your car? The wedding? The offer to go to Australia, surprising me at the sugar house, and... last night? What the hell was last night? Ian–you played me!"

"No. It's not like that, Hastings. I genuinely like you. I'm attracted to you, and–"

"But you *used* me!"

"Absolutely not. I was trying to protect you from Burke."

"You *are* Burke! As far as I'm concerned, Ian, you hurt me *more* than Burke!"

He looks like I slapped him.

"My marriage was dead, Ian. We were business partners for the last year we were together. Nothing more. The man wouldn't sleep with me! Do you know how degrading it feels to know he had five wives and I was the one he *didn't* bother touching? And then you come along, Mr. White Knight, telling me a story about being attracted to me all these years, how Burke didn't deserve me, blah blah–"

"That was real, Hastings."

"You're a liar! You're a con man and a liar. You conned me, just like Burke."

"I was helping you. Protecting you."

"I never asked for that! Why would you do that?"

"Because *I love you,* DAMN IT!"

The roar of anger rises up Ian's throat, pouring out of his mouth in a thunderous vibration that slips between my ribs, shaking my heart in place like an electroshock.

"I love you and didn't want you to be hurt. Men like Burke are snakes, all over the financial industry, and I could tell something was wrong with him years ago. I got physical evidence and I went to the Feds. They asked me to help build a solid case against him."

"You've been investigating Burke behind my back for... how long?"

"Not investigating. Just sending info when I came across it."

"You're an informant?"

He nods.

"And you've loved me all these years?"

"No," he confesses. "Not in the beginning. Attraction? Yes. Love? Not until we started dating–"

"We had one date, Ian. ONE. And it was a wedding where you half-dumped me at the end." I close my eyes. "That was it, wasn't it? When you said 'It's me,' you meant *this*, didn't you? You were working the investigation. Nothing about your feelings was real."

"Your attention to detail is normally charming, but right now, Hastings, I don't give a rat's ass how you categorize my emotional state. I just told you I love you."

"You love me. You *love* me? This is your idea of *love?* You're really messed up in the head, Ian. You collude with the Feds to set Burke up, then you–"

He lets out an angry sigh. "I did not collude. I made a vow, years ago, that if I ever saw anyone cheating people out of money, I'd find a way to stop them. My grandparents lost their dairy farm in Wisconsin because of a man like Burke."

"What does a farm have to do with–"

"They were conned, plain and simple, by an 'investment advisor' who convinced them to dump tons of money into a sham system. A Ponzi scheme. We used to call it 'pulling a Madoff' but now it's 'pulling an Oonaj'."

"Your grandparents got taken and you're some sort of financial vigilante for justice?"

"My grandfather died from the shame of what happened to him, Hastings."

"He… did he..."

"No. He didn't *literally* die from it. Or take his own life, though plenty of farmers do when they're driven into bankruptcy. But he lost the farm, the land in his family for four generations. His heritage. *My* heritage. All because of a financial scammer who decided farmers like him were suckers and easy pickings."

"How did you figure it all out with Burke?"

"You."

"Me?"

"You took out a Small Business Administration loan at one of the regional banks I was partnering with. I'm on the board, and your name was floated. I thought it was odd that you would have a loan, because at the time, you worked for Keating Xin Luis. You made good money and you were in private equity. Why would you need a loan intended for beginners? It didn't make sense."

Images of the boxes of financial records my lawyer pored over, that I didn't even know existed, flash through my mind.

"Burke did that. Forged my name. Opened shell companies using my social security number, then created EIN numbers for the LLCs. Delaware and Nevada corporations, with offshore–"

"I know. I know exactly what he did. One hell of a web he spun."

"Of course you know. So the SBA loan made you suspicious?"

"That, and I never liked the guy. Not from the moment I met him."

"You started building a case with the Feds because of a suspicious SBA loan?"

"Never screw over the SBA. Those people are vicious. Auditors with backbones of steel. Once we followed the paper trail, we found shell company after shell company, then a money laundering scheme out of Monaco that took us to Gibraltar, then St. Kitts, and..."

"And then, years later, you finally understood how thoroughly he screwed people over in at least thirty-seven countries."

"Yes. And he lives in one of them." Ian's eyes drift to mine. "And now you have contact."

"I do. And the Feds are listening in on everything." I snort. "What am I saying? You *are* the Feds."

"I don't work for them. I just work *with* them."

"Fine, *Agent McCrory*," I say coldly. "You got what you wanted."

"I'm not an agent. And what I want is *you*."

"I'm off the table. You don't get to lie to me and expect me to forgive. Fool me once, shame on you. Fool me twice–"

"I haven't fooled you twice."

"Not yet."

"I will never, ever lie to you, Hastings."

"You already did!"

"It was a lie of omission."

"OH. MY. GOD. Those were Burke's exact words just

now, Ian! Do you big-money guys have a playbook you work from? Swap a deck and PowerPoint your way through crushing people's souls?"

"I just told you I love you, Hastings. Crushing any part of you is the last thing on my mind. Especially your heart and soul."

"Too late. Too damn late."

Leaving is an option, but I stand my ground, shaking my head.

Finally, I say, "So how are we doing this?"

"Doing what?"

"I'll do whatever I need to do to help find Burke. We have a lead now. He expects me to wire him money."

"Those numbers are useless. The real payoff is in how you lengthened the conversation. You're good," he tells me.

"All I had to do was pretend my self-worth is in the gutter and I'm nothing more than an object to be used for a man to achieve a goal. How is that 'good'?"

"I'm sorry the conversation with Burke was that bad."

"I wasn't talking about *Burke*," I spit out.

The federal agents come back in, the woman's mouth twisting with a smile. "Really good work, Hastings. We got background sounds that helped us pinpoint his location to a specific cluster of islands off the coast of Colombia."

"How?"

"Bird calls and the ship's horn. He spoke Spanish. He's in a port of some kind in a distinct geographical zone. We'll work on getting him in custody, but also on closing down his financial options there. The noose is tightening, and it's all thanks to you."

"I just answered a call and played along."

"You did more than that. We'll be in touch."

Their departure is as abrupt as their arrival.

My hands are on my hips and my body is shaking. Ian

stands tall, staring at me with an intensity that reveals he has no shame.

Not one drop.

"You can leave, too."

"I'm not going anywhere until we talk this out."

"There is nothing to talk about."

He stays in place, watching me, the clock ticking between us, marking time.

Marking my heart's place as it descends.

"I mean it, Ian. Leave. You want to talk now? The time to talk was a long time ago. You lied to me."

"I did it to protect you."

"I think you did it to save your ass. Maybe you're not such a Boy Scout after all. Maybe you were forced to work with them because you did something wrong and this is how you get out of it."

"Absolutely not."

"You chose to work with the Feds for good reasons. The moment you kissed me, though, this became something else entirely."

"No, it didn't. Kissing you didn't change anything other than my heart."

"Our entire relationship has been one big conflict of inter-est, Ian."

"Is that all? Nothing more? You feel it, too, Hastings. I suspect you felt it before, when we couldn't be together. Long ago, even before I learned about Burke's shady dealings."

"We talked about this. I am monogamous. Burke might be a cheating opportunist, but I take my vows–even if they turn out to be bogus–very seriously."

"And I take my feelings seriously. There is no conflict of interest when it comes to those, and you're not married now. I love you, Hastings. I love you when you're angry with me. I love you when you're figuring out a complex financial problem. I love you when–"

I hold up my palm. "Cheesy declarations of emotion aren't going to work. Neither is some grand gesture, or a kiss that knocks my socks off, Ian. You lied. I feel conned. You knew that one of my biggest fears was being a sucker again, and you did it to me. You turned me..." My breath catches, the sob taking me by surprise, "...into a mark."

"I did no such thing. I made a series of decisions that made sense at the time, but hurt you in the end. And for that, I am so sorry, Hastings. I truly am."

Easy.

It would be so easy to do what feels comfortable, retreat into old patterns, shut myself off after being hurt by Burke. To wallow in the self-righteous swamp of being the injured party.

Easy.

It would also be so easy to tell Ian off, make him the bad guy, blame him for everything that's happened to me at Burke's hand. I could drill down and make him the source of my pain.

Easy.

And it would be even easier to quit my job with him, to cut him off, to banish him from my life and live in a rage-filled state of judgment, because being destroyed by Burke's mess gives me the right to do that.

Mom wants me to find a life that's easy.

Ian's staring at me, giving me space and time, opening himself up and taking whatever I throw his way. He's not leaving. Not running away. Not escaping.

Not abandoning me.

He's facing the consequences of his choices and still–*still*–wants me to be real with him.

So, I'm choosing hard.

A *hard* life.

"Why do you love me?" I challenge, needing more than my own acquiescence to feel the complexity. "And none of that Hallmark crap. Lay it out there."

"I love you, Hastings, because I have never met another soul who lights up my brain like you do." His abs curl in with a single laugh. "Body, too, but that's secondary."

There is nothing secondary about Ian McCrory's body, but I keep my mouth shut.

"When I am with you, I feel elevated. We can talk to each other in shorthand. Nothing's pretentious, even when *you* are."

"You really suck at this, if your goal is to woo me."

"That's not my goal."

"Then what is?"

"To tell the truth."

"Go on." I frown. Something's... off. I'm forgetting something. Radar in the back of my head makes me feel itchy, like...

"Because, Hastings, I–"

"OH MY GOD, THE CHEESE!" I scream, running past him through the back door, the giant drum of boiling milk a mess as it bubbles over, at least a gallon on the ground, ruining Dad's lawn. I grab the huge wooden paddle and stir, hoping it's not overcooked.

"Can you still use it?"

"Maybe. If it's overcooked, the cheese will be rubbery. The butterfat won't remain. Damn it," I curse, stirring. The only saving grace is that I didn't feed the fire under it, which has gone largely to coals. Calibrating small batches means being intensively present, and Burke's texts and calls distracted me.

Not to mention the seventy-six inches of hot distraction in my face now.

"Can I help with anything? Need some muscle?"

"I need to know what to believe."

"Believe me. Believe that I love you. Believe that my apology is sincere."

"I do," I whisper. "I want to. And I'm grown up enough to also know that you were just trying to help me."

"No 'just' about it. I was trying to help. Still am. I worked with the Feds for my own reasons, Hastings. They were good, moral ones. Being able to protect you, even just a little, came after."

"I know. And I do appreciate it."

A war is being fought inside me.

Team Easy vs. Team Hard.

He reaches for my hand, the one not holding the paddle. The soles of my shoes swim in boiled-over milk, ewe's musk heady and overwhelming in the air, mixing with the woodsmoke from the fire. There is no music. No electric hum from a device. No pretense.

Nothing but us.

"I want to be with you, Hastings. I don't know what that means, and I don't want to push you. Every second I spend away from you is filled with your presence. You take up a lot of real estate in my mind, you know."

Mr. Minsky's cat appears suddenly, nose twitching as it starts lapping at my shoe tip, then moves to the milk. Another one, an orange tabby, slips in with his calico compatriot.

Ian sneezes.

I bend down to reach for one of the cats and he grabs my arm.

"Please don't. I'm ah–ah–ah–"

He sneezes again.

"Allergic?"

He nods, stepping back from the cat.

"That bad?"

His answer is a sneeze.

"The great Ian McCrory has a weakness?"

"I also sunburn terribly and cannot stand Tori Amos' music."

"Well, now, those are dealbreakers." I move up from my kneeling position and face him square on.

"I promise to wear sunscreen, and I can take Benadryl for the cat issue, but I draw the line at Tori Amos. Sorry, Hastings. That's my hard line." Sliding his hand under my cheek, he asks softly, "What's yours?"

His phone buzzes. So does mine.

We ignore them.

"Tacos."

"Excuse me?"

"How do you eat your tacos?"

"Is this a euphemism for oral sex?"

"No. I'm asking about actual tacos."

Please don't say soft. Please don't say soft. Please don't say–

"Hard shell. Spiced beef. Fresh salsa, not canned, with more jalapeno than cilantro. Bibb lettuce, shredded really small, though iceberg's fine in a pinch. Never romaine. Monterey Jack cheese, sour cream, sometimes guac but the balance has to be–"

"Just right," we say in unison.

Just right.

❧ 2 1 ❧

"**T**wo hundred and twelve people came through this 300-square-foot store, and I sold out," I tell a very naked Ian as we stare up at the exposed-beam wood ceiling in the sugar house, our bodies tangled in an old sleeping bag I unzipped and threw on the ground for an improvised christening of the Anderhill Cheese store.

"You didn't save any?"

"There's a small wheel in the cooler. Dad asked me to set it aside for him and Mom. Other than that, no. Except for the batches that are still aging."

"Good grand opening," he says, tonguing my nipple. "Congratulations. The only grander opening is the one between your legs."

"It's not *that* big."

"It's not? I don't remember. Let me check it out and see if it jogs my memory. I'll use this handy measuring stick."

"The one attached to you?" I squeeze it gently.

"It's very convenient, isn't it?"

"It gets lots of use."

"Made in the USA. Genuine craftsmanship. Built to last."

My laugh turns into a moan as Ian moves over me, my thighs parting, ready for another round.

And then.

And then–a scream. A man's yelp.

"Oh, sweet merciful mighty Jones!" my mother shouts.

"My eyes! My eyes!" I hear Dad bellow.

I look up to see the main door of the store cracked open, the back of Dad's head visible, with shoulders up to his ears.

Ian discreetly moves me to the edge of the sleeping bag, then covers our naked bodies like a burrito.

"We, uh, came back for the cheese you set aside for us," Dad explains.

"We were planning on a wine and cheese dinner after your wonderful debut, honey!" Mom chirps from in front of him, her shoulders shaking. Is she crying?

No. Worse.

Laughing.

"Never thought we'd get dinner *and* a show," Dad mutters as he walks backwards into the store, my horror mounting.

"Dad? What are you doing?"

"Getting the cheese." He reaches into the cooler, back to us, fishes around in the back, and gets the small wheel. As he leaves, his left arm snakes out and nabs a bottle of red.

"Not that one, Roy," Ian says calmly. "You want a good Médoc instead."

"What are you doing?" I hiss at him. "We want them to leave. Now! You're prolonging this."

"I can't let the man make a poor wine choice with cheese that good."

Dad plunks the bottle down, searches through the bottles on the table, and grabs another, one that's half full. "This one okay, Ian?"

"Yes, sir. Good choice."

"Thank you. I respect your ability to put together the finest pairings."

And then he turns around and winks.

Winks!

"DAD! LEAVE!"

"ROY!"

"What? They're covered up now. I saw the reflection in the window. Besides, Sharon, the man's right. This will be a better choice with the pecorino..."

Their voices fade out as they leave.

Ian stands, nude and confident, and locks the door after them.

"I love your parents," Ian says with a chuckle.

"I love you," I say softly, my fingers on his cheek, memorizing the line of his jaw.

"So I've been told."

"Have you? Do I say it enough?"

"Do I?"

"Yes."

He pulls me to him, the sleeping bag askew, afterglow destroyed by *parentus interruptus*.

"Where were we?" he asks.

"You were attending my grand opening."

"There's quite the party in there. Someone even brought noisemakers and confetti."

"You have very high expectations for my vagina, Ian."

"You're an overachiever, Hastings. You set the bar high."

"Takes one to know one." I grab his personal measuring stick. He grins at me, a stray lock of dark hair floating over his brow, his body loose and free with mine. His hand strokes my hip, moving back to caress my bare ass. Our hands connect our separate, naked bodies with a languid sensation.

My store is open.

My business has been launched.

I am in love with my former arch rival.

Bzzzzz

We both turn toward the sound, my purse behind the store counter, Ian's phone in the back pocket of his pants. Both buzzed at almost the same time, the slight delay making the near-simultaneous notification seem urgent.

"Ignore it," he says.

And then both our ringtones follow.

"Shit," he mutters, reaching for his phone while I go to get my purse, rooting around in it, finding my phone. It's weird to walk around naked in my store, but dusk has settled in, and it's private enough here.

I drop to the ground and pull the sleeping bag over me.

It's Perky.

"Hey, Parker," Ian says from his pile of clothes, a mystified tone in his voice. He joins me, crossing his legs, cocking his head as if to ask me if I know what's going on.

I shake my head.

"Perky?" I ask, dispensing with formalities. "Why is Parker calling Ian?"

"Are you two together? Good. Because you're going to need some support."

"Support? What's wrong? Is someone hurt? Mom and Dad just left here. Were they in a car accident? Oh–"

"It's Burke."

"Is he dead?" Ian raises one eyebrow at my question.

Maybe there's a wee bit too much eagerness in my tone.

"No!" she shouts with glee. "That's the best part. He's captured, but alive!"

"What?"

"That call, the one where you kept him on the phone? It let the investigators figure out where he was. They were zeroing in on him, but the dumbass beat them to it."

"Beat them to what?"

"Hastings!" Ian says, Parker's voice a steady baritone through his speaker. "There's news about Burke."

"I know! Perky's telling me."

"Parker's telling me."

"Hold on. Perky, are you with Parker?"

"Yeah."

"Then let's do speakerphone," Ian says, pointing to mine. "Turn that off. We'll use the call with Parker."

"Got it!" Perky says, then my phone drops the call. Ian puts his phone on the wood floor, cranking up the volume, as Parker's voice comes through clearly.

"I shouldn't be doing this, but I'm on a burner phone and can give you some basic details. Burke Oonaj was taken into custody a few hours ago."

"Oh, my God," I gasp. "He's really caught."

"THAT'S NOT THE BEST PART!" Perky screams, giggling.

"Why are you so happy?"

"Because he's rotting in a South American jail, Hasty. He's not in U.S. custody. The idiot screwed over a high-ranking Colombian government official and really pissed the guy off. He's charged with a bunch of crimes in that country!"

My head turns into a buzzing chainsaw.

"Parker, can you explain?" Ian asks, his hand going to my waist, his warm, slow, even breaths helping ground me enough to listen.

"It's what Persephone is saying, but here's a rough outline: Burke has been in hiding on a small island off the coast of Colombia. He began to run out of money, so he started a scheme there. Schmoozed his way into some high circles, plus he has dirt on enough wealthy, high-powered people that he pulled in some favors and got access. Convinced a few to invest in some oil scheme. One of those guys is a–wait. Hold on. I can't reveal the government official's position, but let's just say the guy has enough power to arrest Burke on the equivalent of multiple felony charges. *And* it's a grudge arrest, because apparently, Burke slept with his daughter."

Ian's face is a tight mask of disbelief. I let out a long puff of air, taking it all in.

"So," Ian finally says, "he's not being extradited."

"No. The Colombian government was clear on that. He's in their jail system, being held without bond or bail until trial, and... well, it's not looking good for Burke Oonaj."

"He screwed over the wrong person," Ian said. "Someone with enough power to make him suffer the consequences of his own actions."

"Tell her the rest, Parker!" Perky whispers.

"Oh. Right. He was found with a particular piece of jewelry on him, according to some agents who have access to police info. It was the heirloom engagement ring you've asked about."

A piece of my heart lodges itself in my throat. "That rat bastard. He did have it! Great-grandma's ring. All along."

"He offered it to the arresting team of police officers sent by the minister of–ah, sent by the government official he swindled."

"I can't get it back, can I?" I ask, knowing the answer. At least now I know he *did* steal it.

"It's long gone, Hastings. Impossible to get our hands on. I'm sorry. Someone just noted it in the report. An informant mentioned it because of where it was found on Burke."

"What do you mean?"

Silence. All we hear is Perky snickering.

Parker clears his throat. "It was discovered during a cavity search at the jail. That's when he offered it as a bribe."

"Now I *really* don't want it back!" I sputter.

Ian calmly reaches for my abandoned wine glass and the

half-full bottle we started before making love, pours himself a glass, then hands me what's left of the bottle.

Which I proceed to chug.

"Oonaj is contained, then," Ian says to Parker and Perky. "Done. He can't wreak havoc anymore."

"Any other guy, I'd worry he could use connections to weasel his way out. And he *will* threaten to turn informant on people. That would work here in the U.S. It's anyone's guess if it'll work in Colombia, but given the amount of money he took the government official for, and what he did with the guy's daughter, I'd say you're right. He's contained and done."

Done.

"Thank you," I choke out, wiping my mouth with the back of my hand after following Ian's suggestion and yes, drinking straight from the bottle, which is now empty, thank you very much.

"You're welcome, but I didn't do anything. Burke did it to himself."

"No, Parker, you did plenty. You and Ian. You worked together with authorities to figure this all out. Information is as important as action. Knowing Burke's facing justice takes some of the bitterness out of the collapse of my life."

"Congratulations, Hasty!" Perky says, glee in her voice. "You had your successful grand opening, and your douchebag ex is festering in hell. I'd say that makes for some perfect karma!"

Ian strokes my thigh, his smile evaluating me, checking for emotion, figuring out how to help me integrate all this.

"Thanks. Burke got what he deserved."

"And so did you," Ian says sincerely, bending over to kiss me.

"Sounds like you two have lots to celebrate now," Parker says, clearing his throat. "Persephone and I will leave you two to whatever you were up to."

"Bet they're screwing on the floor of her cheese shop, Parker," Perky says.

"That's none of our business if they are, Persephone, and it's a bit rude to–"

End.

Ian hits End Call.

"Well," he says, pushing the phone aside, reaching for me. "That was unexpected."

"Definitely."

"Are you okay?"

Are you okay? What does that mean? Am I? Burke's capture means closure. An end to wondering. A cap on my anger, as justice is served to him, in whatever form it takes.

But am I okay? What do I really feel?

"I'm happy," I whisper in his ear as I kiss his cheek, moving my hand around his waist, pressing his chest to mine, inhaling deeply of him.

"You are?"

"Yes. Truly, deeply happy."

"That is your greatest achievement, Hastings."

"Being happy?"

"Mmm hmmm."

"Then I need a new goal."

"Let's be happy together."

"We are!" I pause my touch. "I... I assume you are? Happy with me?"

"Couldn't be happier."

"Well, damn."

"You're upset I'm happy with you?"

"No, no, I'm thrilled. It's just... what do we do now? We need a goal."

"You're right. We do. What comes after happiness?" he asks, kissing me slowly, softly, hands everywhere, chest broadening, breath going deep and rasping.

"I don't know, Ian."

"How about we find out?"

"How do we do that?"

"We start here." His hand goes to a very specific place.

"Ohhhh, I like here."

"And here."

"I like that second here even better."

"I'll go here, there, and everywhere with you, Hastings."

"Everywhere?"

"Let me start with your body as a map." He touches a particular spot that makes me gasp. "We'll begin at You Are Most Definitely Here."

EPILOGUE

*ne year later*

"WHAT DO YOU THINK?" IAN ASKS AS I STAND IN FRONT OF A rolling hill covered in green, the contours shaped by iceberg and water millions of years ago, but landscaped now by teeth.

Sheep's teeth.

"I think it's beautiful. And pungent. Which means the land is fertile." A border collie, a blur of white and black, barks once at us. She's an old girl, gone thick in the waist, and when I give her face a better look I see plenty of gray.

Gone are her days of herding sheep. Instead, she herds us.

"Plenty of milk here," he says in a voice that isn't quite as smooth as usual, his back to me, one hand in his front right pocket, the other on his hip. We're staying at a gorgeous bed and breakfast nearby, right on the New Hampshire border with Maine, the kind of place you don't know exists unless you know someone who knows someone, the establishment kept intentionally out of the public's eye. Ian, like plenty of other obscenely wealthy people, likes to travel quietly sometimes.

A network of obliging small business owners are happy to make that happen for a pretty penny.

For this trip, Ian brought his Range Rover, one of the three cars now garaged at the house he bought in Gloucester, right on the ocean, built atop of craggy cliff. We've been together for a year now, and my cheese business is profitable.

And I don't sleep with Lisa Frank looking over my shoulder these days.

"The Cordais family doesn't sell their sheep's milk to small businesses like mine," I tell him, surprised he doesn't remember. "They're locked up in contracts with bigger entities."

"Not anymore."

His words don't make sense, and as I approach him, I can't help but take a good, long look at his body, the old jeans molded just right to his ass, the tall rubber boots barely able to fit around thick, muscular calves, the rugged feel of flannel across broad shoulders willing and able to do the hard, physical work of farming, but not needing to.

"What do you mean?" I ask, my fingers tentative for some reason I can't explain as my heart begins to gallop, his shoulder steady as a rock as I touch him.

"The milk is yours."

"You negotiated a deal? The Cordais family produces ten times more than my current supply, Ian! I'll be able to scale up like crazy! How did you get them to crack? I've tried and tried. They're about to sell out to agri-business. I can't remember the conglomerate, but they'll be swallowed soon, and — "

"I know," he says, turning around, one hand going to my chin, tipping it up. Those deep brown eyes, wild with excitement that makes my heart join in, telescoping, pulling me inward, inviting me to be a part of him.

"You got the contract when I couldn't? This is a gloat, isn't it? You beat me to it. Are you going to turn this into a competition?" I joke. My hand goes to his chest, right over his heart, his eyes intense and loving, never moved from my gaze. Under his skin, his heart beats like crazy, the feel of it jarring.

What is going on?

"How about a merger?" he says, voice thick with emotion, as he pulls his hand out of his right front pocket and shows me a velvet box.

A velvet box.

"A merger?" I squeak as — oh, *oh!* — he drops, slowly, to one knee, eyes never leaving mine, only the angle of his look changing. Suddenly, I'm the one bent down, he's turned up, and his hand out, the box flipped open by his thumb.

And what I see makes the world stop and spin out of control, all at once.

"The ring!" I gasp. "How did you get my great-grandma's ring back! Oh, Ian!" I pause. "Please tell me you had it really, really, *really* cleaned."

"It's not the original, Hastings. I wish I could get that one back. But I took pictures Roy gave me and had a jeweler re-create it. It's not your family heirloom, but it's a damn fine version."

"Like me," I whisper, eyes crawling all over his face, the border collie barking twice as if to assert its power, a herd of sheep in the distance all following a hay truck like they're imprinted on it.

"Every version of you is damn fine, Hastings. And I want to marry every damn fine version of you. Will you do me the honor of being my wife? My one and only wife? And will you make me your only and *only* husband?"

Yes, I want to say, but the moment is too perfect to rush, a breeze blowing the hair off his brow, making him blink just once, the magic of the moment so delightful, so precious, so perfect I need to embed it in my bones with a long, slow breath that stops time.

Until finally, I say what needs to be said, all of the versions of me, indeed, damn fine.

"Yes, Ian. Of course, yes. Always, yes."

"You'll marry me?"

"Yes. Was there ever any doubt?"

"No." He laughs, a resonant sound that I feel in my marrow. "I just wanted to hear you say it again."

Now, he shakes.

Now.

His boyish nervousness is what finally makes me cry, his fingers struggling to slide the ring on my left hand, the fit perfect. He's paid attention, hasn't he, sizing my finger before this moment, choosing a verdant, green sheep's farm as the sight for our proposal, to forge our new life together.

The guy knows me so well. He even buttered me up with a new milk contract.

But none of that matters as I bend down to kiss him, pitching into his arms, Ian moving us so he's on his back and I'm straddling him, much to the border collie's consternation. With a backdrop of barking dog, baaaaaahing sheep, and a wind that doesn't judge, we kiss for eternity, the solid weight of the ring Ian's given me as a sign of commitment tethering me to the land.

He breaks away, forehead against mine, eyelashes so long.

"And for clarity's sake, I didn't get the contract for the milk."

"What?"

"There's no contract for the milk."

"Then what did you mean when you said, 'the milk is yours'?"

He smiles, the look of an achiever who has pulled off a careful plan, a long-game with moving parts and risks that don't pay off until the end. I know that smile.

I adore that smile.

"It's yours."

"Ian!" I smack his chest lightly. "What does that mean?"

He lifts me off him, then stands, offering a hand, our palms grasping as I join him upright, the sun glinting on my new ring, making me smile even harder. His arm goes around my shoulders and he rotates our bodies in a panoramic arc, looking over the beautiful land. A wind kicks up, blowing my hair behind me, everything so fresh, so old and new at the same time. Green, lush hills roll out before us, begging to be admired for what they are: pure, true, authentic.

Then he kisses my cheek and whispers, "The milk is yours because I bought the farm for us. Welcome home."

THE END

Thank you so much for reading *Hasty*, by *New York Times* bestselling author Julia Kent. Hasty is the final book in the Do-Over series, so if you haven't read *Little Miss Perfect*, *Fluffy*, *Perky*, and *Feisty*, now's your chance to go back and read the whole series.

But if you already have, consider moving on to Julia Kent's Shopping for a Billionaire series, a *New York Times* bestselling romantic comedy romp as billionaire Declan McCormick meets mystery shopper Shannon Jacoby in the men's room of one of his stores while she's evaluating customer service... and so much more.

Start with Shopping for a Billionaire 1, which is free (in ebook) right now on all retailers: Click here to download your copy.

OTHER BOOKS BY JULIA KENT
SUGGESTED READING ORDER

Shopping for a Billionaire Boxed Set (Books 1-5) (a New York Times Bestseller!)

Shopping for a Billionaire's Fiancee

Shopping for a CEO (A USA Today bestseller)

Shopping for a Billionaire's Wife (A USA Today bestseller)

Shopping for a CEO's Fiancee (A USA Today bestseller)

Shopping for an Heir (A USA Today bestseller)

Shopping for a Billionaire's Honeymoon

Shopping for a CEO's Wife (A USA Today bestseller)

Shopping for a Billionaire's Baby (A USA Today bestseller)

Shopping for a CEO's Honeymoon

Shopping for a Baby's First Christmas

Little Miss Perfect

Fluffy (A USA Today bestseller)

Perky (A USA Today bestseller)

Feisty

Hasty

Our Options Have Changed (with Elisa Reed) (A USA Today bestseller)

Thank You For Holding (with Elisa Reed)

Her Billionaires: Boxed Set (A New York Times Bestseller!)

It's Complicated

Completely Complicated

It's Always Complicated

Random Acts of Crazy (A New York Times Bestseller)

Random Acts of Trust

Random Acts of Fantasy

Random Acts of Hope

Randomly Acts of Yes

Random Acts of Love

Random Acts of LA

Random Acts of Christmas

Random Acts of Vegas

Random Acts of New Year

Random Acts of Baby

Maliciously Obedient (A USA Today bestseller)

Suspiciously Obedient

Deliciously Obedient

ABOUT THE AUTHOR

Text JKentBooks to 77948 and get a text message on release dates!

New York Times and USA Today bestselling author Julia Kent writes romantic comedy with an edge. Since 2013, she has sold more than 2 million books, with 4 New York Times bestsellers and more than 19 appearances on the USA Today bestseller list. Her books have been translated into French and German, with more titles releasing in 2019.

From billionaires to BBWs to new adult rock stars, Julia finds a sensual, goofy joy in every contemporary romance she writes. Unlike Shannon from Shopping for a Billionaire, she did not meet her husband after dropping her phone in a men's room toilet (and he isn't a billionaire she met in a romantic comedy).

She lives in New England with her husband and three children where she is the only person in the household with the gene required to change empty toilet paper rolls.

She loves to hear from her readers online.

Visit her at http://jkentauthor.com

Made in the USA
Coppell, TX
03 January 2022

70747269R10194